THE
Charmed
WIFE

Also by Olga Grushin

The Dream Life of Sukhanov

The Line

Forty Rooms

THE
Charmed
WIFE

Olga Grushin

G. P. PUTNAM'S SONS
New York

PUTNAM
—EST. 1838—

G. P. PUTNAM'S SONS

Publishers Since 1838

An imprint of Penguin Random House LLC

ISBN 9780593085509

Printed in the United States of America

Book design by Ashley Tucker

To my mother, Natalia Kartseva,
and the memory of my grandmother Tamara Tomberg—
the first storytellers in my life

Cinderella and the prince
lived, they say, happily ever after,
like two dolls in a museum case
never bothered by diapers or dust,
never arguing over the timing of an egg,
never telling the same story twice,
never getting a middle-aged spread,
their darling smiles pasted on for eternity.
Regular Bobbsey Twins.
That story.

Anne Sexton, "Cinderella"

Even a fruitful magic by degrees
    Can wrap us in a dubious spell;
Tales that articulated mysteries
Now offer only ways of looking back,
    As though across the ocean's swell,
Or down alleys through the pine and tamarack.

Timothy Steele, "Summer Fairytale"

THE
Charmed
WIFE

A Story with No Ending

Once upon a time, there lived a man who had a wife and a daughter. His wife was loving, his daughter sweet-natured, and his trade successful, and for a while all went well with him. But one day all his ships sank in a storm, then his wife took ill and died, and he had nothing left but his little girl. He wanted to do right by her, and so, after grieving for a year, he married again to give the girl a new mother; but his second wife turned out to be haughty and cold. Soon the merchant himself fell sick and died, and his daughter was left all alone in the world, with no one but her stepmother to take care of her. The woman had two daughters of her own, from an earlier marriage; like their mother, they were proud and unkind, and disliked the pretty little girl on sight. While her father still lived, they had been afraid to abuse her openly, but one week had not passed since his funeral when the three of them began to treat her like a servant, forcing her to clean the house and cook for them. She never complained but worked at her menial tasks with a smile and a song, and in a few years blossomed into a beautiful maiden, yet so dirty and ragged was she from her daily labors that her sharp-tongued stepsisters gave her a mocking new name.

"Cinderella!" my daughter would always cry at this point in the story, beaming at me, and I would smile back, right her

sliding blanket, and go on. The rest was soon told: years of drudgery and obedience passed, none too quickly, and then came a
fairy godmother, and mice that turned into horses, and a pumpkin carriage, and, at long last, a ball with its handsome prince. In
due course the palace clock chimed midnight, and the glass slipper was lost and the lovestruck admirer gained; but before I could
come to the royal wedding itself, my daughter would ask about
the dresses of the guests at the ball, and did the ladies' skirts
have those long puffy trains that looked like meringues, and if so,
didn't the cute little pages with their scarlet stockings and silver
trays trip over them and fall and spill the drinks all over everyone, and what kind of sweets did they serve anyway, did they have
the peach ice cream, her favorite, or make do with the lemon
sorbet instead, which tasted like sour water—and not once could
I arrive at the ending, for amidst the giggles she would soon drift
off to sleep.

She never wanted any other story told, only this one, and she
never wanted it told in any other words. She had learned it by
heart by the time she turned five years old, and would catch me
out in any verbal departure, no matter how trivial, and demand
the "real truth" on the verge of tears. After a few slip-ups, some
accidental, some less so, I knew not to alter a single sentence. I
must have told it dozens, no, hundreds of times; but while the
story stayed exactly the same, her questions changed. When she
was six, she no longer asked about the ruffles and the desserts but
wanted to know if the glass shoes were not terribly uncomfortable
to dance in and whether the stepsisters were not upset to have
been tricked. Those I could answer, smiling still; but one night
shortly after her seventh birthday, she told me: "Nanny Nanny
says that love is like a plant, it grows little by little, it needs to have
light and water and time to get tall and strong. So how was there
enough time to fall in love if it was only one ball?"

Her west-facing bedroom was aglow with the setting sun, everything pink and sweet. I could hear a lonely siren crying far away. My daughter was looking at me with no trace of her usual smile, eyebrows raised in a triangle of expectation. I bent to adjust her rose-tinted pillows as I scrambled for the right words in my mind, thinking all the while that if I were able to be more forceful in my dealings with hired help, I would chide Nanny Nanny most severely.

When I straightened, I took her small, hot hand in mine. A second siren had joined the first by now, and then another, and yet another—familiar wails heralding distant disasters, fires or wrecks or even death somewhere out there—but not here, not in my world, for everything was tranquil, everything was special, everything was charmed in my world.

"Love is not always like a plant," I said to my child in a measured tone. "Sometimes it is, but other times, it is more like lightning, it strikes all of a sudden. You look at someone, and there you are, in love."

"But isn't lightning a bad thing?" asked Angie, frowning.

And in that moment, I had no answer for her.

Her younger brother, at two years old, required much supervision, so I began to use my exhaustion as an excuse for ceasing my nighttime visits for a while after; I would only come by the flaming room at sunset, to kiss her forehead and wish her pleasant dreams, then depart with a rushed swish of silk. And when, some months later, I was finally ready to resume the telling of the story, I found that she had moved on.

"Tell me of Cousin Jack and the Giant Beanstalk," she chanted as she bounced up and down on her bed. "I like Jack, he's so much fun, we should have him over for a playdate."

I tried telling the story to her brother as well when he was little. He tolerated it briefly, although with him, too, I could never reach the ending before he interrupted, curious about the colors of the mouse horses' coats and the uniforms of the guards at the palace gates. But after only a few times, he started to grow impatient with it.

"Really, don't you know any other stories?" he drawled one evening, bored, his eyes wandering over the painted clouds of the nursery ceiling.

I knew that my children could be cruel just like any other children, in spite of having been blessed by the fairies in manifold ways, but it came as a painful pang all the same. Perhaps I should have chastised him, but I merely smiled in silence, as I tend to do when I am truly hurt, and thought: Well, but maybe he's right, maybe it simply isn't the kind of story that bears a lot of repetition. So I told him about a vagabond soldier and three magic dogs. I did not omit any of the frightening bits, and Ro fell asleep with a look of satisfaction on his face.

After that, I never mentioned the slipper or the ball to either of my children, nor indeed to anyone else—for whenever I tried, my daughter's small voice would ring out clear and merciless in my ear: "Love is like a plant, it grows little by little." I thought of other replies I could have given her. Love for a child is nothing like a plant, I could have told her; it is instant and complete, a full and sure surrender, like falling into deep, deep waters that close over you. At times the waters are warm and tranquil, familiar like an all-enveloping blanket, a one-eyed teddy bear, a worn-out bed-time story, the milky smell behind a baby's tiny seashell of an ear, and they carry you through your days in somnolent, animal peace; and at other times, they turn roiling and fierce, taking your breath away with fears and worries, tossing you about on sleepless nights—yet this love is always there, always whole, needing no light to feed it.

But whenever I thought this, another voice, much older than

that of a seven-year-old, would steal into my mind. Ah, but love for a man is nothing like love for a child, it would say in a sly, silky whisper. It is more like the sun that burns bright in your eyes, is it not—and when the sun is gone and you close your eyes, defeated, its afterimage is blackness.

The afterimage of this kind of love is hate.

—

Part One

—

The Scissors:
Close to the Beginning of the End

Hate is a clenched fist in my heart. It keeps my nerves numb as I lie in the dark, pretending to be asleep, waiting for my husband's breathing to grow slow and even. It takes some time; he tosses and mumbles before falling still at last. Once I know the draught I poured into his wine has done its work, I slide out of bed and dress as soundlessly as I can, and oh, I can be very quiet indeed— I am well practiced in silence. I do not light a candle. The room is pitch black, for the fire has long since died in the fireplace, but I have no need of sight to find my clothes, to skirt the perils of invisible corners: this has been my bedroom for the past thirteen years—thirteen and a half, to be precise—and I have measured its every inch in hours of wall-to-wall pacing. And a candle might wake Brie and Nibbles, who are such nervous sleepers.

The shoes, the lightest among a hundred ballroom pairs I own, are lined up by the dresser, and the borrowed cloak, the color of shadows, is waiting folded on the chair. As I put it on, I grope for the sewing scissors I slipped into its pocket earlier in the day, and the touch of cold metal reassures me. Ready at last, I tiptoe to my husband's side of the bed—and at once, without warning, I am rattled by a memory of our wedding. The moon was enchanted that night, white as the richest cream, bright as the brightest candle, as is traditional on similar momentous occasions; once he slept, I stared at his profile, outlined by the moon's brilliance against the pillow plush with the Golden Goose down, and cried tears of joy at my great fortune. But tonight, there is no moon, and all I can see is a pool of denser darkness in the dark. For a minute I stand unmoving, just listening to him breathe, until I become aware of the scissors' edge cutting painfully into the palm of my hand. And now I want to cry again, if for a vastly different reason. I do not cry. I bend lower instead and feel amidst the moist swirls of satin sheets. When I alight upon his curls at last, the perfumed waviness of his hair is soft, so very soft, under my fingertips.

I swoop down upon him with the scissors.

The mice do not stir in their walnut-shell beds as I creep out of the bedroom, the snipped lock of hair tucked away in the pouch concealed at my hip, next to a few other things already there: a bunch of dried flowers tied with a fading lavender ribbon, a miniature portrait in a bejeweled locket, a sapphire brooch that I will hand over as payment when all this is over, and fingernail clippings from my husband's left hand.

"It must be the hand he uses to shoot," the witch told me the night I went to see her.

"Shoot?" I repeated, confused. "Shoot what?"

"How should I know?" she snarled. "Stags, swans, sirens, whatever it might be his pleasure to shoot. They all shoot something, dearie."

I stayed quiet then, because the echo in the witch's cave filled all words with a cold, hollow menace and I felt afraid of the treacherous sound of my own voice, and also because I never like to contradict anyone, but I thought: My husband doesn't shoot, he just signs papers—still, as some of them are execution orders, perhaps it comes to much the same thing? And at dawn of the fall equinox, as instructed, I gathered the yellowing crescents of his left-hand nails off the floor of his changing room before the Singing Maids got to them, hoping it would be enough.

I carry my lantern unlit under the plain gray cloak as I hurry along the corridors. Out of the corner of one eye, I catch the reflection of an escaped blond strand and a pale cheekbone in the glass of a grandfather clock, and pull the hood lower, so no one will wonder where I am going at this late hour. But the hallways are deserted, which is just as it should be, for here, all things run on schedule. Every afternoon, at five o'clock on the dot, porcelain teapots bustle through the palace, knocking on doors with their gleaming spouts, splashing tea into dancing teacups wherever required, after which chandelier crystals begin to tinkle in all the ballrooms, chamber orchestras commence playing repetitive waltzes, and courtiers twirl, one-two-three, one-two-three, and gift one another with fatuous smiles, and dine on roasted quail and little cakes with apricot icing, and talk about the new fashion for pastel-colored gloves. Then the music winds down and they curtsy and part ways until breakfast the following morning, when the busy flock of teapots flits through the hallways once more, steaming with tea, not too strong, plenty of cream, plenty of sugar, every day, every month, every year, over and over again. At this late hour, so close to midnight, everyone is long since in bed. Only once do I meet a solitary candle sprite hurrying to an assignation with a candle burning somewhere, but it is too aquiver to pay my passage any heed; for love makes everyone blind, as simpering court storytellers are forever fond of intoning, quite as if blindness were a happy circumstance in which we all long to share.

Storytellers are dangerous fools, and my eyes are wide open now.

I sweep past dim expanses of reception chambers, past mirrored staircases leading down into multiplied shadows. As I near

the Ancestor Gallery, I slow my steps, but the portraits are doz-
ing, the kings snoring mightily, their beards rising and falling, the
queens making thin, delicate noises through dusty smiles. No an-
cestors of *mine*, I tell them soundlessly as I slip by. In the Great
Hall, candelabra are ablaze along the walls and two guards stand
flanking the iron-bound doors. I freeze, my heart lurching, then
see that they, too, are asleep, helmets drooping over ceremonial
lances, the gargantuan visitor log book sprawling unattended between the ostentatious flower arrangement and the old-fashioned
apparatus on the slumbering concierge's desk. Sliding a little on
the marble floor, I steal across to the doors, lean on them with my
shoulder, gather all my strength, and push.

The doors do not creak. The guards do not wake.

I step over the threshold.

Light from the hall has fallen onto the ancient slabs of the terrace in a great rectangle the color of honey. Beyond it, autumn
lies in wait, chilly and damp. I can just see the ivy-clad banisters
of the Grand Staircase starting their descent into the garden and
the stone arms of a nymph holding out a mossy basket of prim-
roses, the rest of the statue lost to darkness. I pause to light my
lantern, and now my hands begin to shake. It takes four tries and
a burn on my finger before a tiny wild flame careens into being.

The lantern lit, I linger in the golden doorway for yet another
minute. The night before me smells of leaves and rain—and something else, too, a troubling yet exciting smell I fail to recognize.
The palace at my back smells of all things small and familiar—
candle wax, cakes, parquet polish. This is all I know, all I have
known for thirteen long years—thirteen and a half, to be precise—
and I feel sudden fear at the thought of walking away. Then I notice my shadow lying on the ground, and the shadow is dark
within the light, cut from the same cloth as the night beyond. All
at once I say to myself: Oh look, my shadow is growing impatient

with me, it wants to go home to its own kind. And somehow this poor little jest gives me courage, so I draw the cloak tight against the chill and push the doors closed behind me. They come together with a dull, heavy thud, like some massive volume slammed shut when the story is over.

The brilliant light is extinguished at my feet.

I am halfway down the stairs when the chiming from the clocktower overtakes me. At the first stroke, a swarm of memories dive after me like shrill, sharp-toothed bats. I cannot let them catch me, so I walk fast, faster still, then break into a run. I skip over steps, slip on stones, slide on leaves, trip over roots, until the palace is only a pale haze of lights shimmering behind me, until the rain-splashed park with its cupids and fountains falls behind as well, and, at last, I am through the gates.

The rutted road stretches before me, black fields on both sides.

I run. My lantern beats against my thigh, my pouch beats against my hip, my heart beats against my chest. Winds pick themselves off the ground in my panting wake, shake themselves off like enormous gray wolves, and lope after me howling. Their ferocity makes me feel brave. Side by side with the winds, I run all the way to the crossroads.

The witch is waiting for me, her cauldron already smoking.

The Cauldron:
Closer Still to the Beginning of the End

The world is black and red—black of the night, red of the fire, black of the cauldron, red of the potion. The witch, all warts and hook nose, her eyes gleaming from within the sinister cave of her cowl, her fingers dark and agile like spiders, lurches around the cauldron in a jagged jig, flinging pellets and powders into the bubbling brew, muttering under her nose: "One horn of a poisonous toad. A pair of wings from an unhatched death's-head moth. Eyeballs of a blind three-eyed newt. Four ground claws of a lame baby dragon. Five scales of a wish-granting pike . . ."

At midnight, the crossroads is a place where the skin of the world has worn thin, and great underground powers are pressing against it: a place of disorder and flux, an in-between place at an in-between hour. Untamed shadows crowd upon it from all sides, low clouds threaten rain, and the prowling pack of winds that have followed me here stalk it on heavy gray paws. Whenever one of the winds throws back its grizzly head and howls, dead grasses rustle in abandoned fields, and flames under the cauldron waver wildly. I wind the cloak tighter about myself. My courage, such as it was, has seeped away, little by little, until I feel trapped in an ugly dream from which I ache to wake up in my blue-and-white bedroom overlooking the park, with my collection of porcelain poodles lining the mantelpiece and the night kept at bay behind the lace of the curtains—yet I stay where I am, and the winds keep on howling and the frightful old woman goes on reciting her lists of strange poisons that fill me with dread.

"Nine tails of rats that met lonely and violent ends. Ten coals from the hearth of a freshly hanged strangler. Eleven drops of the essence of insomnia. Twelve words of venom that broke a woman's heart. Thirteen lies that tore apart a kingdom. And, for the crowning touch . . ."

Her mumbling grows too low to hear as she drops the final ingredient into the potion. When she looks up, her cowl has fallen back, and the pupils in her deep-set eyes are two slits of molten fire.

"Your turn now, girlie." Her voice is a cackle. "First order of business, a treasured piece of your childhood."

My hands unsteady, I loosen the pouch, reach for the dried nosegay of forget-me-nots from my mother's garden, tied with her hair ribbon, and hand it to the witch without speaking. She flicks it into the cauldron. As I watch the faded petals become consumed by the boiling turmoil, a dull old sorrow cuts my heart.

"And a smidgen of your blood. No need to get all pale and wide-eyed, duckie, it'll be but a little prick, I'm sure you know all about those, most princes sport them . . . There, all over now."

My ring finger stings where she has pierced it with a rusty pin, but her touch is surprisingly gentle. She squeezes one drop into the cauldron, and it falls with slow gravity, much heavier than a single drop of blood has any right to be.

"And the nails of your husband's killing hand? Good, good. And now, his portrait. You did remember, dearie, it must be the most recent one you've got?"

I nod, my mouth too parched to speak. The witch does not know who I am. I came to her cave an anonymous petitioner, a wronged woman without a name, common as tears, plain as despair—and I myself am common indeed, but my lot is far from it. I fumble in the folds of my gold-tasseled pouch, pull out the locket. The initial R on the lid is inlaid with rubies, and as the light of the greedy flames falls upon the stones, it looks as if I have trapped a rivulet of fire in the palm of my trembling hand. The witch's breath rasps in her throat, and when I see the hungry curve of her mouth, I am seized by the cowardly urge to close my fingers tight over the locket's secret and cry that it was all a mis-understanding, an honest mistake, that I meant none of it—then run, run with my husband's fate, with my old life, safe in the plush velvet nest at my hip, run all the way back to the palace.

It comes to me then that I always think "palace"—I never think "home."

"Here," I say, and click the locket open.

We look at him together.

The night is black and the fire unsteady, but even in the vacil-lating of shadows there is no denying how handsome, how incred-ibly handsome, he is. The strong lines of these cheekbones, the chiseled jaw, the easy set of his not-quite-smiling, not-quite-serious lips, the flight of the proud eyebrows, dark and glossy like strips of luxurious fur, over these narrowed blue eyes—so radiant is he with beauty, in fact, that the glinting circlet of gold in his chestnut curls seems merely an afterthought. The witch lets out a whistle, and her eyes jerk away from the locket and swoop onto my face.

My husband's most recent portrait was done at his coronation.

"Well, now," says the witch, "this is quite unexpected." Her tone is dry and businesslike, all traces of cackling gone, her words stiffly formal, no more "girlies" or "dearies." "It appears that someone was withholding vital information. Had I known who your husband was, madam, my terms would have been different. Queens do not pay in trifles like sapphire brooches. Queens pay in things of true value—their firstborn child or their youth or their voice. Surely you know the rules?"

And I do, indeed I do. We live by rules in our land, and the rules are exacting and many. Trials and wishes come in threes, glossy fruit should be avoided, frogs must never be kissed unless you are ready for a commitment, and princesses, at least the warbling kind, should be ever so mindful of their mood swings—it is sunny when we are cheerful, dreary when we are sad, and stormy when we are driven to consult heinous hags in furtive matters of maleficent magic. And stern justice binds us all, high and low, young and old, good and evil, as some invisible but ever-reliant presence keeps strict tallies of trades and exchanges, rewarding bashful boys' kindnesses to small animals with beautiful brides, punishing laziness with slugs dropping out of shamed slatterns' mouths. All magic indeed must be paid for—yet the payments do not always come as violent wrenches, as scourging stabs. There are gentler ways, there are kinder stories. My own life was transformed by magic once before, but nothing was torn from me in exchange for my sweet reward: I earned it instead, scrubbed floor by scrubbed floor, washed plate by washed plate, unvoiced grievance by unvoiced grievance, through many slow, industrious years of patience and misery. I have been hoping that my past stock of exemplary behavior would stretch to pay for this as well.

I see now I was wrong. This is not the same story.

My porcelain poodles, my palace, my park, my predictable past—all of it belongs to a life well thumbed with familiarity and repetition, and no longer mine; and in any case, my once-happy ending has proved to be only another beginning, a prelude to a tale dimmer, grittier, far more ambiguous, and far less suitable for children than the story I believed mine when I was young.

Silent, I stand at the crossroads, twisting and untwisting the hem of my nondescript cloak.

The old hag's eyes are shrewd and flinty, but when she speaks, her tone is a study in indifference. "Madam, I am a busy woman, and there are few things more odious to me than my time being wasted." She shakes her wrist out of her sleeve, glances at it. "As a matter of fact, I have another client, a spurned miller's wife, coming shortly, so I must proceed to my office without delay if we are all finished here. I suggest you make haste to return to your husband before your absence is noticed and he grows incensed. Wives must be obedient. Good night to you, madam."

The first drops of rain splash on my shoe, on my cheek. Turning her back upon me, the witch starts to gather her pungent satchels and gruesome bundles, sort them with fastidious efficiency, and pack them away in the crevices and furrows of her robe. In mere minutes, I see, the crossroads will cease to be the hallowed place howling with four-cornered winds and pregnant with the workings of destinies, and revert once again to a barren stretch of stunted land where a few gray brambles struggle in the desolate dust and one potholed dirt road runs across another, both leading from nowhere to nowhere.

I hear someone ask: "What do you want?"

And it is my voice, it is I who have spoken.

Instantly, the witch swings back upon me, her eyes alive with glee, her rags swirling, her knees popping, her mad hair snaking, the crossroads crackling with restored magic.

"What do I want, what do I want," she croons as she dances around me. I wait, imprisoned by the chilly drizzle that falls harder and harder. "The spell you've asked for, it's ancient, it's dark, and it doesn't come cheap, not for the likes of you. What I want is a royal-sized payment. Let me see, let me see here. Your youth is gone, your voice won't be missed by anyone, and your firstborn is only months away from a woman's curse, more bother than it's worth . . ." She stops and laughs, a sharp, baleful laugh like the crack of a whip. "Ah, I know just the thing."

"My soul," I whisper, with doomed certainty.

"Not your soul, silly girl, of what earthly use would your soul be to me? Brimstone and damnation are ever men's unsubtle threats and crude bargains, and they're welcome to them. What I want is your life's spark."

I stare at her through the rain that has become a thousand daggers of cold stabbing me over and over.

"Your spark," she repeats with impatience. "Your warmth. Your passion. You know. You'll get your wish, you'll go back to your life, and you'll go on, sure as rain, but from now on, everything around you will seem deadly dull. Flat, like. The cheer of singing, the taste of good food, the touch of a lover—you can have them all you want, but they'll be like pages from a book in a tongue you don't speak, like a tedious aunt droning on and on about her dressmaker's cousin's ailments. Like that children's counting rhyme: *A garden with no flowers, a summer with no sun, a forest with no birdies* . . . Well, you know how it goes. I want your joy. Ah, I see by the look on your pretty doll face that you understand. So, what say you, my pet chicken? Yes or no?"

No, I want to scream back. No, no, no! But I never scream at anyone, I do what people tell me, I bend to everyone's will, an obliging sort of woman, am I not—and just as I think that, the hate in my heart unfurls its great burning wings, and smashes and smashes anew against my rib cage until I cannot breathe, until I cannot think, and the wolf winds are howling, and the storm is raging around us, and the world is black and red, black of my fear, red of my anger—and "Yes," I say. "Yes. Take it all, take it now."

I close my eyes.

"That's right, keep them closed, my precious, it'll all be over in a moment," the witch sings out. "And it won't hurt a bit, or perhaps it will, but only a little, only a stab, one teensy-weensy little stab, a little pinch in exchange for a lifetime of no pain at all, not such a bad bargain—"

I have never had much physical courage. I brace for the violation, my eyes screwed shut, my face dissolving, the water and the tears all running together. But the moment stretches, and stretches, and stretches, and nothing is happening. The rain has become a deluge; all is dark, wet misery. The witch is hemming and mumbling, fussing about me. I am suddenly conscious of my satin slippers swiftly growing soaked through; my toes are quite frozen, and a sneeze is creeping upon me.

"Well, now," the witch mutters, and she is close, so close I can smell the stench of her breath. "This is peculiar. Very peculiar."

I sneeze and, gingerly, open my eyes. Her nose almost pressed against mine, she is squinting at me through the downpour, which is starting to abate, ever so slightly. I wait, hardly daring to breathe.

She makes a noise in her throat and moves her face away.

"How big is that sapphire of yours, anyway?" she asks gruffly.

Without a word, I plunge my hand into the glacial water flooding the pouch, and fish for the brooch, and show it to her; and the stone is quite big indeed, the size of a phoenix's egg. She considers it briefly before her spider fingers pounce upon it, and it vanishes somewhere in the soggy crannies of her robe.

"And that locket with rubies. One fine-looking man, your husband."

She explains nothing, and I know better than to ask questions, for it is unwise to pry into the caprices and causalities of magic, the give-and-take of fate. I will never know what has just happened, why I have been spared. Feeling limp with relief, I hand her the locket. She scratches at its inside with a crusty nail to dislodge the enameled oval of the portrait, drops the picture absently into the potion, and pockets the locket itself.

The rain has dwindled to a trickle.

"And the trinket on your finger," she says now.

I gasp. The diamond has been in my husband's family for

many a generation, has served as a boon in many a royal quest. Shell-encrusted sea monsters have swallowed it, only for its dazzle to be revealed beneath a curlicue of parsley in the mouth of a garnished bream on some king's dinner platter; prophetic golden-eyed eagles have flown off with it, so that some bewildered maiden with bleeding feet could climb a glass pinnacle to retrieve it from a hungry fledgling's beak and later, limping still, exchange its hard brilliance for her pocket-sized happy ending; sorcerers with indecipherable accents have sworn dreadful oaths on its flawless facets. He will surely notice its absence, and he will be furious, I think in an agony of indecision—and then remember that, once I am done here, he will never be furious with anyone, not ever again.

I twist the ring off—and it requires much effort, for it has been on my finger for thirteen years (thirteen and a half, to be precise). I am not sorry to see it go.

"Well," the witch says with a shrug, "this isn't much, but it will have to suffice. One must always make the best of a sorry deal. And now, for the spell."

She turns to the cauldron. Dead coals smoke, splutter, and burst into vigorous flames. The rain has stopped. My feet are miraculously dry again.

The Spell: At Last, the Beginning of the End Proper

"Magic's not strictly a science, it's more of an art," the witch says as she stirs the cauldron. "There are laws, to be sure, but every case is unique and, with a potion this powerful, we can go in any number of directions. First off, there is the trusty old eye-for-an-eye approach. He's caused you pain, and you can repay him in kind— say, make him break out in boils and hives, or go lame, or develop a bad case of hemorrhoids, well, you get the idea. No doubt satisfying in its own barbaric way, but I can't recommend it, because, let's be honest here, if you're having trouble with him now, just wait till he is hurting good and proper. Ever had your husband stub his toe? Those princes are all manful bluster, of course, when it comes to skewering ogres or hunting down maidens—or is it the other way around?—but they're such insufferable babies when faced with the least physical discomfort." I can tell that she has given this speech countless times before, for her words have grown fluid and remote, like pebbles worn smooth by the ceaseless attrition of the sea. "So, then, moving on, you can make him fall back in love with you, relive the romance of your honeymoon, flowers, kisses, all that maudlin sop. And it works, and some of my clients do opt for it, but I always tell them, 'Dearies, there is a catch.' No potion can change his nature, so whatever lousy thing he did to you in the past, he will do it again in the future, as soon as he tires of your kisses, which he certainly will if he has once already, and in double time now, because let's face it, you are no spring chicken. No, not a long-term solution, a year won't pass before you'll be dropping by my cave, begging me to curse him all over again."

The more she talks, the smaller I feel, as if my story is just like every other story, a commonplace, and I a lifeless cardboard cutout, in control of nothing, made to go through motions to illustrate some preordained, banal conclusion. A grain of resistance starts to form deep, deep inside me, tiny yet stubborn, insidious like a pea under a suffocating pile of mattresses to which a fellow princess was once subjected in an insulting parochial trial. Oblivious of my mood, the witch carries on. "A better way, by far, is to target the root of the actual problem. Does he treat you with cruelty? We can make you invisible. Does he gamble? We can turn all the coins in his pockets into cobwebs and leaves—a cheap fairy trick, that, but quite effective. Does he drink? Any wine he puts in his mouth from now on will taste like troll piss. Are there other ladies involved? We will cause him great difficulties in this department, if you get my drift, heh-heh-heh, just say the word—"

And I do, after all my years of silence. And the word is "No."

"No," I say, in a loud, clear voice. I feel myself flushing, not with embarrassment but with anger. "No, I do not want any of that."

The witch looks startled, and I am startled, too, for I have never spoken to anyone with such force before, not me, not the sweet-natured girl who never argues.

"No," I repeat once again, just to prolong the unfamiliar sensation that has awakened in me. This new sensation is heady and large, its edges harsh and defiant, not like any of the plaintive, aggrieved, stealthy sensations I have carried inside me for so long they have grown soft and worn-out with a decade of use, like crumpled old handkerchiefs soggy with old tears. This sensation is one of power—of having him in my power at last, of holding the smiting sword of justice raised above him, not some impersonal fairy-tale justice meting out brides and slugs, but my own, very personal, long-overdue justice, about to crash down upon his handsome curly head.

"Well, it's your spell," the witch says cautiously after a pause. "What *do* you want, then?"

I know just what I want.

"I want him dead."

A strike of lightning, perfectly timed, accompanies my words. I do not flinch. I see everything clear and frozen in its purple flash— the witch, her scraggly eyebrows lifted in surprise, the cauldron with its revolting blood-tinged concoction, the wolf winds lying in prone submission at my feet. Then the world winks out again.

"It's your spell, madam," the witch repeats, but a novel note sounds in her words, one I am not accustomed to hearing from anyone. I wonder if it could be respect. "Well, then. If you're sure."

"Do it," I tell her.

And the night is black and the fire red and the commencing spell long and extravagant and full of awe-inspiring sound effects, complete with growls and howls and rolls of mighty thunder. A dark, stormy stretch of the heart-pounding eternity passes before the witch throws her arms up and screams the closing words of the incantation. Another impeccably timed bolt of lightning strikes the cauldron, and I am blinded. When I can see again, I look at the old woman with a new appreciation. I am grateful to her for matching the magnificent pitch of her magic to the magnitude of my marital disappointment.

Anything less might have made me less certain of my intent.

"Now it's yours to complete," says the witch. "Get the lock of his hair. How long have you been married?"

On any given day, I know the exact duration of my marriage

as surely as I know my husband's collar size (sixteen), the ages of my children (eleven and six, soon to be twelve and seven), and my own age: thirty-five, soon to be thirty-six, then forty, then fifty, then—while he grows only more attractive, a graying lion with his imposing stride, commanding gestures, and the fierce geometry of cheekbones—then just another bent and wrinkled hag, not all that different from this warty old woman.

"Thirteen years. Thirteen and a half, to be precise."

She takes the soaking chestnut curl from me, deftly peels off thirteen single strands, counting under her breath, then breaks another one in half, and tosses away the rest, and drops the thirteen and a half hairs into my readied hand.

They lie on my open palm, wet and seemingly harmless in their insignificance.

"Just throw these into the cauldron, one after another, and when the last half goes in, spit after it. Spit with feeling, mind. And then—poof!—you're a widow."

Something seizes within me at the matter-of-factness of her words. My fingers stiff with cold, I separate one hair from the soggy bunch, stretch my hand over the cauldron.

"Well, go ahead, drop it, drop it!"

I release it. Together we watch it drown.

On the surface of the potion, images bubble and flit.

The Beginning of the Beginning
(After the Happy Ending)

Once upon a time, in a distant land, there lived a merchant who had a wife and a daughter. The wife was soft-spoken, the daughter pretty, and his trade successful, and for a while all went well with him. But then all his deals went sour, his wife took ill and died, and he had nothing left but his little girl. He thought to start fresh and moved with her to a new land, and there married a local woman who seemed kind to him but was not. For in truth, he barely spoke the new language, and he knew the new customs so poorly that he understood very little of what his new wife said and did. Soon the merchant, his spirit broken, sickened and died, and his daughter was left all alone in the world, with nothing to her name but a dried bunch of forget-me-nots from her childhood garden and no one but her stepmother to care for her. The woman had two daughters of her own; like their mother, they had no patience for people different from themselves and disliked the pretty little girl for her heavy accent and her foreign ways. One week had not passed since her father's funeral when the three of them began to order her about and give her chores around the house. She never complained but worked in stoic silence and, after years of drudgery and obedience, blossomed into a beautiful maiden. And then, as was only proper, came a fairy godmother, and mice that turned into horses, and, at long last, a ball with its handsome prince. The prince fell in love with her, because he had absolutely no reasons not to: she was ornamental, blond and pink, and ever ready with expressions of gaiety, attention, or solicitude, whichever was called for. And so they were married and the envious stepsisters properly chastened, and she came to live in the palace, which looked and smelled like a vanilla cake, white and light, with blue icing.

(In a quick aside, her originally murine, briefly equine, now permanently murine best friends, Brie and Nibbles, moved to the royal quarters with her. Brie was a dainty she-mouse who swiftly acquired a profusion of refinements, such as a taste for sweet cookie crumbs and a habit of wrapping her whiskers in golden foil. Nibbles was of an earthier nature, a jovial glutton whose simple conversation invariably turned to cheese. Whenever he attempted to discuss the gastronomical superiority of camembert over brie, Brie squeaked in mock indignation, "Oh, you beast!" and slapped him with her tiny perfumed gloves. When Nibbles laughed, his entire stomach wobbled like blancmange, and ever more so as he learned his way around the kitchens. He only hoped that their princess was no less at home in her palace life; he worried about her, they both did, and with good reason, and her happiness was the sole subject of contention between them. At least her new father-in-law had welcomed her gladly.)

The old king was kind to her, and she liked the mirrored buttons that were always close to popping on his soup-stained vests and the apologetic manner in which he spoke to his grooms. The courtiers, flamboyant in their flounces, ruffles, and ribbons, were overall interchangeable, employed as they were mainly for atmospheric backdrops and humorous relief. And while it was true that the queen was no longer alive, or perhaps she had vanished— well, something or other had happened to her—her passing (or else disappearance) was not, as everyone was quick to assure her, a cause for melancholy, for it had happened quite a while before and was largely a matter of convention. And in any case, deep feelings were not a likely possibility here, for in this kingdom all souls appeared to be more or less one-dimensional, with just the slightest hollow at the center, for fleeting frustrations (not enough sugar in the morning tea!) and exclamatory enthusiasms (new stockings! new kittens!) to perch ever so briefly, splash in the shallows, then take off again, no depths stirred in their passage.

This was, of course, pleasant and proper, and she felt that she was one of them, that she belonged. During the day she stayed busy being happy, and when she slept, she had no dreams but saw a sheet of solid blue instead, spreading on the underside of her eyelids, flooding her mind with peace. The prince—he was called Roland, though she had not thought to inquire after the name before sliding her little hand in his, looking deep into his cornflower-blue eyes, and whispering, "I do"—was all a prince should be, gorgeous and courteous, and he adored her. He threw balls in her honor, serenaded her with the finest musicians, showered her with sweet-voiced songbirds, soft-pawed puppies, and other tokens of princely fondness, whose very uselessness demonstrated the full extent of his devotion. If they did not finish each other's sentences, it was only because they were not in the habit of holding protracted conversations: true sentiment had no need of verbal expression. Her love for him was all flowers, and waltzes, and a great sense of relief at things having worked out just so. And just so, they lived happily ever after, for one whole year.

By the end of that year of bliss, she was with child.

A sudden white flash rends the night over the crossroads, and I close my eyes, thinking it another bolt of lightning. Then I smell lavender soap, and my spirits sink, for I know just what—just who—it is.

"Well, look what the cat's dragged in," the witch says darkly.

I open my eyes to find my fairy godmother bearing down upon me, wringing her hands, smothering me in her laundered pink robes and fresh lilac smells, almost knocking me off my feet as she slams into me with the full impact of her unwavering goodness. I have never seen her apple-cheeked, double-chinned face look so distraught.

"My child, my dearest child," she wails, "what are you doing here with this villainous wretch? Oh horror, what horror! Thank heavens I've arrived in time to save you from making the greatest mistake of your life!"

The witch spits at the fairy godmother's feet.

"You can't stop her, you know. Rules are rules. It's her spell, and she is the only one who can end it. Madam, do you wish to continue?"

"She wishes nothing of the sort!" My godmother shakes me, none too gently. The top of her agitated, bobbing head barely reaches my shoulder. "You don't know my darling like I do, drastic change will never make her happy. She just needs a good cry, that's all, a good cry, a lovely cup of tea, a cuddle with her pillow, and things are bound to feel better in the morning. Let's take you home without delay, my precious child, you'll catch your death out here, in the cold and the damp, what with your delicate health. Come along now, there's my girl." She steps back to give me a sweet, encouraging, anxious smile. "My finest accomplishment."

Her slightly protruding eyes are round, white, and moistly gleaming, like two peeled hard-boiled eggs, and I see myself reflected in them, a fragile ornament that has somehow rolled out of the box and needs to be repackaged with care in its soft, padded nest, where it will keep safe and untouched, asleep for a hundred years.

Anger scalds my insides. I twist away from her.

"I want him dead," I say through gritted teeth.

The witch looks grimly triumphant.

"And I want him dead *now*. Do we really have to dole out the hairs one by one, or can I drop the whole bunch in at once and just be done with it?"

The witch ponders. Both of us pointedly ignore the fairy god-mother's gasps.

"I don't see why not," the witch announces at last. "Of course, traditions are, well, traditional, but allowances can always be made for exceptions. Go right ahead, it will be sprightlier this way."

My heart takes off in a gallop—almost there, almost free . . . I step up to the cauldron; the two women follow. As I bend over the brew, I see the shuddering reflections of our three faces in the tumultuous mirror—a hag, a matron, a beautiful girl (who, quite true, is no longer a girl and whose beauty has dimmed, grown saggy here, tight there, yet who can still pass for one in the black of night, in the turmoil of magic, if no one inspects her too closely). I look from the florid double chin on my left to the warty chin sprouting wiry tufts on my right—my future laid out with such cruel clarity before me—and, newly hardened in my resolve, pinch the sorry bundle of my imminently late husband's hairs in my fingers, and raise my hand.

And then, just as I am about to let go, the fairy godmother lurches forward with a stifled cry and makes a grab for me, her plump grip unexpectedly strong. The arc of my gesture goes awry. Only two or three hairs flutter, ineffectually, down into the potion, while the rest remain plastered over my fingers.

"You . . . you meddlesome *witch*!" cries the witch, as our struggling reflections in the cauldron give way to the vision of the royal palace.

The End of the Beginning

She was wan and unwell all through the spring, and the prince was obliged to attend a dozen state balls and dinners by himself. She could not help feeling that she had let him down somehow, but he was full of understanding and begged her not to worry, not even when some urgent matters of foreign diplomacy forced him to travel to a distant southern province without her. To prove that she was ever in his thoughts, he had his fastest courier (the very one, in fact, who had brought the glass slipper to her stepmother's house the previous year) shuttle between them, delivering immense gift baskets of star-shaped purple fruit ripened by the southern sun. It was lovely of the prince to think of her so often on his grueling travels, and she always rewarded the young courier with a grateful smile.

With the advent of summer, her sickness passed, and she began to swell. The prince was more solicitous still upon his return. He had moved his own bed to his study in the west wing to ensure her proper rest, her situation being delicate, but the regular tokens of love that he sent with the servants demonstrated his unfailing devotion. (She did not, in truth, feel especially delicate, but did not dare contradict the royal physician; she felt fortunate to be in his care.) The gifts themselves grew practical in nature, more suitable to an expectant mother: a pair of thick socks to be worn in bed; a book of recipes titled *Mommy, Is Dinner Ready Yet? A Guide to Easy and Nutritious Cooking with Children*; a set of knitting needles, along with a basket of yarn enchanted to never run out. The knitting needles in particular offered hours of useful distraction, and she felt ever so appreciative as she whiled away her tranquil days making sweaters for old King Roland, chatting with her trusty mouse friends, Brie and Nibbles, and daydreaming of the prince's next visit.

(Incidentally, Nibbles was courting Brie now, for Brie's personal charms had come into much greater clarity once she had ornamented her whiskers with golden foil. Brie, however, felt rather torn, for she had met Falstaff, the pet mouse of the Marquise de Fatouffle. Unlike Nibbles, who was an ordinary brownish gray, Falstaff was perfectly white, and the insides of his ears glowed delicate pink, which Brie admired greatly. Too, Falstaff was exquisitely polite and lived in a beautiful cardboard mansion furnished with the softest little sofas and the loveliest little rugs, which he had inherited from a broken porcelain doll of the marquise's youngest daughter. On the other hand, Brie had known Nibbles her entire life, and his cheese jokes and tummy rumbles made her giggle. For a time, distraught, she took to wandering alone in the garden, plucking daisies the size of her head, tearing off petals and muttering, "Falstaff—Nibbles—Falstaff—Nibbles," into the spring breeze. When the gardener's dog jumped out at her from behind the statue of a one-eyed queen, Brie only just made her escape, with a petal still crumpled between her paws and Falstaff's name on her lips.

She was so badly shaken that she saw it as a sign, and that same night she scratched on the door of Falstaff's mansion and allowed him a great many liberties on the plushest of his sofas. Immediately upon taking the liberties, however, Falstaff kissed the tip of her paw and said theirs was a most pleasant acquaintance and he sincerely hoped that she had not misunderstood his intentions, which were honorable, of course, but had to take into account the regrettable circumstance that he was the Marquise de Fatouffle's beloved pet, and she, much as his soul protested against it, was only a common gray mouse—even if her whiskers were wrapped in golden foil. "You understand, my sweet," he said, and set to brushing his immaculate fur.

She said she did, in a small, small squeak, and, still in the middle of the night, slunk away, and crawled back to Nibbles. She was relieved to hear her friend's hearty snores continue uninterrupted as she snuggled up to his warm side and, there and then, through her tears, decided that she would accept his suit in the morning. And when she did so, Nibbles was overjoyed, even though he had only pretended to snore the night before. For he had always known where her heart truly belonged, in spite of her fancy whiskers, which, after her six seconds of misguided passion on the dollhouse sofa, she stopped wrapping in golden foil in any case. And if their first litter of mouselings were born with lighter coats than strictly necessary, Nibbles loved her enough to say nothing about it. There would be many more litters in their happy future, for they were blessed that way, unlike their poor princess, who was still carrying one single baby after all these long, long months.)

In August, the prince placed his hand on the rise of her belly, and in September, he rubbed her feet. Her love for him was all complacence, and comfort, and embroidered handkerchiefs. In October, pleasantly aflutter, she was in the midst of preparing for another of his monthly appearances and had just greeted her hairdresser when the baby made itself felt. The prince's visit was speedily canceled, and thirty-seven hours later, Angelina arrived.

And then her world grew exhausting and warm, and everything smelled of baby formula and laundry detergent, and she was ecstatic, and she was apprehensive, and she was overwhelmed, and she was never alone, which felt oppressive at times, but she was also never, ever lonely. She held the baby close to her heart through vague afternoons and restless nights, for hours and days and weeks. The baby cooed, babbled, and gurgled—mostly—but every so often the baby cried, and then she would tickle its toes, blow soap bubbles, and have Brie and Nibbles dance funny little jigs on the rug. And her diversion tactics worked—mostly—but on occasion they failed, and then she felt as if her world might just split at the seams with the robust wails.

One morning found her lying in bed, limp with fatigue, surrounded by stuffed rabbits and beady-eyed teddy bears in varied shades of pink, with her head throbbing and the baby in her arms still going strong with stalwart howls.

"She will not cease," she marveled aloud in a kind of dismayed wonder. "Nothing I do will make her cease."

"Have you tried telling her stories, milady?" asked the teapot of white porcelain with a blue bird on its lid, which, just then, happened to be filling the cup on her bedside table.

"Stories? She's too little for stories."

"Not true, milady," the teapot said, primly and a bit disapprovingly. "Stories are good at any age."

"But I don't know how," she confessed.

"Oh, it's easy. You go like this—and make your voice melodious-like: 'Once upon a time, there lived a blue bird.'"

"And then?" she asked, in astonishment, for at the teapot's singsong words, the baby had stopped crying and was cocking her head, listening.

"Why, then it simply tells itself," the teapot replied, gathering the creamer and the sugar bowl around her like a mother hen her chickens. "Excuse me, milady, we must rush before I cool off, the marquise likes her tea steaming."

And so she tried, and it was indeed a miracle, for, as long as the stories kept coming, the baby kept quiet, gazing up at her, spellbound, with milky eyes, eventually drifting into dreams. She had never told stories to anyone before, and the nightly ritual of saying "Once upon a time" felt deeply soothing, like settling into a favorite armchair with a bit of knitting. She told her baby about a poor miller's daughter who lost her hands but was so virtuous she got to marry a king, and he made her new hands of polished silver, which the queen liked even better. She told her about a beggar girl who hid her beauty under a donkey skin, but her beauty shone through the disguise, so she got to marry a prince. She told her about a poor miller's son who had a clever cat and got to marry a princess. Best of all, she told her sweet baby about a poor orphan girl who was so good and so pretty that she got to marry a prince—a story that, at first glance, seemed much like the other stories (all of which seemed much like the same story over and over again)—save that it was the one story that really mattered, the only story that was entirely true, the story of Mommy and Daddy, of their fairy-tale love and happily ever after in the beautiful snow globe of a charmed world.

And thus seasons came and went, in stories and feedings and naps, and her waist shrank little by little and color returned to her cheeks. On Angie's first birthday, as tradition dictated, the royal baby passed into the care of the ever-capable Nanny Nanny, and all at once she had time on her hands. She invented amusing ways to spend her days. She trilled with songbirds, stopped to chat with gardeners and cooks, twirled through the palace dispensing smiles and minor kindnesses. She met the spirit of a long-dead minstrel who haunted the Great Hall and listened to him recite his militant epics, knitted a pair of mouse-eared slippers for the sweet old King Roland, sent homemade preserves to Archibald the Clockmaker and Arbadac the Magician, better known as Arbadac the Bumbler, the elderly brothers who lived at the top of the palace tower and labored over the great clock, which had, for some reason, stopped chiming on the hour and taken to marking random stretches of time instead. In the evenings, she played dominoes with Brie and Nibbles, using gnawed chunks of cheese in place of tiles. *(Unbeknownst to her, these Brie and Nibbles were not the original Brie and Nibbles, for, sadly, mice—even those in fairy tales—do not live all that long. Brie and Nibbles the Second were siblings, two of the numerous children of the original Brie and Nibbles, who, when close to dying of satisfied old age, designated the best-mannered and the fattest of their off-spring, respectively, to play their parts, so as not to upset the princess with their passing. The second-generation Brie and Nibbles, in truth, did not re-semble their parents all that closely, neither in appearance nor in character. Brie the Second, scrawnier and much less garrulous than her mother, did not give any thought to the state of her whiskers, found dollhouses confining, and liked to spend her evenings by the fire in the kitchen, listening to Grandfather Rat sing of the brave deeds of bygone mouse kings. Nibbles the Second, larger and slower than his father, had one all-consuming passion—sleep. They did their best to follow the many detailed instructions of their beloved progenitors—"Brie: collapse in giggles every time you hear Nibbles burp. Nib-bles: partake of cheddar daily"—but failed time and time again, and were perennially worried that the princess would discover their ruse. But the princess never appeared to notice.)*

The prince was frequently absent, traveling the land on mat-ters of state, and when back in the palace, he continued to stay in his private quarters: he worked long hours and professed himself reluctant to disturb her rest. Yet whenever they chanced to be together, he was unfailingly attentive. On their third anniversary, ever grateful, she reflected on their matrimonial harmony. There had not been a single disagreement, not a single harsh word ex-changed between them in all three years—nothing less than per-fect, in fact, that she could recall, apart from, perhaps, one entirely insignificant misunderstanding some months before, which had stayed in her memory for the sole reason that it demonstrated, yet again, Prince Roland's forgiving nature.

Sometime in the course of her solitary rambles through the palace, she had discovered an unfrequented passage in the east wing that dead-ended in a curious tapestry, so old and faded it was impossible to tell exactly what it depicted. When a shaft of sunlight pierced a nearby stained-glass window and the air in the corridor grew briefly bright, she thought she could discern blushing youths out for a stroll or ladies strumming delicate lutes; most of the time, though, the image remained shapeless and gray, with one puzzling dash of threadbare red in the middle. She felt drawn to the mystery and, hoping that one day the light would be just right for the meaning to reveal itself, paused here often on her way from the nursery.

One afternoon, as she neared the tapestry corridor, she heard a woman's low laugh and a man speaking softly. She could make out no words, but something about the urgent yet amused tone of the man's voice froze her in her tracks. She listened intently—and then knew the voice to be that of Prince Roland, though not as she herself had ever heard it. Her blood quickened as she braved the corner, expecting to see she knew not what; but there was nothing, there was no one there, only the faded old tapestry hanging still and inscrutable against the stone wall.

That night, she sat opposite the prince at a long, elaborate table. The dinner was held in honor of the Duke and Duchess von Lieber, visiting from a neighboring kingdom, and as a special compliment, Arbadac the Bumbler, the court magician, had enchanted all the courses to match the unusually intense green of the duchess's eyes. The results proved rather unappetizing, however, and she found her throat closing up at the procession of bright green venison steaks and bright green loaves—or perhaps it was her lingering sense of unease that made her unable to eat. On her right, the jolly duke was telling her some interminable hunting story with much enthusiasm and spittle, shouting "Bam!" in imitation of every shot, slamming his hand vigorously against the table, so that bright green potatoes on his plate jumped. She smiled and nodded and tried to watch the prince at the other end of the hall, but his face was obscured by the many smoking tureens and made shimmery by the many wavering candles between them and she could not catch his eyes all night.

After the poisonously green pears had been cleared away, the guests turned to her, expecting her to give the customary signal of the dinner's conclusion. Making up her mind, she stood and crossed the hall instead. The prince, ever the polite host, was listening to the Duchess von Lieber, who prattled with animation, the woman's small, pretty, slightly monkeylike face liberally sprinkled with velvet beauty marks, the woman's eyes every bit the shade of an unripe pear.

She placed a quavering hand on the prince's shoulder.

"Darling, I'm sorry to interrupt, but what were you doing in the east wing's second-floor corridor this afternoon?"

She tried to speak softly, but the room had grown quiet and her words carried. She sensed the duchess's astonished gaze upon her.

"An east-wing corridor, my love? But I haven't set foot in the east wing all day. I was working in my office until they rang for dinner." He smiled at her. "And now, my precious dear, would you please escort the honored duchess to the after-dinner tea?"

He spoke with his habitual kindness, and instantly she saw that she had indeed been mistaken, that the voice in the corridor, whatever it had been, had sounded nothing like this civilized, gentle voice, the voice of her husband. And then she heard the whispering behind her back, and understood that she had broken the courtly etiquette with her impulsive, childish question, had embarrassed her dear prince in front of all these foreign dignitaries. The prince, seemingly at ease, motioned for everyone to rise, and the awkward silence broke, filled with the scraping of two dozen chairs, the shuffling of four dozen feet. Still, she felt flustered and could not quite recover her poise during the ladies' tea that followed, even as she played a conscientious hostess to the chatty duchess. But later that evening, she sat by Angie's crib, singing a bedtime lullaby, when the prince paid an unscheduled visit to the nursery. He kissed them both tenderly, bounced the child on his knee, asked about her day. He did not allude to her faux pas at dinner, but his gestures, his words, were full of loving reassurance, and at last she was able to see the unfortunate episode for the trifle it had been. She looked at the two of them, her kind, considerate husband, her daughter giggling in her father's arms, and thought: This moment, right here, right now—I want to hold this moment perfect and whole in my memory, so that even decades from today I will be able to see it, undimmed, undiminished, and know just how lucky I was.

The night. The crossroads. The cauldron. The witch. The fairy.

The witch and the fairy are snarling at each other.

"You can't interfere, you bully, you must let her make her own choices!"

"*You* are the bully here, taking advantage of the poor darling in her fraught state! *I* am only helping her see the truth. Love will always triumph in the end. But I don't expect *you* to understand, you bitter old prune, no one has ever loved you, no wonder you hate all men." The fairy godmother faces me, her hands clasped in supplication. "I beg you, sweet child, cease this rash foolishness. Let me take you back where you belong, back to your happy marriage."

"Two or three happy years don't yet a happy marriage make," interrupts the witch.

"Well, of course, one must be a bit more flexible after a decade together," the fairy godmother admits, somewhat deflated. "Marriages are work." She makes a visible effort to rally. "Still, whatever happened later, my child, I'll help you move past it. The important thing is, you and the prince had such love between you once. You just need to keep the memory of that beautiful beginning alive in your heart."

She has a gift, it seems, for saying precisely the wrong thing.

I am newly seared with anger.

"Does anything other than platitudes ever come out of her mealy mouth?" the witch asks with disdain. "Just throw in the lot and be done with it, madam."

"No, child, no!" the fairy godmother wails. "Think of your little angels if nothing else! They need a wholesome family, they need their father!"

And just like that, the long-forgotten vision of Roland with little Angie laughing on his knee thrusts itself, unbidden, vivid, into my mind.

My fury is dampened. I look down at my hands.

One, three, five, eight, ten. And a half. Ten and a half hairs left.

Perhaps I should count again, just to be sure.

"Well, what are you waiting for, madam? You still want him dead, do you not?"

I do, indeed I do; but my daughter's laughter continues to sound in my ears, guileless and carefree like her very childhood, which I want to protect with all my heart—which I am trying to protect, in truth, by doing this.

But what if this destroys her childhood, their childhood, instead?

Would they even understand I am doing this for them?

Would they still love me?

Anxiety tightens my throat.

"Perhaps not all at once?" I mumble.

"Once you decide to cut off a dog's tail, you don't hack it away chunk by chunk," the witch notes with disapproval. "Moreover, my rheumatism is starting to act up."

"Whatever happened to letting her make her own choices?" the fairy godmother cries. And immediately they are squabbling again. All at once I am starting to slide toward panic. I close my ears to their bickering, and next I close my eyes—and, with a feeling much like stepping off a roof, toss a bunch of hairs into the cauldron, without counting, without thinking.

Then, my heart pounding, I open my eyes to see what I have done.

Five or six strands are spiraling down into the potion.

Less than half are now left in the palm of my hand.

The Beginning of the Middle

Time had a mysterious habit of flowing faster the fewer events occupied it. The palace shone blue on summer mornings and glinted white on snowy afternoons. She turned twenty-six. Princess Angelina turned three. Prince Roland took frequent trips. She gained some weight, made preserves, presided over mouse polkas on her fireplace rug. Life was peaceful, pleasant, and predictable. On the occasion of her twenty-seventh birthday, Angie gave her a charming present: a tiny ballroom shoe that the child had painstakingly, if rather unevenly, carved out of pink soap. She ran to the west wing, to Prince Roland's quarters, to show him, only to be told that he had departed on a mission to a nearby kingdom and was not expected back for several days. She stood before the closed door to his study, feeling the unaccustomed sting of disappointment, chewing on her lip. Then she clapped her hands in delight—she knew what she would do. She would give in to the marvelous spontaneity of this day.

She would surprise her husband.

And so, she ordered a carriage, kissed Angie good-bye, and, gently cradling the child's soap carving in her hands, left for the neighboring kingdom, with just one aged groom minding the horses and only her trusty Brie and Nibbles in attendance. *(These mice were cousins in the next generation. Brie the Third was much fussier than her mother, always anxious about everyone's health, constantly nagging Nibbles to wear warm scarves and beware stealthy drafts. Brie was badly frightened at the prospect of leaving the palace, but Nibbles magnanimously promised to protect her. He thought her infantile and helpless, and saw himself as a fierce, even heroic, mouse; and indeed, his squeak did sound much like the roar of a lion, albeit a tiny one. Needless to say, he was thrilled to venture out into the unknown. He nurtured a secret hope that the princess might get ambushed by some ruffians along the way, and he would enter legend by rescuing her in some spectacular fashion.)*

It was a bright winter day. The road snaked from the palace gates and past the town. Beyond it, landscapes became unfamiliar. There were frozen streams to be crossed on rickety bridges, falcons swooping over snowy meadows, copses of silent trees with icy branches glittering clear and sharp in the sun. Now and then, a dazzling unicorn pranced by, or a thin needle of some solitary wizard's tower rose tall on the horizon. She sat leaning far out the window; she had forgotten to wear a hood, and her ears soon burned with the cold, yet she did not heed Brie's admonitions to draw the curtains closed but looked and looked, drinking everything in with something much like greed—for it suddenly came to her that she had never traveled anywhere, anywhere at all. By the time the old groom guided the horses through another town, up another hill, to the gates of another palace, she was in a state of childlike excitement.

When she was announced, there appeared to be some confusion as to the prince's whereabouts, and she, in turn, was surprised to discover that this was the domain of the Duke von Lieber, the jocular nobleman who had paid them a visit some seasons before. The duke himself was away on a weeklong hunt, she was informed by the pomaded butler with a measured gait who showed her in, but the duchess would be overjoyed to see her imminently, or almost imminently, once Her Grace arose from her midday rest. Alone she sat in the reception chamber (Brie and Nibbles had gone off to explore the kitchens) and smiled, imagining with what delight the prince would greet her. The butler brought her a cup of weak tea with too much sugar in it; once the man's departing steps faded away, there were no sounds save for the ticking of a clock in the corner. The thrill of the ride through the brilliant countryside was still making her blood run faster. And as the minute hand crawled to mark another quarter of a drowsy afternoon hour, she did something out of character: she set down her empty cup, and rose, and walked out of the room, mischievous laughter bubbling up inside her.

No clear goal in mind, she followed a corridor, went through a double door, crossed a hall, passed under an arch, climbed some stairs, turned some corners. She soon discovered this palace to be quite unlike her own—its spaces darker, its air warmer, its furnishings soft and opulent, its lines lithe and sinuous, its colors lush, jewel bright, emerald and crimson and midnight blue—so different from the light-filled, pastel-tinted geometry of the clean, cool, clear expanses to which she herself was accustomed. In a heavily curtained chamber on the second floor, she came upon a low table with curvaceous candelabra twinkling at either end and the remains of an interrupted meal. Her silent laughter died away as she picked up a peach with an imprint of small, perfect teeth in one downy side, trailed her finger along the rim of a goblet, one of two, filled with ruby-red wine. In the next room, dimmer still, velvet pillows lay scattered on the floor, a lyre leaned against the wall, and in a shadowed niche, a cage gleamed dully.

At her approach, the cage exploded with screams.

She clutched at her heart to keep it from leaping away and blinked at the large green bird with eyes of molten amber. The bird was screaming still when a door flew open in the upholstered wall, and Prince Roland strode in. She had just the time to notice that his hair was disheveled and the top two or three buttons of his shirt were undone, when he spoke, and everything else was driven from her mind.

"You! What are *you* doing here?"

She had heard plenty of shouting in her youth, but no one had ever addressed her with such venom. Stunned, she stared at him. His eyes had gone dark, his face was rigid. He looked like someone else, someone she did not know. She pressed her hands to her mouth, and turned, and fled, pursued by the bird's strident screaming; and it seemed as if the screams had words in them, some words meant just for her.

She ran—ran through chambers of startled maids, chambers of nasty statues, chambers of stalking cats, until she found herself in a room more frightful than the rest, a badly lit, cavernous place deceptive with the quivering of candles. The air here hung stuffy with some musky perfume, and a monstrous bed stood drowning under storm-tossed waves of scarlet silk. The bed—the bed was horrible, the bed was obscene—and oh, was it possible that someone was hiding under the sheets, breathing, stirring, *giggling*?

For one lost minute, she felt that she herself might be asleep, she herself might be dreaming, for nothing was what it was, nothing was what it seemed to be. She flew away again, a soundless cry frozen in her throat, her mind in turmoil, down long carpeted corridors, past numbered doors, and still the nightmare went on, and sudden rips ran through the fabric of things all around her, revealing snatches of dangerous half-truths beneath, and she almost lost all hope of ever finding her way out, when an unexpected light grew before her, and there was the yawning O of the concierge's mouth, and bellboys hurtling out of her way, and the revolving lobby doors—and at last she was outside.

She scrambled into the carriage, repeating, "Go, go, go!" to the old groom, who rushed to put out his cigarette and groped for the keys, raised eyebrows all but vanishing in the nest of white hair. She expected the prince to burst out of doors after her then, to chase her limousine down the street—yet he did not. She lowered the curtain on her window and sat staring straight ahead with dry, unseeing eyes. It was not until the last gas station on the outskirts had remained behind that she realized she had forgotten Brie and Nibbles in that terrible place. At that moment, they seemed to her the only true friends, the only loyal souls, the only ties she had to anything familiar. She thought of a dozen sleek cats she had glimpsed prowling through scented shadows, and had no choice but to order the groom to turn around. As the carriage bounced back over the cobblestones, she remembered her actual reason for coming here and, with a sickened start, unclenched her tense, sweaty hands, only to find her daughter's darling soap slipper half melted, deformed out of all recognition. She pressed it to her heart and cried, heavy with humiliation, all the way back to the palace.

Prince Roland, fully buttoned now, was standing outside. He watched her as she went in, waited stony-faced while she explained about the mice to the confused butler. It took a long, a very long, time to find Brie and Nibbles. *(The reason for the delay was simple, if rather unfortunate: in the kitchen of the von Liebers' palace, Nibbles had been eaten by a cat. Brie had not wanted to go to the kitchen at all, for she had a queasy feeling in her tummy, but he mocked her for her cowardice with such booming laughter that she ended by gathering her tremulous tail in her paws and creeping after him. Once there, Nibbles made an obnoxious racket, clanging lids on the pots, shouting out the contents of the pantry, boasting that his nose would lead him to the tastiest cheese in the icebox, clowning for all he was worth, when out leapt an enormous beast with burning orange eyes and gobbled him up, just like that, before anyone could finish saying "Parmesan." In fact, everything happened so fast that there was no possible way to ascertain whether or not Nibbles had died a hero, although it might have seemed to Brie that, in the split second before the murderous jaws gaped open, Nibbles had turned sickly gray and attempted to hide behind her. She had no time to think about it, however, busy as she was bashing the monster on the mouth with a ladling spoon. The cat, momentarily taken aback by Brie's ferocity, recovered quickly and was readying itself for another jump when the entire kitchen exploded in an ear-splitting commotion. A hundred roaring mice poured out of every crack and crevice and attacked the beast, prodding its sides with forks, lobbing rinds of moldy cheese at its head, poking its paws with toothpicks, until it howled and bolted in a malodorous blur of rotten vegetables.*

Brie, gasping for breath, lowered the ladle and saw herself surrounded by creatures wild in appearance, ragged and grim, some missing ears or tails, many sporting horned helmets of crude leather.

"But, but," she stammered, "but you're all girls!"

"Women," the mouse who had led the charge corrected sternly. "Our men were all eaten by foul beasts a long time ago, because men are weak and slow. I am General Gertrude, the leader of my pack. We call ourselves Valkyries. We run free and fight evil whenever we find it. We saw you in battle, and we deem you worthy. Join us, sister."

And the timid Brie, who feared drafts and dust bunnies, looked in wonder from one strong, lean face to another—looked especially long into the bright eyes of a tall warrior with a jaunty red sash around her waist who stood shoulder to shoulder with Gertrude—and felt something equally strong and bright respond in her own breast, and saw another kind of life stretch before her, a purposeful, exhilarating life. Then a faint echo carried the princess's plaintive calls to her ears: "Brie, Nibbles! Brie, Nibbles, where aaare you?"—and her heart broke twice over, for her poor cousin and for the princess's imminent grief. She had to go back.

She explained her predicament to the Valkyries, thanked them for saving her life, and, feeling quite small once again, began the never-ending trudge to the door. On the threshold, a firm paw held her back, and she found herself meeting the bright, steady gaze of the mouse with the red sash.

"*General Gertrude has given me leave to come with you,*" *said the mouse.* "*I will pretend to be Nibbles, to keep your princess happy.*"

"*But . . . but you too are a girl!*" *Brie cried weakly, overwhelmed by amazement, anxiety, and relief all at once.*

"*A woman,*" *the mouse replied with some severity, then added, in a gentler tone, "And would your princess know the difference?*""

And so it was settled, and Captain Brunhilda left her Sash of Blood Honor behind and became Nibbles the Fourth in the royal palace. And in truth, she had no choice in the matter, for, the instant she had beheld tiny Brie fearlessly walloping the duchess's meanest cat squarely on the nose with the ladle three times Brie's size, she knew her own heart forfeited forever. Of course, it would take time and delicate persuasion before Brie herself shared Brunhilda's certainties, but after a few particularly chilly nights when the fire in the princess's bedroom died early and it seemed only natural to huddle closer for warmth, Brie would understand that everything she had learned in the course of her hitherto conventional mouse existence was merely one possible way of going about life, and that, moreover, they could always adopt. And from then on, Brie the Third and Nibbles the Fourth would live happily ever after. Their furry bliss, however, was still some weeks away when the princess picked them off the floor in the duchess's kitchen and, silent tears streaming down her face, slipped them inside the pocket of her traveling cloak, where Brie, thrust into immediate proximity to Brunhilda's bristly coat, started to tremble, as she had not trembled in the face of death an hour before.)

With her best friends recovered, the princess wiped her tears and walked stiffly to the carriage. The prince followed her, saying nothing. They did not speak all the way back to their palace, and when they arrived, she left the carriage without looking at him and went straight to bed. The next morning, the wintry sun shone into the bedroom and Prince Roland bounded in, smiling hugely, bearing a tray of oranges. She still had not risen, in spite of the late hour; she had slept poorly, cried much, and was suffering from a headache. He pounced onto her bed, her starched, white, modest, girlish bed (nothing like that other bed, rumpled and red, candlelit and musty, wanton and savage), and sang out: "And how is my beautiful little princess today? Tired from yesterday's ride? It was so sweet of you to come. I'm sorry if I wasn't quite myself. I was traveling to King Julius's court, you see, when I was overtaken by some passing sickness, and the Duke von Lieber's servants, who happened nearby, were kind enough to take me in. Of course, the duke and the duchess themselves were away on a hunt, but their physician saw to my comfort. When you arrived, and so unexpectedly, I was running a fever and hardly knew what I was doing or saying. If I seemed out of sorts and offended you, I am so very sorry. It was a joy to see you, my love. It always is."

She rose on one elbow and looked at him. His beauty was breathtaking as ever, his teeth blinding, his blue eyes clear; dimples appeared and disappeared in the smooth planes of his cheeks.

"But the butler said," she began. "The butler said the duchess would see me."

"No, my love, you misunderstood. Have an orange. Wait, let me peel it for you."

And she took the orange, and tried to think, but her temples throbbed, and she did grow uncertain, for the butler had indeed mumbled and she had been distracted, and in any case, fairy-tale princes never lied. The orange was sweet. Prince Roland was sweet. Their life was surely sweet. And look, there were cavorting pink-cheeked cupids painted on her ceiling and tiny blue flowers embroidered on her snowy eiderdown, and the sun slanted joyfully through her lacy blue curtains, and things were now firmly back in their places, just where they had always been. Her love for the prince was all abating bewilderment and deepening relief. While she ate the orange, he played with her golden ringlets, and the tips of his fingers smelled of sweet juice.

By the time he left, she was smiling again, if a bit wanly.

.   .   .

"'Overtaken by some passing sickness'!" the witch snorts. "Doesn't matter what they actually tell you or how plausible it is, it only matters whether you are willing to believe it. And you are, and you are, and you are, until one day—snap!—you aren't. And here we are, up to our elbows in toad skins and newt eyeballs."

"Ah, don't listen to her, my darling," croons the fairy god-mother. "You were simply overexcited by that green-eyed lady's admittedly vulgar approach to interior decorating, and you for-got proper etiquette. Surely, a visiting princess must quietly await her hostess instead of barging through rooms without knocking on doors? Of course, such an embarrassing display of poor man-ners would cause some coolness between you and your husband, but that's far from tragic." She gives me one of her patient smiles. "And just between us, my heart, it pays to close your eyes to mi-nor missteps. A man is not a supermarket, you know, you can't just stroll down the aisles with a basket on your arm, picking and choosing whatever you please. Still, a spoonful of tar shouldn't ruin a barrel of honey. I see no reason to resort to murder."

I make no reply. The woman's middle-aged certainties are all of a kind, belonging to a world of nighttime cups of warm milk, herbal remedies for both toothaches and heartaches, sensible commonplaces, and reduced passions, and I am already too old and still too young to believe in such placid wisdom.

"Not altogether romantic of you, now, is it," the witch says mildly as she stirs the brew, "suggesting that poor put-upon wives ignore their spouses' transgressions with such vigor, all in the name of pragmatism and material comfort?"

"In the name of peace and love," the fairy godmother says firmly.

"Is it, though? Is it, really?" The witch shrugs. "Well, you are the resident expert on love around here, I just clean up the mess afterward. Still, from where I stand, it seems much more pleasant to be eating éclairs amidst silk cushions in some lovely little palace than to be getting soaked at a crossroads. It pays to be oblivious, wouldn't you agree, for as long as you can take it—or should I say, fake it?"

"I don't see what you're implying here," the fairy godmother blusters.

I do, though, and my breath hitches with a sudden sense of unease.

"Please." My voice breaks a little. "Please. Can we just get on with this?"

The surface of the potion has continued to flicker all the while.

When we look down, it is already spring in another year.

The Middle of the Middle

In her twenty-ninth year, she began to have unsettling dreams, of herself drifting lost—and, shockingly, naked—through dark, scented places where no walls ran straight, no angles were right, but everything curved and wavered and candles quivered and peaches dripped and cats streaked softly past her bare calves. When she awoke, her rib cage heaved as if something untamed were beating against it from the inside, and there was a hot heaviness somewhere at her core, at the bottom of her stomach, perhaps, that she did not understand and did not like. On such mornings, she threw on her dress, ran to the nursery, and, relieving Nanny Nanny (who was shedding just then and welcomed rest), drew princesses and built cardboard castles with Angie, then, after putting her down for a nap, sat by her bed and told her about the ball, about the slipper, hurrying just ahead of the child's questions in her scramble to reach the happy ending, again and again.

"And they danced together all night," she would say in a rush, "until the clock began to strike midnight. Then she fled as fast as she could, and in her haste lost one glass slipper on the stairs. And the prince declared that he would marry the girl whom it fit. And all the girls in the kingdom tried it on, but it fit no one, until the courier came with it to our house. My ugly stepsisters did their best to squeeze their big, ugly feet into it, but they failed. And then the courier got down on one knee and put the slipper on my foot, and of course it fit perfectly. They took me to the palace, and dressed me in beautiful clothes, and held the royal wedding, and then the prince and I lived happily ever after, while the stepsisters got just what they deserved. Gloria, the older one, never married at all and became a bitter spinster, while Melissa married someone so poor she now spends all her time scrubbing floors and washing dishes!"

But as she told the story over and over, it grew leached of inner meaning, as a word might when one repeated it too often, and she started to find it oddly lacking. What if the slipper *had* fit someone else—would the prince have married the other girl instead, would he have even known the difference? Was she, in fact, all that different from every other maiden with a sweet singing voice and a patient disposition? What exactly had he liked about her at the ball—the way she waltzed, the cut of her bodice, the childlike size of her feet? Why hadn't they asked each other's names, or, failing that, favorite colors at least, or favorite ice cream flavors? Also, and most disconcertingly, why did the recollection of the young courier kneeling before her—the brief pressure of his hand upon her bare instep as he had helped guide it inside the slipper, the golden brown of his gaze that had lingered one moment too long on her lips, the soft burr of his accent (like her, he had come from a distant land as a child)—why did it make her feel so profoundly unsettled?

It was at this point in her ruminations that she rose and, blushing, went to see her husband. They had not been alone in quite some time. The guard at Prince Roland's door muttered apologies while trying to bar her way into the study, but she distracted him with her most radiant smile, ducked under his elbow, and pushed the door open. The prince sat behind his massive oak desk, his elegant fingers steepled, his eyes closed, a thoughtful look on his face, while one of the Singing Maids—they only ever employed singing maids in the palace—appeared to be crawling in search of something underneath the desk, her ample uniformed rump protruding beyond the desk's carved phoenixes and vines, undulating in some hurried rhythm.

At the slamming of the door, Prince Roland's eyes flew open, his eyebrows flew up, and he said, his usually smooth voice rather husky: "Esmeralda, you may stop looking for that thumbtack now, my wife is here."

She heard a choked exclamation, a rustling of clothes, and presently Esmeralda emerged from under the desk, a bit rumpled and red-cheeked, her mouth slack, her small black eyes running about her face like startled beetles. She gave the maid a polite nod, then, once the door closed behind the woman, went and sat in Prince Roland's lap, entwining her arms about his neck.

"I love you," she said. "Do you love me?"

Without replying, he pulled her closer with a jerk. She gasped. His gaze seemed both intent and unfocused, and before she quite knew what was happening, his lips were devouring her neck. And then that persistent warm, heavy feeling somewhere at her core flared up, and everything grew urgent and new and vastly surprising, and she was lost in the fumbling tangle of skirts, the helpless, eager need to undo his britches (which had somehow proved already undone—but no matter), the awkward struggle to accommodate their arms, their legs, their rocking to the confines of the chair, to the shamelessness of the afternoon light flooding the windows, all of it so rushed, so vital, so unlike the few (so very few) nighttime, chaste, brief, sweet, embarrassed, blanketed, invisible, horizontal couplings of their first year of marriage (and none at all since she had found herself with Angie—which she had always assumed to be the proper way of these things—so why now, why this?—but no matter, no matter) . . . A button popped, the chair groaned, he groaned, she felt something unexpected rising in her, something overwhelming, akin to a powerful command to close her eyes and fall backward, trusting some great new sensation to

break her fall—a sensation so unfamiliar, so freeing, so impera-
tive as to be almost frightening. But just as it had started without
warning, so now, without warning, it was over, everything was
over, and, still poised on the brink of that fall into the unknown
that she had not taken, that she sensed she would never take now,
she felt something inside her shifting, tilting, growing unhinged
and unmoored.

He tipped her off without ceremony, adjusted his clothes. His
eyes came into focus and were absent. Hurriedly she dropped her
skirts to the ground, to cover her shame—and, to her terror, dis-
solved into sobs.

"Please," he said, frowning. "I must work now. What is it?"

"It's nothing," she said, and pulled herself together, then added
in a small voice, "I love you, Roland."

"I love you, too." There was a barely perceptible pause. "My
dear."

He began sifting through papers on his desk.

She fled the room.

In later months, as she lay sleepless, stroking the dome of her
belly where the baby was kicking, she found herself haunted by
that anonymous endearment, by that pause in his words. And
since she did not wish to give in to her unease, she began telling
tales to the baby growing inside her, whispering familiar old stories into the mound of taut flesh. Yet now the comfort fare of the
miller's son, and the miller's daughter, and the beggar girl all
marrying their princesses and princes failed to soothe her, even if
it still made her feel just as if she were settling down to knitting in
her favorite armchair. And her unease grew, until one night, as
she stood by the window, watching a pale moon rise above the
black park, listening to the distant wail of a lonely siren, she realized that, quite simply, she no longer wanted to do any knitting in
any armchairs.

What she wanted was to leave on a journey through mysterious twilit woods full of uncanny creatures and unexpected encounters.

And so, she began to invent.

She invented a world unlike anything she had ever known, anything she had ever heard of. She was used to small villages and bustling market towns where everyone greeted everyone else by name, so she invented an improbable city—a city so immense that all the passersby were strangers to one another and every chance "Good morning" could become the beginning of an exhilarating adventure. She was used to frivolously ornamental palaces that looked like baroque wedding cakes overflowing with frills, curls, and lace, so she imagined the lines of her city to be sleek and simple, all glass and metal. She was used to rigid fairyland rules dictating every move and every outcome, so she made life in the outlandish world of her fancy fantastical and unpredictable, for in that world there existed true magic—the magic of choice.

The ease of her invention took her by surprise: it was almost as if she were describing a place she had seen in some intense, vivid dream.

"Once upon a time," she would tell her belly, "there lived a man who had a wife and a daughter . . . But no, that's not the right beginning, it's not about the man at all. Let me start again. Once upon a time, there lived a little girl whose parents loved her, and she was happy until her mother got sick and died. Then she grew so sad that her father decided to take her somewhere far, far away from all the sadness. They climbed onto a magic silver bird, flew across the ocean, and came to a great city, and she soon knew it for the most magnificent city in the world. Astonishing things happened there day and night—and nights were as bright and full as days, for the city never slept and it never grew dark. Enchanted lights floated above pavements, palaces stretched a hundred blazing stories into the sky, the streets were full of shiny carriages that moved without horses. Thousands of wizards who knew the secrets of the universe and could turn paper into gold and dirt into diamonds jostled one another on the sidewalks, leopards and monkeys cavorted in a great menagerie in the city's wooded heart, pictures of beautiful princesses flashed on and off above broad squares, and there were treasures to look at everywhere you turned—necklaces and shoes and toys and roses and oh, so many things, dogs, jugglers, pigeons, churches, bridges, balloons, guitar players, parks, guardsmen, marching bands, pretzels, stone lions, fortune-tellers, people laughing, people crying, people fighting, people kissing, people *living*."

The girl's father found work doing handyman's jobs in an elegant inn. The widow who ran the inn smiled at him whenever she met him in the hallways, and after a while he and the woman married. But he was not happy, for the glitter of the city was making him anxious, and one day his heart gave up and stopped beating, just like that.

And so the little girl was left all alone in the world, with no one but her stepmother to take care of her. And the stepmother was bossy, and the stepsisters uncaring, and when she turned fourteen, they made her clean after the guests who stayed in the inn. Morning and evening, she carried her bucket and broom down long corridors, knocking on doors and calling "Maid service," entering to change stained sheets, mop bathroom floors, wipe steamed-up mirrors. She did not mind the work, but she longed to go outside, into the streets, where the magic of life was sweeping through without cease. Sometimes she would press her nose to a window and, from the height of the third, sixth, tenth floor, spy on the world below. One spring, one of those enchanted pictures, larger than life, was always blinking on and off on a building across the way, and she watched it light up, over and over, in childlike wonder. It showed a lovely woman in a flowing white dress who stood in a half swoon, her back arched, her eyes half closed, her swanlike neck exposed, while a gorgeous man all in black was bending over her, swirling some mysterious potion from a glowing blue bottle into a glass he was holding up to her half-open lips. There was something about the expression on the woman's face, the slackening of the woman's mouth, that made the girl catch her breath every time the picture flashed up. The woman seemed to belong to some other world—a world out of reach for mere mortals, a hidden, thrilling world of beauty and happiness.

One day, she promised herself, she, too, would live there.

And in time, the girl in these secret predawn stories did grow up and go to a dance and have a wedding, just like the girl in the oft-told romance Angie demanded now at every bedtime; but the sequence of these events was much less certain, the girl had decisions to make, and every tale was different in some small, subtle way that yet made her feel more alive in the telling. In none of these stories was there a fairy godmother who popped out of nowhere, nearly stabbed her in the eye with a wand, and trapped her in an insipid blue banality shaped like an upside-down cupcake. No, she had saved what modest wages she had received for helping out in the hotel—the stepmother was stern but fair—then went to a splendid shop that stretched over several lustrous floors and there found a beautiful dress all her own. In some versions, the dress was black, long, and elegant and clung to her hips just so, and in others, yellow, short, and sassy, shot through with sparkle. And when she tried it on in the bathroom she shared with her stepsisters (who were, incidentally, selfish as all teenage sisters were wont to be, but hardly the insensitive monsters of the familiar story), she loved the girl who looked back at her from the mirror, for the girl's lips were those of a woman and the girl's eyes shone with a great desire to live.

The dance was an annual gala held in the hotel ballroom, and she sneaked in without an invitation, using her knowledge of service corridors. Unlike the other ball, this one had many princes, and she chose the one she liked best. She chose him before he chose her, and not because he was rich or desired by all but because she liked the boyish shyness of his golden-brown gaze, the soft cadence of his accent, the warmth of his hand when it found its way into the small of her back. But of course, the man she picked would change with each retelling, too, just like the dress. Sometimes he would be blue-eyed, suave, and dazzling, and other times mysterious, silent, and dark. In all the versions, though, she fell in love without a doubt, and her love was like the home she had always dreamed of having, warm and thrilling and filled with shared understanding—and reflected, just as deep and certain, in her beloved's brown, or green, or cornflower-blue eyes.

The girl in these stories, needless to say, did not go about losing her footwear like some silly strumpet, nor did she need to be recovered like some misplaced piece of luggage. They had a proper courtship that spanned days, weeks, months—not mere hours. They dined on spicy fare in the imaginary city's ethnic restaurants. They went to the opera, where their souls soared in unison with the music. They took long drives through the countryside, and she laughed when falling leaves brushed her face. She knew the prince's name. She met the prince's family. She approved of the prince's hobbies and forgave him his foibles, whatever they might have been. She was asked whether she wanted to be married, and she chose to say yes.

These stories, in short, were nothing like the familiar story, and this girl was nothing like the familiar girl: this girl was special. The only thing, perhaps, that the two had in common was the presence of the two mouse friends, Brie and Nibbles— although in this new world the girl had purchased them, with her own money, at a neighborhood pet store.

(There was, as it happened, great unrest among the mice during this time. Brie the Third and her companion, Nibbles the Fourth—formerly Cap-

tain Brunhilda—had adopted twin mouselings, a boy and a girl, who had been orphaned in the kitchen when the fattest of the cooks had slipped on a lemon rind and landed with her voluminous backside on top of their hapless mother. To the adopted children, in due course, passed the mantle of the Royal Companions and the titles of Brie the Fourth and Nibbles the Fifth. Young Nibbles settled into his new life of chocolate delights and musical pastimes with perfect ease, but young Brie soon began to chafe against the silky restraints of her role; having been raised by Brunhilda with a strong sense of civic duty, she bridled at having to dance polkas to the princess's listless clapping and thought her passionately serious nature better suited to combatting poverty among the recently migrated field mice.

She was not alone in considering herself unfit for her position. Among the direct descendants of the original Brie and Nibbles, there arose a mouse with an uncommonly long tail, by the name of Maximilian, who believed that the exalted life of mouse royalty belonged to him and his by sacred birthright. His great-great-great-grandparents, he told anyone who would listen, had been Chosen by the Higher Power and the distinction should never have been allowed to pass out of the family, first to a foreign upstart with unnatural proclivities and later to some kitchen riffraff whose genealogy could not even be traced beyond one threadbare generation. Having gathered a number of like-minded followers about him, he led an efficient nighttime raid, which became known in the Murine Historical Annals as the Five-Minute Mantelpiece Coup. Upon waking one morning and finding herself and her twin brother trussed up and surrounded by an agitated mob led by Maximilian, who wielded a thumbtack, Brie was frankly relieved, and promptly abdicated in order to devote the rest of her life to the pursuit of social justice among the underprivileged inhabitants of the palace sewers.

Nibbles, however, had grown enamored of his goosedown pillows and breakfast sweets, and, too, at this sudden encounter with violence, the more militant lessons of his adoptive mother Brunhilda stirred in his breast. He determined to offer resistance. "Blood is a mere accident of birth," he preached from inside the pumpkin in which he had been imprisoned. "It is merit alone that should be rewarded—and no one dances the mouse polka better than I!"

Two of the mice set to guard him were swayed by his eloquence, helped him escape, and became his Right-Paw and Left-Paw Captains in the eventual civil war of the Mouse House against the usurpers Nibbles the Sixth, formerly Maximilian, and Brie the Fifth, formerly Lady Bruschetta, Maximilian's sister and concubine. In the end, the Blood Faction prevailed, albeit after many violent battles and regrettable casualties. Unluckily, Maximilian himself perished of his wounds in the final skirmish, and it was his son who assumed the title of Nibbles the Seventh to rule with his mother (and aunt) by his side. Maddened by their loss, the victors showed no mercy to the defeated and had the headless body of their enemy, the unfortunate Nibbles the Fifth, flung into the sewers. A hushed crowd of sorrowful rats brought it before their beloved Sister Charity, formerly Brie the Fourth. Heads bowed, they stood around her in the underground dimness, as she cradled what was left of her twin brother and lamented the senselessness and cruelty of the world.

"Oh, my dear heart," she cried, her fur matted with blood and tears, "do you see where your foolishness has gotten you? And all for what—the love of chocolates and a few absentminded pats from a frivolous, moody princess who can't tell any of us apart and treats us like wind-up toys, just because we are little? I do not blame Maximilian—like my poor brother, he, too, was a misguided fool, and he paid for his own mistakes dearly. No, I blame her, I blame her!"

She moved her eyes along the wall of silent mourners, her piercing gaze burning into them with unmouselike fire. When she spoke again, her tears had dried and her voice was a low, fierce chant: "My brother's blood is on her hands. All of our blood is on her hands. And I curse her, I curse her, I curse her. As long as she walks the places turned red with the spilling of our lives, she will never know a day of peace but will be gnawed by discontent, fear, and sadness, just as we gnaw our daily bread. I bind her to her misery by the truth in our blood.")

The princess hoped that her unborn child would be a girl who might benefit from being thus imbued, while still in the womb, with brave examples of free and unconstrained living. Yet when the child was born, it was a boy. They named him Roland, after his father the prince. Since the old king, too, was Roland, as the king's father, grandfather, and great-grandfather had been before him, it made her son Roland the Sixth. She felt secretly disappointed, even a little betrayed, as if all her marvelous inventions had been wasted—more, as if she had made some vast, courageous effort to do something different and it had been in vain.

And seemingly out of nowhere, despair descended upon her.

"'An insipid blue cupcake,'" the fairy godmother quotes, her voice frosty. She has seated herself in an ample leather armchair she has summoned out of thin air and is brushing invisible specks off her cloak. "I never took you for an ungrateful kind."

"As much as I hate to admit it, I agree with the busybody here," the witch says as she stirs the potion. "Also, I must tell you, it's not very reasonable, expecting the prince to remain eternally enticed by you no matter what. Because, let's face it, you did not exactly overwhelm him with personal accomplishments or depths. Preserves and polkas, did you say?"

"But." My eyes are stung with unexpected tears. I blink them back, quickly. "But that is what princesses are supposed to do!"

"Is that so? Well, I don't claim to be an authority on princesses. All the same, it might have done you some good to develop a real interest or two along the way. You could have studied astronomy. Just for instance."

"Or practiced watercolors," the fairy godmother chimes in suddenly.

"Or become a rock climber," says the witch after a beat.

"Or founded a charity that rescued homeless dogs," adds the fairy with a sniff.

"Or learned another language."

"Or discovered a new species of butterfly."

"Or played in a band."

The witch is ticking off the items on her fingers now, and they are nodding at each other.

"Or opened a bakery."

"Or gone to law school."

"Or taken piano lessons."

"Or gotten involved in local politics."

"Or volunteered at a school."

"Or—"

"Stop!" I cry. "Stop! I—"

And then I, too, fall silent. The realization that neither of them seems to like me all that much is surprisingly painful, and I want to justify myself somehow—but I do not know what to say. When I try to catch their eyes, neither woman will look at me. Everything is very still around me. The winds have long since abandoned the crossroads. The grasses are not moving in the fields, the flames under the cauldron have become coals. The world seems perfectly flat and gray, all dust and weeds.

"Well, like I say, you get out what you put in," the witch concludes dryly. "Let's move along, then, shall we."

"By all means," the fairy godmother says. "None of us are getting any younger, and some of us have real things to get back to. Like clients who appreciate what we do."

Feeling deeply ashamed, I return my gaze to the cauldron, in whose turmoil another stretch of time has already passed.

The End of the Middle's Middle

One morning, as she lay on the sofa in her godmother's visiting chamber, her tea grown cold, she drew a breath and made a shocking confession.

"I'm not very happy, Fairy Godmother."

The matronly woman looked up from her knitting, her bulging eyes amplified even more by the rainbow-colored butterfly-framed glasses.

"Don't be silly, my dear. 'And they lived happily ever after,' remember? The story is very clear on that point. Another cup of tea?"

She shook her head. "I know I *should* be happy. I've done everything required, I've followed all the rules. Only I'm often sad, and the prince never seems to be there, and sometimes . . . sometimes I even wonder . . ."

"Yes?" The fairy godmother stared without blinking, one knitting needle poised like a pen in her rosy hand.

"It's . . . hard to explain."

"Do try, my dear. Verbalizing your feelings helps with tension reduction."

"Oh." She crumbled a scone into dust on her plate. "Well, sometimes I wonder if this story hasn't . . . hasn't gone *wrong* somehow. Because sometimes I almost feel like I don't belong in it. Like maybe I'd be happier in some other story—even in some other world, a really *different* world, if only I could figure out how to get to it . . ."

Her anxious voice trailed off.

The fairy godmother sighed.

"My dear child. There is no other world. There is just this world. And in this world, I assure you, stories never go wrong. All of us get exactly what we deserve. Villains have their punishments, heroes win their princesses, and if your story has a happy ending, then it is simply your matrimonial duty to be happy." She paused to ponder. "Still, you know, stories don't always run in a straight line. There could be something you're overlooking, some twist to the plot. Of course, all twists are properly catalogued in the royal library. I'm afraid our hour is up now, but I want you to read up on fairy tales this week, and we'll continue at our next session. As always, Tuesday at eleven. Let me jot it down for you, you've been a bit forgetful lately."

"Yes, Fairy Godmother," she said meekly as she accepted the appointment card.

That very afternoon, she walked to the palace library.

The library was a light-filled room with cream-colored armchairs, cream-colored curtains, and four slim white bookcases, one along each wall, with carved daisies on the sides and books neatly arranged behind glass; it was most often used for midmorning tea parties. Professor Dagobert, the scholarly dwarf librarian, grumbled, as he showed her in, about the lack of dark wood paneling, blackened fireplaces, illegible manuscripts, and overall air of arcane knowledge and insomnia. He found the gilded compendium she required, explained how to use the index, and left her perched on an ottoman next to a small display cabinet whose shelves contained a modest collection of magical treasures, with a tiny crystal shoe in the place of honor.

Resolutely not looking at the shoe, she moved her finger down the columns of words, whispering under her breath: "Apples, as emblems of patriarchy. Apples, golden delicious. Apples, as weapons of destruction. Beasts, as allegories. Beasts, as bridegrooms (see under 'Frogs,' 'Stags,' 'Swans,' 'Swine, abusive,' 'Swine, adulterous,' 'Swine, alcoholic,' 'Swine, lying,' 'Swine, not pulling their weight around the house,' 'Swine, unemployed,' 'Wolves'). Children, desired (see also 'Children, unwanted,' 'Motherhood, ambiguous,' 'Stew recipes'). Children, grown up into monsters (see under 'Parenting, poor'). Children, royal, as ciphers with no distinguishing characteristics, used to further the plot . . ."

For a while, it was quite slow going; but when she came to "Spells, false brides," she read, with growing excitement, the entry on lawful wives being deprived of—or rather, this still being the land of deserved conclusions, temporarily diverted from—their happy endings mid-story, by scheming, envious women who plotted to marry the husbands after plunging the wives into slumber, rendering them mute, turning them into fowls or fawns, and otherwise befuddling and bewitching them in such a way that their normally faithful princes became blind to their charms and virtues. She was not by nature mistrustful, but something about this malevolent notion sent shivers of potential revelations through her mind, and she went to bed that night harboring a grave suspicion.

Was it possible that she was under some sort of spell? Could that be the reason for her feeling of *wrongness*—and for the deepening chill between her and the prince?

When, after much tossing and turning, she fell asleep at last, she was trapped in her old recurring dream of dim, scented places where she wandered as before, lost and naked, only this time, a giant green bird with eyes of burning amber flew after her, shrieking, "You fool, you fool, you fool!" It was barely light when she bolted upright in bed, wide awake, reeling. She thought back to

that afternoon in the reception chamber of the Duchess von Lieber: the ticking clock, the muttering butler, the tray tremulous in
his gloved hands as he had pressed a cup of tea upon her. She had
drunk the sweet, watery offering to its last drop, courteous guest
that she had been. She remembered, too, her deepening sense of
confusion as she had dashed through the low-ceilinged maze
filled with luscious fruit, ruby-colored potions, and slinking cats
fit to be some wicked witch's familiars—and at the end of the
maze, Prince Roland looking at her with cold eyes, the eyes of a
stranger.

Truth struck her like a thunderbolt.

The tea—the tea had not been tea.

She had been most cruelly poisoned.

Minutes later, she tossed on some clothes and was pelting
down hallways, alarming teapots on their brisk breakfast errands,
causing havoc among a clump of gossiping maids who squealed
and scattered at her passage. "Your Highness, your slippers don't
match!" one of them cried, and the babble of scandalized voices
followed her all the way to the fairy godmother's door, upon
which she proceeded to bang in the most unladylike manner.

"Fairy Godmother! Fairy Godmother, I must speak to you!"

There was a moment of startled silence on the other side, before a muffled reply reached her: "Not now, my child, I have a
visitor."

"But I need you, I need you *now*, I'm under a spell, you have
to fix me, he won't love me if you don't!" she wailed, and, in a
move even less ladylike, flung the door open. She heard an abrupt
squawk, saw the edge of a robe (or, possibly, a mantle edged with
ermine) and the heel of a shoe (or, perhaps, a mouse-eared slipper)
disappearing into the wall through some secret passageway, and
found herself face-to-face with the fairy godmother, who looked
highly indignant, and not a little disheveled.

"Dear child, this isn't proper, there are appointment books," the fairy began, hurriedly doing up a butterfly-shaped button of her salmon-colored blouse—but she had already thrown herself onto the soft matronly bosom and wept, and the fairy godmother abandoned her scolding and started clucking.

An hour later, she walked back to her room, her pockets bulging with multicolored vials. "A pink spoonful at breakfast, for mood improvement," she whispered to herself. "A green sip before bedtime, for insomnia. A blue drop every other day, for . . . for . . . No, the blue one at breakfast, for anxiety, and the pink one . . ."

The fairy godmother had promised that the potions would work as antidotes to the perfidious spell, setting her right in a matter of weeks—months at the most. Having a list of concrete steps to follow made her feel newly hopeful. Her love for the prince became an earnest resolve to cure herself of the evil malaise until she was, once again, the wife he deserved. She obeyed her godmother's instructions with steadfast adherence, and, for a while, things did get better. Her days, true, grew a bit muffled, as though swaddled in cotton; but her nights were dream free at last, as if someone had stretched a peaceful black cloth over the nocturnal agitation of her mind. She spent her waking hours playing complacently with her children (though she now left all storytelling to Nanny Nanny, who favored simple tales of the animal kind, with foxes being cunning, chickens naive, and wolves malicious; love did not enter into them in any guise, only the most basic needs to eat and not be eaten). And whenever she saw Prince Roland at state functions, she smiled a slightly loopy smile in his direction, patiently waiting for him to notice the positive change in her nature and rekindle their romance.

Yet seasons passed, and still the prince came no closer. Her patience wavered. To speed up her cure, she began to down the potions two or three at a time, grouping them by color, or on a whim. Her days grew wobbly then and ill defined, now stretching until prolapsed, now shrinking to taut compression. Sometimes she woke up, after not being asleep, and was thrust into the midst of foggy conversations with the frowning Nanny Nanny or the Marquise de Fatouffle, who gaped at her rudely over a teacup. On one occasion, she discovered old King Roland hovering above her, in hushed consultation with the court physician, and thought she could make out, amidst their whispers, an oft-repeated phrase: "Nervous breakdown, nervous breakdown . . ." She was unbothered by it, for she had started to sense a kind of gap between herself and everything around her, not unlike the jolting sensation one got when one failed to notice stairs coming to an end and attempted to place a foot on yet another step, only to have it hit the floor with shocking abruptness—and in that gap, she would glimpse, at times, disjointed fragments of that other, imaginary, world, streets thronging with multitudes, roads honking with hurtling monsters, gilded musical boxes sliding up and down the metal spines of needle-like buildings, everything loud and bright and sharp-edged, and somehow so much more present than her actual life in the palace. Her feeling of dissociation grew, and grew, until she did not feel at all herself. One day, she drank three pink potions in rapid succession, then sat before her mirror, watching a pasty-faced, overweight woman who glared at her with hostile eyes, when it occurred to her that, quite possibly, she was *not* herself—could not be herself—for her true self, her lovely, lovable, thin, happy self, must have been spirited away by the wicked enchantress, hidden, perhaps, in some dream-spire of steel and glass—and the unlikable woman in her mirror was none other than the *evil impostor* in person.

Horrified, she cast about for ways to rid herself of the hateful creature. She stopped leaving her room altogether in an effort to keep the false wife away from the prince, hoping that the villainess would see the futility of her designs and go back whence she had come; yet the wretched woman did not budge. Next, she thought to scare her away with violence, and went about smashing teacups and pressing china shards into the tender skin of her arms and thighs; but invariably she found the pretender wife unperturbed and herself howling with pain. Desisting, she decided to starve the impostor instead, and tried to stop eating; yet always she broke down and accepted a cracker or a cluster of grapes that Brie and Nibbles pressed upon her, then felt ashamed of her weakness.

(As it happened, the descendants of Maximilian the Long-Tailed were no longer in power. The dynasty had developed an extravagant taste for luxury along with an imperious sense of entitlement. Not content with styling themselves mere Royal Companions, they had demanded to be addressed as Their Majesties and claimed an ever-growing number of prerogatives, from taxing all cheese consumption to exercising the droit du seigneur. King Nibbles pinched the backside of every passing mouse, whether nubile or old, simply to remind them all of his authority, while Queen Brie expected everyone she encountered on the daily inspections of her domains to prostrate themselves before her, and was always preceded by two pages, one of whom heralded her approach by blowing into a peapod, while the other walked backward unrolling a ribbon of crimson silk under her paws. And tyranny and oppression only worsened with time, even though rulers themselves changed rather frequently: numerous members of Maximilian's family, seduced by the heady prospects of impunity and overindulgence, vied for the throne and deposed one another with clockwork regularity, by means of varied brutality that ranged from plying siblings with poisoned truffles to pushing grandmothers off staircases, and not excluding an occasional bout of surreptitious infant strangling or a more elaborate ploy involving a dozen young cousins who were invited to a birthday party only to find themselves in a locked room with a famished cat. There had, in fact, been so many assassinations and coups that no one paid attention to the regnal numbers anymore.

Still, as long as the royal contenders kept all the murder in the family, the masses grumbled quietly; but when one of the pages tripped while unrolling the ribbon before one of the queens and stepped on her toe and she had him beheaded, the grumbling grew louder. Sewer rats were the first to voice their discontent openly, and the working kitchen mice joined them shortly. In the end, the entire indigent population rose up, led by the intrepid Provolone the One-Eyed, overthrew the tyrants, and liberated their fabled stores of chocolate.

A general democratic election to the positions of Brie and Nibbles was then held in the kitchens. Victory was carried by a landslide by a team of two brothers, Snufflebit and Snifflebit, who were young and carefree, and had won the favor of the electorate by running a hilariously improvised campaign, complete with stand-up comedy, blueberry juggling, and riding along pantry shelves on bottle caps. Grandmothers' tales had led the brothers to believe that the job would entail hours upon hours of board games, musical diversions, and much merriment, and they were eager to test their dancing skills. Soon after moving to the royal mantelpiece, however, the Mice Elect discovered, much to their dismay, that no dancing was required and that, far from being an enviable boon, the role of the Royal Companions was a grueling charity. It appeared, quite simply, that the princess was not overly intelligent and needed someone sensible to take care of her, day and night, or she might forget to eat, neglect to sleep, and have unfortunate accidents with assorted sharp objects. Less than a month into their one-year term, Snufflebit and Snifflebit grew so wan and thin that their family, alarmed, called an emergency meeting in the broom closet. The brothers were absolved of their duties, and a weekly rotation was set up among volunteers—a week, it seemed, was all it took before even the most stalwart mouse felt utterly worn-out.

As summer days cooled into fall evenings, it became harder and harder to find volunteers. Then someone remembered that in the rat-infested sewers deep below the palace, there was rumored to live an incredibly ancient seer by the name of Sister Charity, so beloved and wise that even the most murderous rat bandits grew as gentle as hairless mouselings in her saintly presence. Many argued that it was only a legend and no such mouse existed, but eventually a

*rat was found willing to show them the way to Sister Charity's abode in ex-
change for a ration of sausages, and a small, nervous delegation with Snufflebit and Snifflebit at the helm was sent down below to ask the venerable seer
for guidance.*

*They found her seated in the darkest underground chamber, telling a quiet
story to a circle of mesmerized baby rats at her feet. She looked older than the
very stone foundations around them, and in the unsteady halo of light cast by
the candle stub in Snufflebit's shaking paw, they saw that her eyes were milky
and blank, for she had gone blind in her great age. Yet when she turned to face
them, they felt that she was looking directly at them—looking directly into
their souls.*

*"I know why you've come, o mice from above the ground," she said in a
voice like a rustle of leaves, like a creaking of trees. "I see the pleading in your
hearts, and your hearts are pure. So be it. For your sakes, I declare the old debt
paid, and I release her. Let all her mistakes be her own from now on. You will
be free of your toils at the advent of winter.")*

At the advent of winter, a messenger came to the palace with
a letter from Melissa, the princess's younger stepsister, informing
her that her stepmother had died. She felt distraught at the prospect of leaving her room. On the day of the funeral, she stood in
the front row of mourners, her face buried in the fur of her collar,
her eyes hidden behind oversized sunglasses; she had drunk three
or four potions to calm down, and now her features felt as if they
were both numb and melting. Melissa, on her right, was crying openly, but Gloria held herself with her usual haughty self-
possession. It was Gloria who, her mouth hard, her back ramrod
straight, tossed the first handful of earth onto their mother's cof-
fin. Afterward, Melissa and Gloria walked off together, Gloria's
arm wrapped protectively around Melissa's heaving shoulders,
but she herself had slipped the tightening noose of sisterly embrace and trailed a few steps behind. As she stumbled through
the frozen cemetery, headstones beckoned to her, angels leered

suggestively through marble tears, and at last the path buckled beneath her feet, which she was now surprised to find liberated of shoes.

A hand grasped her arm, and there was Melissa helping her to a bench, saying, "Here, sit down for a moment. Are you feeling all right?"

"I'm fine," she replied, or tried to reply; her words had grown larger than her mouth and would not quite fit there. The world was swimming, and everything felt hot, and her stepsister was peering at her with eyes that had gone wide and solicitous.

"You don't seem well," she kept repeating. "And why are you barefoot?"

She straightened, tried to focus. They had not seen each other in almost a decade, not since the royal wedding, in fact, though she presently recalled that Melissa, who had ended up marrying the king's woodsman, had persisted in sending her holiday cards, dutifully answered by Prince Roland's scribes, as well as stork-bordered birth announcements for her numerous children, five or six by now, she was not certain exactly how many, but however many they were, she decided in a burst of resentment, Melissa had grown far too dumpy and her life was far too pathetic for her to have the right to offer any kind of sympathy, to visit any kind of judgment, to be looking at her betters with such condescending concern while living, it wouldn't surprise her, in a shoe in some backwoods with her badly washed brood, eating porridge morning, noon, and night, telling time by the crowing of a rooster, and now Melissa's eyes were once again brimming over, almost as if she were voicing all these awful yet indisputable thoughts aloud, which of course she was not, which she was almost sure she was not, until Gloria took her under both elbows with unwomanly strength and, lifting her bodily from the bench, passed her to a slack-jawed footman and ordered, rather grimly: "Her Highness needs to go back at once. She is upset. And speaking of shoes, do find hers."

The last things she remembered were her younger stepsister's glistening cheeks as she sobbed, over and over, "I forgive you, you aren't yourself, you aren't yourself right now!"—and her own dignified reply, while she was being manhandled into the carriage: "Well, *of course* I'm not myself, the evil sorceress sent *me* away a long time ago!"—and the hush falling among the mourners. Then everything turned black and still until, without any transition, there she was, sitting on a sofa in her reception room, possibly on a different morning, her hands cradled in the gentle warmth of Melissa's grasp.

"I came as soon as I could, we're all so worried about you, you must tell me what's wrong," Melissa was saying to her, must have been saying for some time. And suddenly she was crying on her stepsister's shoulder, talking about the treacherous butler, and the prince's cold eyes, and the overweight, overwrought woman in the mirror who would *not* go away—oh, and the potions, the endless potions that brought no cure—her words coming out all at once, in a soggy, incoherent jumble.

When she collapsed into exhausted silence, Melissa sat stroking her hand, carefully, lightly, as though it were some trembling, skittish animal.

"Show me what you've been taking," she said at last, her tone guarded.

They went into the washroom. The potions were stored in a secret cabinet behind a painting of a lotus. Together they looked at the formidable army of green, blue, pink, yellow vials. Then, without warning, Melissa reached in and swept all the bottles off the shelf, and they shattered in a many-hued explosion of glass, noise, and magic on the stone tiles of the washroom floor.

"Oh no, what have you done, why have you done this!" she

cried—but already the spilled vapors of spells and enchantments were billowing toward an open window, and in their swirling turbulence she glimpsed green imps, blue dragons, pink flies, yellow cockroaches with jaws loosened in toothy grins, a nebulous phantasmagoria of grotesques, all vile, all filled with some dark, dangerous essence. Growing quiet, she watched them seep and seethe past the windowpane, then dissipate in the cold wintry light. And when the last polluted whiff was gone, she felt a weight lift from her shoulders, and the world grew sharper and brighter, as if drained of some subtle yet pervasive poison.

Melissa was holding both her hands, squeezing them tightly.

"No more dark magic, promise me, promise me! You've been ill, and no wonder. I just don't understand why your prince didn't smash them all ages ago."

"But he couldn't have," she mumbled. "He didn't know."

"How in the world could he not?"

She shook her head, not looking up.

"I prefer not to trouble him with my problems. He has so much on his mind. And it's hard to find a private moment to talk, really. Whenever I see him, at official functions, there are always so many important people he must talk to first . . ."

"But I don't understand. You see each other every night after the day is done."

"Oh, well, no, to be honest, I mean, he travels so much, and he works so late, and I'm such a light sleeper, you see . . . Of course, it's a big palace, and the west wing is more convenient for him, so after the first year or two, he just . . ."

She broke off. Her stepsister was staring at her.

She felt a need to defend her husband.

"He is busy, you know. He has a kingdom to run."

Melissa pursed her lips. "Well, pardon *me*, I just live in a shoe, but at least Tom and I see each other daily. We talk. We sleep in the same bed. If I ever got into a state like this, he'd be the first to notice. Your prince is rich and handsome, no argument there, but he doesn't strike me as a very nice person. Cold, he always seemed to me. Shallow. Uncaring. But to each her own, I suppose. You chose him, so clearly, compassion and compatibility matter less to you than his other, more visible, qualities."

This was much like the Melissa of their teenage days, when they had gotten into spats over homework or chores, and she felt briefly reassured by the familiarity of her sister's sour expression. Yet after Melissa left (full of sympathy once again, having exerted from her the promise to stay clean), she knelt to sweep away the empty orange bottles, the debris of all her crushed, drowned pills, and, as the last of the drug-induced haze lifted from her mind, thought about her life, thought about her marriage, and saw some truth behind her sister's words.

She and the prince were overdue for a heart-to-heart talk.

She just needed to go on a strenuous diet first.

It is the fairy godmother's turn to keep her eyes averted.

"Really?" the witch spits out. "You stupefied her with potions for *years*? What, do the Powers That Be pay you a commission for each happy ending that doesn't end up at my crossroads?"

"I will have you know, it is perfectly within magical regulations." The fairy godmother's voice is pitched too high. "Of course, I could see there was no curse upon her, some women are just taken that way after a baby, but I thought it would be more beneficial to her cure if I allowed her to stay within her preferred frame of reference. And it isn't dark magic, not strictly speaking, not unless misused to excess, and had she but followed my directions . . . Self-medicating can lead to all sorts of trouble. I feel terrible, truly terrible, but you understand, I had no idea—"

An anemic half-moon has just risen over the fields, and in its pasty light, the fairy godmother's pale, plump hands keep fluttering like weak moths. I want to reach out and arrest their nervous trembling.

"Fairy Godmother."

She will not look at me.

"Fairy Godmother, it was not all your fault. Not your fault at all. It was just . . . I was just . . ." I want to reassure her, but it is hard for me to stare back into my personal darkness, so I fall silent and watch the sickly moon. It is moving in and out of low, billowing clouds, and sometimes it seems as though the predatory clouds are chasing after it while it struggles to escape them, and other times as though it means instead to seek shelter behind their woolly softness, hide from the emptiness of the stark autumnal skies. "It just felt easier to run away. And I guess I kept running for a while. For a long while. And not just with the potions . . ."

"Yes, well, reality can be a bitch," the witch interrupts. "And here we are, all full of remorse and weeping into our hankies. The night is halfway done, madam. Are you ready to finish this? Do you still want him dead?"

The moon has now climbed above the clouds—or else the clouds have abandoned it to its lonely, cold, naked fate. In the sudden brightness, I look at the hairs remaining in my hand.

One, two, three, four, five. And that little half.

Only five and a half hair-thin seconds separating his life from his death. And I still want him dead, I do, of course I do, I want him dead because of everything he's done to me, nothing has changed . . . I stretch my hand over the cauldron, and wait, holding my breath, wait for the fairy godmother to try and stop me, but she only gives me a grateful, sheepish glance and stays unmoving and silent. And all at once, in the absence of her protests, I feel the full weight of my decision crashing down onto my shoulders, no one else there to share my burden. I am truly alone.

I bite my lip and let the hairs fall.

One.

Two.

Three.

Four.

Five.

And then—and then I close my hand, trapping that last half-hair in my clenched fist, keeping it safe, postponing the moment of reckoning, for just a tiny bit longer.

The Beginning of the Middle's End

One morning in late spring, a thinner princess walked to the prince's quarters. The guard looked puzzled at her approach but made no effort to stop her. She scratched at the heavy door, then waited nervously. Only upon hearing an impatient "Yes?" did she edge into the study.

She had not been here since that memorable afternoon three or four years before. Once again, Prince Roland sat behind his imposing desk, fingers poised under his chin, but he was alone now—or nearly alone, for on the wall behind him hung a life-sized portrait of him, which she had never seen. The prince in the painting was likewise seated behind the faithfully rendered desk, his hands held in the same elegant gesture, his eyes raised at the viewer. At her entrance Prince Roland glanced up, and her breath stilled at the unexpected sight of the two of them, one directly above the other, looking at her. The resemblance was quite extraordinary in every detail, save that, unlike the original, the painted man was smiling broadly, his blue eyes frank, his expression full of welcoming benevolence.

"How can I help you?"

She tore her attention away from the painting.

"Please, my love, I need to talk to you." Her words came out more like a wheedling plea than the somber demand she had practiced.

"Now is not a good time." He turned a page of some report, picked up a sharp black quill; unlike his father the king, he favored porcupines over geese as the source for his writing implements. "Perhaps if you came back tomorrow. Or better yet, Friday. Yes, why don't I tell my secretary to put you down for the second Friday of the month."

His face was impassive, all polished planes of cheekbones and chiseled chin; in truth, he appeared far less lifelike than the portrait behind him. She was oddly unsettled by the radiant man floating above the head of her distant husband, so much so that she found herself forgetting everything she had come to say.

"Please, when was this done?" she asked instead.

"I beg your pardon?"

"Your portrait, when was it painted?"

His mouth appeared to tense. He regarded her in silence, stabbing his ferocious quill at a curl of parchment.

"I do not recall," he said at last. "I am always followed around by that clown of an artist, it is such a nuisance. I regret to tell you I am busy now, the Unicorn Pact requires immediate action." Still he looked at her, frowning. "You are starting to show your age," he added presently. "Thirty-one already, are you not? Perhaps you should schedule an appointment with a beautician or something. People like their betters to keep up appearances. Good day to you."

She curtsied, then flushed dark, and turned, and ran, Prince Roland's parting words ringing cruelly in her ears, the glorious vision of the painted smile nestled in her breast, warm and startling.

That night, she had trouble falling asleep. She listened to the clock on the tower striking at random times and Brie squeaking in a dream. *(Incidentally, ever since the mice had been freed from their backbreaking labor of minding the princess, they found themselves in possession of much leisure, and they began to dedicate their energies to higher pursuits. Grizzled philosophers stretched on couches fashioned out of bread crusts, imbibing wine from thimbles and arguing over the meaning of life from moonrise till sunrise; among the young, a secret religious cult sprang up around a mysterious blind mouse rumored to live in the sewers with a band of cutthroat rats; and arts flourished throughout the community, especially music and sculpture. An indisputable genius by the name Gouda staged vastly popular performances in which he fashioned miniature cats out of pieces of his namesake cheese, then nibbled them away to the accompaniment of savage squeaking, varying the order each time, starting now with the ears, now with the tail, to add suspense to what he called his "primal happenings"; a treatise about his technique was being gnawed into a candle by a prominent art critic for the edification of murine minds. General education, too, made giant strides, after the first mouseling school had been formed in the pantry. One of the courses, Human Studies, included, as part of its curriculum, a weeklong internship on the princess's mantelpiece. The class, however, was not nearly as well attended as other seminars, for instance Wax Whittling or Linguistic Inquiries, which included stimulating discussions of such expressions as "raining cats and dogs" and "When the cat's away, the mice will play." The prospect of spending a week in the presence of royalty had seemed intriguing at first, but now only the most scholarly of the young chose to pursue the discipline, for it had quickly become known that the princess, regrettably, did very little of interest.)* For minutes she lay braiding the edge of her covers, wearing her hands out with restless worry and watching the moonlight move across the rug. When it pooled inside her slippers, she threw the blankets off, slipped her feet into the cool blue glow, lit a candle, and, still in her nightdress, tiptoed out the door.

Never before had she been out of bed so late at night. At this hour, precariously poised between midnight and sunrise, the palace seemed an altogether unfamiliar place. Chandelier crystals swayed softly as she hastened by the ballrooms, yet the tunes they played now were not the customary waltzes but eerie snatches of slow, languid songs she failed to recognize. When she paused on the threshold of the Grand Audience Chamber, she thought she saw translucent figures moving with sinister grace in the mirrors along the walls, their spectral limbs coming together with sinuous undulations that made her blush and hurry on. The shadows through which she passed were likewise not the tamed little puddles to which she was accustomed, but deeper, mysterious pools that condensed into secretive presences she could not quite make out behind curtains or underneath clocks. Magic hung thick on the air, almost visible, like a sheen of green moonlight that made everything slightly distorted, shimmering and shifting—and she sensed this magic to be completely unlike any she had known before. For the ordinary brand of godmother magic was thinly spread, civilized as a powdered wig, harmless as a drop of liqueur after a four-course meal, whimsical as glass footwear, and entirely pedestrian in its dabbling, domestic purposes of comfort and matrimony. This magic felt uncanny—denser, older, much more hidden, and much less certain; though whether it was light or dark, she could not tell.

Briefly she stopped and thought of turning back; but the pull was too powerful. She walked onward with quickening steps. The empty corridor leading to the prince's quarters echoed loudly with her footfalls. The presence of the wild old magic grew stronger here: it was now a thrumming pulse that sent troubling reverberations through her soles and into her stomach, until her whole body vibrated in some primitive rhythm. As she approached the study door, her heart bobbed like an egg in boiling water. She tried the knob, half hoping to find the door locked.

The door crept open.

She stole over the threshold.

The room lay deserted, its bulky furnishings looming in the dark, harsh and immense, like slabs hewn out of rough stone. She neared the desk, raised her candle. The painted prince met her gaze. And perhaps it was only the flickering flame of the candle in her unsteady hand, but it seemed to her that his eyes sparkled with liquid life and his smile grew more luminous still as the two of them stared at each other.

The magical thrumming was all around her now, breathing, pulsing, throbbing. It was coming, she realized, from whatever lay on the other side of the door in the far wall—the door that led to the prince's bedroom. She inhaled, and walked toward it, her hand raised for a hesitant knock, when a voice spoke behind her.

"Help me."

She whirled around.

The room lay dark and still, yet there it was, once again.

"Help me. Please."

The voice was pitiful and gentle, and the sound of it shook her heart. Fearful of what she might see, she threaded her way back through the dead mass of officious armchairs and cabinets, gathering a bruise high on her left thigh from one of the desk's brutal corners, and, once more, shined a timorous light at the portrait.

The man in the painting was no longer smiling, his hands stretched out toward her, his eyes brimming over with some mute, tragic appeal.

"Who are you?" she whispered, nonsensically, for of course she knew who he was—the beautiful man she had fallen in love with at the ball all those years ago. She tried again. "*How* can I help you?"

His lips moved, and her heart came to a stop in her chest like a pendulum that had wound down in its swinging and was now waiting for the next push before it started in a new direction—but before she could hear his answer, she found herself sitting up in bed, her chest stabbed through by a shaft of moonlight, her pulse erratic, and there were the porcelain poodles on her mantelpiece, and Nibbles twitching in his sleep, and her slippers lined up on the bedside rug, precisely as she had left them.

Only a dream, she told herself—it was only a dream—but her heart would not slow down.

She dozed fitfully for the rest of the sunless hours. When morning broke at last, she felt unable to settle to anything. After a wash that failed to cool her burning skin and a breakfast that left no taste in her mouth, she climbed to the nursery, but Nanny Nanny took one good look at her and sent her away. "Go ba-a-ack to be-e-ed, Your Highness," she bleated with some severity, "and have them bring you chamomile te-e-ea and a hot-water bottle."

Nanny Nanny was no different from Fairy Godmother, both practical, bossy, and of limited understanding, she thought as she stormed away, fuming at having to take orders from a goat, even such an old and sage one. And since she was feeling rebellious, she did not go back to her room but went for a muddy stroll in the rain-sodden garden instead, then had her eleven-o'clock tea brought to her in the library, against her usual custom, and sat sullenly contemplating the few odds and ends inside the library's unimpressive display cabinet.

A thin coating of dust covered the whole sorry collection: a red apple with a bite taken out of its lacquered side, a dulled handheld mirror, a delicate chess piece carved out of ivory, a great rusty key with traces of something that might or might not have been blood along its jagged teeth, and, on a shelf all its own, a tiny glass slipper. She cast a furtive look around and pulled the cabinet door ajar. A cloying smell of rotten fruit escaped in a pale puff. The slipper, weightless as a moonbeam, easily fit in the palm of her hand. She unlaced the mud-caked boot on her right foot, wiggled out of it, and jammed her perspiring toes into the precious shoe.

It was at least two sizes too small.

Openmouthed with disbelief, she examined her heel hanging over the glittering edge. Then, all at once worried that someone might come in, unlikely as the possibility was—none of the courtiers made a habit of reading, for, naturally, one did not need stories if one was already inhabiting a story as good as any—she hurried to wrest the unforgiving crystal monstrosity off her aching, pinched toes, and was just putting it back in the cabinet when her eyes fell on the shelf below, and a surprisingly simple idea popped into her mind. After the briefest of hesitations, she upended her untouched cup of cold tea into a nearby pot of geraniums, slipped the handheld mirror between the ruffles of her skirt, and left the library at a barely suppressed trot.

Alone in her bedroom, having accepted yet another unwanted cup of tea, dismissed the maid, and locked the door, for the first time in her life—clearly, it was to be the day for underhanded actions, uncharacteristic emotions, and miniature revolts—she sat on the bed and raised the mirror before her.

"Show me my husband," she demanded, her heart swollen with an unfamiliar excitement, and, when nothing happened, added plaintively, "Please?"

Still nothing happened. She wondered if she would have to be subjected to the indignity of rhyming. In the lusterless glass, she could see a sliver of a pasty cheek, a corner of a bleary eye, a puffy eyelid. The prince had been right (though he could have been kinder about it), she was losing her beauty. Hastily she thrust the glass away from her face, and chanted, all in a rush, drawing on some dimly recalled stock of stories heard in the most remote recesses of childhood: "Mirror, mirror, on the wall . . ."

But of course, it was not on the wall, she was holding it, so she started anew: "Mirror, mirror, in my hand, show me Prince Roland and . . . and . . . and . . ."

It did rhyme, in its way, but obviously something else was needed. She took a few turns about the room, thinking furiously, then tried a more abstract approach: "Mirror, mirror, bring me luck. Show me Prince Roland and . . . and his . . . his . . ."

But the prince kept no pet ducks, "pluck" applied only to

peasant upstarts, and "yuck" did not rightly belong in legitimate poetry. She tossed the mirror onto her blanket, the reflection of her nose skittering along its surface at a wide angle, and screamed in frustration—and, all at once, had the very spell.

"Mirror, mirror, on my bed, show me my spouse, instead of my head!" she recited triumphantly.

The surface of the mirror fogged and billowed.

"That. Was. Simply. Horrendous," drawled a peevish voice. "But you are persistent, I will give you that, and I am really bored."

"Plus the bonus rhyme," she offered readily, anxious to appease the disembodied speaker. "You know. 'Instead.' 'Head.'"

"Well. The previous incantation, had you but completed it, would have been better. More accurate."

"How do you mean?"

But the mirror refused to elaborate.

"Also, technically, this is spying, you are aware," it said after a pause.

"I just want to know him better," she protested hotly. "There is nothing wrong with that! Because I realize now, we were very young when we got married, and we might not have had that much in common. Back then. But our years together have brought us closer. All the things we've shared. Like our children. Only sometimes it feels like I've had our children alone. Oh, of course, he is there for us, he works so hard, and I've always had money and help, I know that, only . . . only sometimes I see these peasant families from the carriage window, a mother, a father, a son, a daughter, having a meal together in some field, a checkered table-cloth, a fat bottle of wine, their dog stealing sausages from their picnic basket, the mother telling a story, the father smacking her cheek with a greasy kiss, the children chasing each other through the grass, all of them laughing, and the sky so blue above them, like a hand cupping them all together, a perfect life, simple yet perfect, you know? Not this—this marble lockbox of a place, the cold ceremonials, the one-two-three dances, the polite agony of loneliness . . . Oh, I don't mean to complain, I'm very grateful for everything, it's just that . . . that . . ."

She stopped abruptly, all at once conscious of babbling— worse, of voicing aloud things that were intimate and shameful. There was an uncomfortable silence. Then the mirror sighed. When it spoke again, it sounded very old and very tired, and for the first time it occurred to her that its voice might just belong to a woman.

"Yes, girl, I know. That's what they all say. You won't like it, of course. But if you are sure."

"I *am* sure!" she cried.

After an interminable moment, the fog shifted in a gesture oddly like a shrug and began to recede. Sucking in her breath with a childlike eagerness, she leaned over the glass, and frowned, then tilted her head, then continued to tilt it, trying to comprehend what it was she was seeing, until her head was jammed all the way against her shoulder and had nowhere else to go.

Her mouth loosened in a wordless scream.

"Ahem. It might be wise to take a break here," the fairy godmother says, her lips pursed as she steps away from the cauldron. "Or shall we just skip this part?"

"Must you be such a prude?" says the witch. "I was finally beginning to enjoy myself. We deserve a bit of excitement after all the dreary dross we've had to suffer through! And in any case, it was my impression that you yourself were indulging in some extracurricular activities with the good old King Roland, or am I mistaken?"

"What gave you such an absurd idea!" exclaims the fairy

godmother, visibly flustered. "That is, he was a client of mine, yes. Depressed for years, if you really want to know, though I shouldn't be telling you that, it is privileged information. Not that there is much harm in divulging it now, poor dear . . . His wife died young, I felt terrible for him, just terrible. But of course, he *was* a widower, so there would have been no harm if . . . Not that . . . I mean to say . . ."

"Human!" the witch cries with savage triumph, poking one gnarled finger in the fairy godmother's direction. "After everything, she, too, is human. Who knew?"

To my astonishment, the fairy godmother blushes, stutters, and looks away.

I blink. Who knew, indeed.

"Might as well get this over with," I say then. "I want you both to understand."

Sighing, the fairy godmother draws back to the cauldron.

In the mirror, the prince was having relations—but no, that was not quite right, the polite euphemism failed to convey the vigorousness and shamelessness of what she was seeing; was copulating, then—but that, too, fell well short of the mark; so, then, was—and there was no other way of putting it—her husband was—a cry of fury born at last, a hand slammed against the wall, a smashed teacup, cold tea running down the front of her dress, a deep breath, a deeper breath, look again, look, do not look away— her husband was fucking two women, one of them the stout forty-nine-year-old pastry chef on an exchange visit from a neighboring giant's castle, and the other, shockingly—as if the rest had not been shocking enough—but yes, still, shockingly—their butler's daughter, who was rosy, long-limbed, lovely, and not a day over sixteen. The energetic tumble was loud with deep-chested grunts (the pastry chef's) and high-pitched moans (the butler's daughter's) and took place on a rich crimson background abloom with royal-blue tulips, which she recognized, after another breath, as the plush oriental rug in Prince Roland's study. The mirror's angle was not sufficiently wide to take in the entire scene at once but offered her a rapid succession of pornographic glimpses of female flesh—pale narrow thighs and puckering pink nipples (the butler's daughter's), reddened gelatinous thighs and massive chocolate nipples (the pastry chef's)—over all of which labored Prince Roland, hard-eyed, trim, and sleek with sweat, looking rather like a circus seal, his teeth gritted with manly concentration, from which he occasionally emerged to demand, in harsh, seal-like barks: "Who's your prince, yeah, who's your prince?"

She watched for a minute, then carefully turned the mirror over, and quietly sat on the edge of her chaste white bed, her hands still and listless like plucked birds in her lap. After a while, she rose, crossed the room to her writing desk, at which she spent a laborious daily hour composing inevitable thank-you notes and invitations to tea parties, and, just as quietly, slid the mirror into the wastepaper basket that stood between the desk's thin white legs. The basket had a border of plump golden cherubs practicing archery all along its edge. The mirror settled on the bottom and was now partially obscured by a small pile of glistening cherry pits, some tangled lace trimmings from an embroidery project, and a draft of a letter to the Marquise de Fatouffle, which she had begun penning on her special peach-tinted stationery the previous morning, before losing a valiant battle with the spelling of "appreciation."

"Thank you," she said, because she had excellent manners and it was customary to offer thanks for rendered favors, even when they resulted in death and devastation, and waited, likewise out of politeness, in case the mirror chose to reply from the trash. The mirror said nothing, however, so she returned to her bed and sat back down. Her hands were empty now. Her heart was empty. She knew the truth at last—but the deeper truth, the truth beneath the truth, was that she might have known it once or twice already and had tricked herself into forgetting. Now she could hide from it no longer. She heard the clock in the corridor outside strike noon, and felt mildly surprised at its being barely past morning, at the curious fact that time was still functioning, still flowing, still meting out the meager minutes, sand grains, bread crumbs, of her life's passing. For just one moment longer she sat pondering the vastness of nothing in her hands, and then, somehow, the room was dark and the pale jellyfish of the moon swam in the inky sky outside the window. Someone was banging on her door, someone must have been banging on her door for a while now, and a chorus of frantic, hoarsened voices, maids, footmen, mice, were demanding to know, more and more shrilly, whether she was fine, whether everything was as it should be.

"I'm fine, I'm perfectly fine," she told them through the door. "I'm napping. Please let me rest until morning."

And they believed her and departed, for, as everyone knows, fairy-tale princes and princesses never lie.

Sometime later that night, she awakened from a dream of crashing trains, shattering lightbulbs, and telephones ringing forever in empty apartments to find herself slumped over in a chair. The moon was gone from the window. Her neck ached, her head pounded, she was wearing unlaced muddy boots and a filthy dress stiff with tea stains. A candle, propped dangerously on the chair's arm, had melted down to a guttering stump and was about to set her hair on fire prior to burning down the entire palace. She blew it out, thus saving everyone from imminent demise— those who deserved to live and those who deserved to die, in equal measure—and went into the washroom. There, she lit every candelabrum until the room blazed, stood before the wall mirror, and stripped naked.

Then she looked at herself.

She had never seen herself naked before, not openly, not wholly. No one had ever seen her naked before. She was shy around her maids, and her couplings with the prince, few as they had been, long ago as they had been, had been nothing like the debauched midday romp she had witnessed in that diabolical mirror—the first few, in the darkness under the covers, and the last, fully clothed. Now she stood before her reflection, and looked at it as if it belonged to someone else. She looked over her neck, her shoulders, her breasts, her belly, her hips, her thighs, the darkening cleft between them. Then, slowly, slowly, she ran her hands along her skin, watching all the while in the mirror, the lights blazing so brightly that her very essence seemed to be burning away in their white, searing glare. She watched the pale, flaxen-haired, disturbingly voluptuous woman in the mirror, as the woman slid her hands down her sides, feeling strange heat beginning to rise from the body no longer her own, touching first her neck, then her shoulders, then her breasts, then her belly, then her hips, then her thighs, then—

Her heart stopped. Her heart stopped, and started again, quickening, racing. Her hands fell away and hung loose by her sides, shamed, still. Because there it was—her thigh. Her left thigh. The bruise, on her left thigh. The bruise, in the shape of a desk's corner, high on her left thigh, just like the bruise she had received in her dream the night before—was it only the night before?—in the uncanny, thrumming dream the night before, the dream in which she had loved the radiant prince in the painting, and he had said: "Help me."

Nothing was as it seemed.

She turned her back on the dissolute hussy with tempestuous eyes and hunger in her belly, rapidly blew out the forest of candles, pulled on her thick woolen nightgown, and slipped into bed. She slept the dreamless sleep of the righteous, and in the morning, she woke up a new woman, a woman on a mission. Skipping breakfast in order not to lose any time, she paid a visit to the court artist in his attic studio crammed with unfinished busts of ghosts and mermaids, and the shabby little man with smears of yellow and red in his unruly hair confirmed what she had already suspected: he had never painted the portrait above Prince Roland's desk, nor did he have the slightest idea of where it had come from.

"I saw it once, though, when His Highness left his door ajar," he confessed with a giggle. "The likeness is exceptional."

Satisfied on that point, she returned to the library and spent weeks perusing weighty reference tomes. Since she was anything but adept at mining nuggets of value from wordy swamps of reading matter, she waded through tedious lists of potion ingredients, arcane discussions of child-to-bird transformations, and incomprehensible interpretations of fairy-tale symbolism with clenched teeth and aching temples, and at times felt the dull, gray despair of excessive knowledge crush her like a tombstone. Still, she refused to concede defeat. And at last, as the muggy summer heat gave way to the crisp chill of autumn, in a dingy little book with a torn-off cover, she stumbled upon a paragraph on enchanted portraits, unsatisfyingly brief and yet enough to reassure her that such things were indeed possible.

A living, warm human soul could, indeed, be trapped in a darkly charmed painting while its empty shell of a body, stripped of all love and understanding, continued to walk, talk, consume pastries with raspberry jam, sign death warrants with self-satisfied flourishes of porcupine quills, ignore concerned family members, and, in its free hours, diddle anything that moved—in short, play at being Prince Roland engaged in the regular business of everyday life.

All the certainties fell into place; but then, in her heart of hearts, she had known the truth—the real truth, this time, deeper yet than any of the other truths, which had not been true, after all—had known it the moment she had seen the bruise on her thigh on that terrible wreck of a night. *She* was not responsible for the unhappy state of their happily ever after—it was he, he alone; but of course, it was not her sweet prince's fault, either. Some years into their conjugal bliss, *he* had been trapped under an evil enchantment. And now—now it was her wifely duty to save him, just like in the stories.

Her love for him was back, alive and generous, and it was all courage, and self-sacrifice, and, in some small measure, rising excitement at the thought of embarking on a perilous quest to rescue her beloved, then having him in her debt for the rest of his life. Energized by her clear-cut purpose, she felt prepared to enter into dangerous camaraderie with wolves, bargain with spoons and chicken bones, beg for help from cantankerous old ladies, even walk to the far side of the wind if need be, in order to break the spell. It was only a matter of figuring out how to start.

She knew that someone suitable should be coming out of the woodwork to provide the required instruction—a wizened dwarf with whom she might share a cupcake, or a bear whose paw she would obligingly rid of a splinter. She also knew herself at some disadvantage, as there was a decided shortage of bears in the manicured park at her disposal, and, too, most quests involved rosy-cheeked maidens in the first bloom of youth, not thirtysomething mothers of two.

Nonetheless, she determined to do her best.

Her initial efforts proved futile. That entire winter, she spoonfed soup to ailing old cobblers in nearby villages, snatched baby squirrels from under the wheels of a reckless carriage (her own, as it happened, but it was the intention that counted), peered into every cluttered closet in the palace in search of an overlooked crone with a spindle who might grant her three wishes, and received nothing for her pains but manifold blessings from teary-eyed peasants, a bite from a chipmunk that had not, it transpired, wanted to cross the road, and a growing reputation for charity.

Eventually, however, cogs of magic started to turn, if a bit sluggishly. One afternoon in the early spring, a scrawny young orphan whom she helped with his orthography lessons directed her to a pond behind a neighboring mill. The pond was choked with lily pads, and in the center of every green platter sat a frog. As she neared the mill, hundreds of liquid eyes swiveled toward her as one.

"Kiss me—kiss me—kiss me," croaked the frogs.

"Thank you, but I'm already married," she demurred with a nervous laugh, hiding behind her parasol. But the frogs stared up at her with their wet, insolent eyes and chanted: "That never stopped nobody before."

She thought them terribly uncouth, and was just turning to leave when the largest frog spoke up from the largest pad.

"Personally, I'm too old to care for kisses," said the frog, and in truth, it did look ancient, warty and fat. "But if you bring me that tasty beetle crawling over there, I will tell you what you desire."

The frog stuck out a pink tongue, fleshy and long and horribly indecent, so she picked up the beetle and carried it to safety; and once the grateful beetle had revived from its faint, it told her about the beekeeper who lived at the foot of the hill.

By the time she reached the beekeeper's place, the sun was already setting, and blue shadows were stretching across the meadow. The beekeeper came out of his cottage, a few bees circling drowsily around his head. He was young and doe-eyed, and when he greeted her, his words carried a soft whiff of some foreign land. He reminded her of someone, but she was too pre-occupied to catch the resemblance in time.

"I should ask you for a boon, it's in the quest handbook," the beekeeper said, and, lowering his golden-brown gaze, blushed in-explicably. "But I will tell you for free, because you were always kind to me."

She did not puzzle over his words but pressed her bright blue parasol as payment upon him—no one should have to break the rules on her behalf—then, just as the round yellow moon the tex-ture of ripe cheese rose in the skies, followed his directions to the dressmaker's shop on the main square of a town across the river, where she spent a week weaving straw roses into bonnets and, in restitution, received an introduction to a gypsy horse thief who was passing through that night and in whose wagon she rode for the better part of the month, learning to cook fiery stews, wear men's clothes, and shoe horses, until they came to the caravan ruled by the gypsy thief's great-great-grandmother, who ap-peared more ancient than the mountains they had just crossed and who—once she had spent the balance of the spring braiding stars into the matriarch's raven-black hair—gave her a Tarot card with the Queen of Swords and the address of a mighty sor-cerer scribbled upon it in rooster blood. She stashed the card in-side her shirt, close to her heart.

The gypsy thief put a ring of beaten silver, two hands holding a heart, on her finger, and kissed her in parting. They stood on a wild mountain peak, the sunset blazed crimson all around them, his sinewy arms smelled of smoke and hay, his dry lips tasted of pepper and freedom, and for one fraction of a moment she saw a different story, pure and fierce, unfolding before her. But when he pulled her against him, the Queen of Swords cut into her left breast, so she freed herself from his embrace, thanked him for his kindness, and, hitching up her britches, trudged down the mountainside already aflame with the vivid colors of summer wildflowers.

The sorcerer lived in a small valley on this side of the wind, but only barely. By the time she arrived, it was early autumn. Nights were growing chilly, leaves were turning red, and her cloak felt much too thin. She found the sorcerer in a neat little garden behind a neat little house, tending to a neat row of gigantic purple cabbages. A tiny old man with sad gray eyes in a furrowed gray face the size of another man's fist, he listened to her with an anxious smile, then asked her to be so good as to speak louder, for he was a bit hard of hearing. She shouted her request, and the tall gray mountains around the little gray valley repeated her words many times over, until all the world boomed with her grievances and her hopes. When she finished and the echoes stopped, the old man shook his head.

"Sadly, my dear," he whispered, "I am retired."

"But you can't be, that's not how it works!" she cried. "I have come from afar to seek your counsel. I have borne amphibian insults, stabbed my fingers with needles and stars, worn out one pair of slippers embroidered with ladybugs, two pairs of sensible shoes, and three pairs of boots, turned my back on the young beekeeper, who blushed so sweetly, and the gypsy thief, who made wild winds blow through my blood. Has it all been in vain? Is there nothing you can do for me?"

The old man thought. The furrows deepened in his small gray face.

"I could give you a few of my cabbages," he said at last. "Nice plump babies sometimes turn up in the patch."

Aghast, she stared at him, then at the cabbages. Autumn was drawing closer to winter now; she saw the first traces of frost on the ground between the orderly rows.

"Thank you, but no, I don't need a new baby. I fear I have not been the best mother to the two I've already had."

And as she spoke, she suddenly knew this to be true. She had been away from the palace, away from her children, for much too long.

Her hand flew to her heart.

"I must get back at once."

She turned to go, firmly, and was halfway to the nearest mountain when the old man caught up with her. He had been running.

"There . . . is . . . something," he gasped. "I've . . . just . . . remembered."

She waited for him to regain his breath.

"I did have a pupil long ago. Not the brightest of the lot, I'm sorry to say, always got his spells mixed up. Still, he may be able to help you—I hear he is a king's magician now, so perhaps he's become less muddled over the years. I must be honest with you, though, he lives a bit far. On this side of the wind, yes, but only just."

Her hope stirred anew, even though she willed it not to.

"Please, where will I find him?"

He drew her a map on a cabbage leaf. She studied it, her spirits sinking. The world scratched into the leaf was broad and strange, bristling with snowcapped ranges, dotted with towns whose names she did not recognize. She thanked the little cabbage farmer, tightened her belt, and set off. As she walked, the eerie blue moon, such as could be seen only at the edge of the world, waxed and waned, winter came and went, hills rose into scraggly peaks and fell into shadowy dales. Her path took her by the gypsy grandmother's caravan, where she stopped for a shot of whiskey and learned that the gypsy thief had taken up with a beautiful dancer and the two had ridden off into the wind on a stolen black mustang, singing raucous songs; she sighed, but not too deeply, for she had her cabbage leaf now. Again the moon waxed and waned, but now it looked less like a wispy blue boat ready to sail beyond the borders of all known things, and more like a head of ripened cheese; and as she continued to follow the map, the landscapes themselves slowly grew more familiar. At the melting of the snows, she arrived one morning in a town by a brown, stately river where merchants' wives wore elegant hats decorated with straw roses. She visited a dressmaker's shop on the main square, to trade her stained britches and crude riding boots for a proper dress and a pair of dainty slippers embroidered with ladybugs (their designs copied, the shop owner informed her proudly, from the clothes worn by a lovely princess who had once stayed there). She paid with the silver ring, two disloyal hands holding a faithless heart, then continued on, her own heart seized with a certain premonition. In the full light of an early spring day, she flew up the hill all abuzz with bees. She would not pause to chat with the young beekeeper who came out of his cottage when she passed by, but she did accept a parasol of faded blue that he begged her to have, and, calling out her thanks over her shoulder, hurried away, leaving him to stand empty-handed and stare after her with a pining golden-brown gaze.

She understood everything now. Her heart in her mouth, she followed the sorcerer's directions past the pond, where the chorus of frogs begged her to kiss them, and around the mill, and across the park with its civilized maze of raked paths and marble nymphs, until the blue-and-white vanilla cake of a palace rose before her. It was marked on her map by a translucent star of the old man's fingernails impressing themselves into the leaf's fleshy pulp with an emphatic crisscross and a scrawl: "Here."

All out of breath and radiant with anticipation, she burst inside at the hour when teapots were just beginning to serve afternoon tea, and dashed up to the nursery, and there were her darling children, Angelina and Roland the Sixth, sitting straight-backed and quiet in their little chairs, listening to Nanny Nanny bleat a nursery rhyme about a cow that flew over the moon.

She pressed them deeply to her heart, first the girl, then the boy, then both of them together. "I am so sorry to have been gone all this time!" she cried. "I have missed you so much, I love you, I love you!"

They pulled away, all resisting elbows and eyebrows raised in surprise.

"Gone?" they said. "Gone where? We saw you yesterday. You brought us cinnamon cookies in bed."

"Bah, Your Highness, but that is ba-a-a-d, ba-a-a-d for their tee-ee-eeth," chided Nanny Nanny, who likewise did not seem astonished to see her.

Stunned, she turned, looked around her. Everything was exactly as she had left it a year before, and she, too, seemed exactly the same as the day she had set out on her glorious adventure, down to her ladybug slippers and her blue parasol (although she thought it had been of a slightly brighter shade). The children paid her no attention. She lingered in the nursery for another minute, then kissed them on the tops of their heads, one blond, one chestnut, and, frowning, left for the tower where Archibald the Clockmaker lived next to his brother, Arbadac the Bumbler.

The winding stairs were long and narrow, with a great many landings. She leaned the parasol (decidedly, decidedly, of a lighter color now!) against the wall at the bottom and began to climb. By the time she reached the third landing, she had forgotten the boat of the otherworldly moon and the little gray man with his cabbages. The gypsy grandmother with the braids spun from the eternal night vanished on the fifth, the gypsy thief's peppery kiss faded on the seventh. The beekeeper with his soft burr of an accent and someone else's face was the last to cling to the edges of her recollections, but at last he, too, slipped into oblivion, and by the time she knocked on Arbadac's door on the seventeenth landing, she was fully certain—and it was quite plausibly the truth of the matter—that only one hour had passed since she had finished correcting the scrawny orphan's orthography lesson.

("Master Archibald's brother is a magician," the boy, who was the clockmaker's assistant, had told her. "He can sure do magic. When he's in his cups, he likes to set all the cogs of the clock dancing. Master Archibald gets horribly mad."

And he had giggled.

"Now, why haven't I thought of him before," she had said to herself. "I'll go speak to him after we get done with this lesson." And, forcing herself to focus: "Write down, please: 'dressmaker,' 'thief,' 'cabbage,' 'destiny.' No, dear, 'cabbage' has two bees. I mean, two *b*s. Oh, this is making me sleepy, I'd better lie down for a bit before going up to the tower.")

After her seventh, rather impatient knock, the door flew open abruptly. From the dimness of the stairwell, she squinted at the tall, lean man who wobbled on the threshold, his wispy hair aflame with the sun setting in the windows behind him. But the light had an odd, fragmented quality to it, and she heard a soft flapping sound, as of hundreds of insect wings beating at once. Just then, sure enough, a stupendous yellow butterfly brushed past her face and sailed majestically out of sight around the curve of the staircase, and another, and three more.

"They're escaping, they're escaping!" Arbadac cried, and before she could collect her wits enough to reply, he pulled her inside and slammed the door shut behind them. She blinked. The chamber shone, tinkled, and flittered. Brilliant sunlight filled hundreds of potion bottles, crystal balls, and specimen jars with many-colored radiance, odd spindly-legged instruments clicked and clacked, and a thick swarm of butterflies drifted through the air. Immediately a full dozen were quivering in her sleeves, tickling her neck, stirring in her hair.

"Is this a bad time?" she asked weakly.

"How's that? Oh. No. No, everything's fine." Arbadac's eyes were the color of fog and had a perennially dreamy look. "It's only that I'm not entirely sure where these pests came from, you see, so it's best to keep them all in here. Just in case, yes. Still, no harm done, thank goodness, not like the other month, Archie was most unhappy, he so dislikes untidiness and explosions, and that hole in the ceiling was a hassle to repair . . . Well. What can I do for you, Your Highness? May I offer you some tea? The cups often turn furry, but it tastes perfectly fine, I assure you."

She refused the offer with hasty courtesy and told him about the prince's enchantment. While she talked, he drifted about, waving butterflies away, his robes floating and billowing around him, his gaze abstracted; she had a distinct feeling that he was not listening to a word she said. When she finished, she looked at him with scant expectation. She was, in truth, feeling rather forlorn.

"Can you help break the spell, then?"

"The spell?" he said, stopping sharply and turning to her with a surprised look. "Ah, yes. The spell. Of course. Yes. Do you know who placed it?"

She had to confess she did not.

"I suppose it could be anyone," Arbadac proclaimed in his airy voice. "All royals are like lightning rods for curses. Well, but you don't really need to know the culprit. What you need is to weave a shirt."

There was a brief pause filled with the beating of wings.

"A . . . shirt?" she asked, faintly.

"A shirt. Give it to your husband on the anniversary of your wedding day. When he puts it on, the spell will be over."

He beamed at her.

She spat out a butterfly and looked at him wildly.

"And . . . that's it?"

"That's it. Except." His smile vanished. He pressed his hands to his forehead and stood restlessly rippling his fingers as though trying to summon a melody on the harpsichord of his memory, likely somewhat out of tune. "Ah. Yes. The shirt must be woven out of bluebells. No, that doesn't sound quite . . . Not bluebells . . . nettles. Yes, a shirt out of nettles."

"Nettles? Are you quite sure?"

"Yes. And you can't talk or laugh the entire time you're weaving it, not until the prince puts it on. Silence is of the essence. If you speak even one word, you must unravel everything and start over."

"Oh."

"And you must weave it only by the light of the full moon. Or in the hour before sunrise." He was gathering momentum now, speaking quickly, his fingers tap-tap-tapping against his forehead, his dreamy eyes gleaming with bursts of inspiration. "And only on Mondays. Though Tuesdays are probably fine, too. Yes. You do need to mind the buttons, of course."

"Buttons?" Her nerves were so taut with her spirits rising and falling by turn that she felt they might snap. "Oh, please, what buttons?"

"But the buttons are the most important part! When you weave the shirt, you must think about the happy years you and your husband had together. Before he was under the spell, do you see, when he was still himself. Sew on a button for each true year, and he will be restored to his true self when he wears the shirt on his birthday."

"On our wedding anniversary, you mean."

"What? Yes, yes, the anniversary, of course . . . You only get one chance at breaking the spell, mind, so you have to get everything right the first time. But as long as you do, I don't see why it shouldn't work, really. May I interest you in some tea?"

Hope palpitated in her heart with the hundredfold motion of

soaring butterflies, and desperate to keep it alive, she declined, once again, the distinctly furry teacup he was holding out to her, thanked him, and ran out the door and down the winding stairs, yellow wings trembling in her hair, just as he was saying: "You might, of course, consider adding the tincture of . . ."

That very evening, she discovered that bunches of nettles were to be had in the kitchens (the head cook favored herbal soups), and she started on the shirt without delay. Her hands were soon covered in blisters, but she did not complain, because she was not in the habit of complaining, and also because she had now ceased to speak altogether, just as instructed. She had wondered how she would explain her precipitous silence, yet no one appeared to notice. Prince Roland never came near her, the old king had grown quite feeble and was napping his days away, Angie was currently answering all her own questions, Ro seemed satisfied with her mere presence in the nursery while he staged epic battles between forks and spoons, servants found her a perfect mistress who smiled and nodded at all their requests, and Brie and Nibbles had recently befriended a family of field mice and left the palace, possibly for good.

(By now, most of the mice had gone. Heady delights of philosophy had failed to sustain them for long, for they soon discovered that puzzling over the meaning of life seemed inversely related to their enjoyment of it: many of their best minds had grown weak from wrestling with the longer words, not a few had died of existential despair, and one sad morning, the most learned mouse of them all was found flat as a pancake, apparently crushed by the weight of her knowledge. As for the vicarious thrills of the arts, it transpired that there were only so many ways to eat a chunk of cheese shaped like a cat. In a desperate bid to restore the flagging enthusiasm for his work, Gouda the artist

abandoned realism and began to add outlandish trunks, horns, tentacles, wings, and warts to his cheese sculptures until his new creations looked so revolting he simply could not bring himself to eat them without retching; and his digestive issues aside, after this infusion of the fantastic and the arbitrary into his themes, the powerful yet simple message behind his early masterpieces— the unequivocal triumph of good over evil—was hopelessly obscured. Eventually even his most devoted fans turned away from him, disappointed, and once the smell of moldy gouda grew unbearable, a youngster named Tuft gathered a few of his adolescent friends, all equally disenchanted with higher pursuits, and led a bloodless raid on Gouda's studio, where they did away with visual arts once and for all.

After that, intoxicated by their success and meeting no resistance—even Gouda appeared relieved—Tuft and his cheering army abolished education, manners, abstract thinking, cutlery, all other kinds of thinking, and much of the vocabulary. Mice should be mice, they shouted gleefully to anyone willing to listen. Their days were short, and they should not waste them lazing about in sunless holes of stone, frightening each other silly with Unnatural Ideas and oohing and aahing over wantonly ruined cheese. No, they should go back to nature and be what they always had been—happy mindless creatures who smelled flowers and one another's behinds, ran through the rain, flexed their muscles, squeaked their animal joys to the skies. And the mice liked what they heard, for it spoke to something deep and furry within them, and they abandoned the palace in droves. Only the aging professor of Human Studies worried about leaving the princess, out of some obscure loyalty he himself had trouble explaining—unbeknownst to him, he was the last surviving descendant of Brie the First on his mother's side and Nibbles the First on his father's; but after a full day of observing her from under her bed, he concluded that mice were not meant to understand the doings of men and that he, too, should follow the call of the wild and revert to a fierce woodland beast, leaving the incomprehensible woman with a sad face to sit alone in her stuffy room and absurdly persist in stinging her fingers with nettles.)

As she worked on the shirt, she thought about buttons and

happiness. She decided on her wedding dress for her prince's lib-
eration: it seemed the appropriate choice. The confectionlike
gown, once her most cherished possession, hung in a cloud of
white tulle in her dressing room. Sewing scissors at the ready, she
stood before it one morning, looked at the pearl-encrusted buttons running down its lacy back, and recalled trumpets blaring,
horses prancing, crowds tossing rice into the warm spring air, her
stepsisters acting huffy and displeased, and the prince lifting her
veil, bending down to kiss her. When their lips had touched, she
had believed that she would float in this tranquil warmth of love
and comfort, shielded from all unhappiness, from all change, forever after. Now she trailed her fingers over the buttons' cool iri-
descence and wondered how many to snip off. Precisely when had
Prince Roland stopped being the attentive, generous man who
had made her feel content and secure and been replaced by the
soulless, hard-eyed automaton who wielded his sharp porcupine
quill and his virile member with an equal self-obsessed, callous
ruthlessness?

For she knew everything now. She had long since retrieved
the magic mirror from the wastepaper basket, brushed off the
cherry pits stuck to the glass, and made sheepish apologies. The
mirror, which had seen it all and took everything in stride, had
accepted her contrition, and she now spent an hour in the morning and another in the afternoon, as well as an occasional hour or
two in the evening, watching the prince's antics; for it seemed
only prudent to keep track of his doings. She found out a great
number of things, all confirming (had she needed any further
confirmation) that this man was not the man she had married.
This man ruled the kingdom with an iron hand, crushing every
disagreement, no matter how minor, punishing every criticism,
no matter how trivial, signing death warrants and exile orders
with no trace of misgivings. In his leisure moments, he worked his

way through the female inhabitants of the palace—and here, once her furious blushing had given way to a horrified fascination at the thoroughness of the curse, his exertions proved rather instructive to watch. The study was the place of choice for his assignations, and he plowed into scullery girls with angular hips and middle-aged countesses plumped up on bonbons, all strewn with egalitarian abandon and in varied combinations on his floral rug; he also not infrequently contrived to couple paperwork with assorted diversions, as a flock of women serviced him under his desk while he perused his reports. The latter revelation shed nauseating new light on that afternoon when she had surprised Esmeralda the Singing Maid in the act of searching for a thumbtack at the prince's feet and had then, so trustingly, alighted in his lap. It made her study her son with fearful apprehension—would the shame of his life's quickening find reflection in his nature? It also confirmed that, by the sixth year of marriage—conveniently, she could calculate the precise date based on Ro's subsequent entrance into the world—Prince Roland had no longer been himself, which brought her back to the pressing question: Exactly when *had* her beloved prince stopped being her prince?

The radiance of their early years together shone undimmed in her mind: the first year, brimming over with dances, roses, and ardent (if properly restrained) affections; the second, when she had bathed in the prince's doting attentions through her long confinement; and the third, when she had learned the ways of the palace, indulged in the innocent joys of poems and tapestries, and basked in her overall sense of belonging.

Without the slightest hesitation, she sheared three buttons from the dress's back.

Then, her scissors yawning in her hand, she stopped and thought.

The fourth year, now—what was she to make of the fourth year, the year she had paid her surprise visit to the von Liebers' palace? The prince had not been entirely kind to her at the time, but he had offered oranges and explanations later. And the following stretch, before the unequivocal afternoon in the man's lap, had not been one of relentless misery, either, filled as it had been with the ups and downs of a regular, albeit not altogether fairy-tale, existence. Was her husband not entitled to some intermittent infelicities, moments of impatience or irritability, and sour moods before she would brand him an accursed monster? At what point would the weight of her cumulative unhappiness signal the innate change in his personality rather than an occasional bad day on his part?

After nearly a year of work, the shirt was finished at last, three buttons provisionally dotting its collar, the day for breaking the curse—their eleventh anniversary, as it happened—fast approaching, and she was still unable to make up her mind. There were only two weeks left now—and then a week—and then, somehow, she rose one windy spring morning to find that their anniversary was on the morrow and yet she felt no closer to deciding. On the verge of panic, she resolved to pay a visit to the von Liebers themselves, to uncover what she could about Prince Roland's long-ago sojourn. The prospect was unpleasant, but she was learning to pursue her aims with a force of will no less steely for her seeming meekness and patient acquiescence, and her poor prince's rescue lay at stake.

And so, she had her grooms ready a carriage and rode over to the ducal palace.

"It pains me to say it, but women are such self-deluding imbeciles," the witch announces. She does not, however, sound particularly pained, and adds after some thought, "Not that I should complain, it's what keeps me in business."

"Well, but hold on a minute," the fairy godmother interrupts. "That year of wandering—was it all just a dream, or wasn't it? And if it wasn't, am I correct in surmising that she went and allowed herself to be groped by some gypsy vermin?"

"Don't get your panties in a twist," the witch says, her tone dismissive. "Of course it was a dream. The girl had clearly developed a bit of an imagination while moping around her palace. A sound survival tactic, too, in my opinion."

"But even so," the fairy godmother persists. "A lady should be better capable of controlling what she imagines. Imagination can be highly dangerous, you know. Deadly, even. And all that mirror business, my dear child, *really!*"

I am grateful for the sudden disappearance of the moon behind new clouds: the conveniently timed darkness hides my reddening face.

"Ah, come now, I'm sure it did her good to stay abreast of her husband's athletic pursuits. She may have even learned a novel move or two to try under the covers in the event her true love found his way back to her bed." The witch pauses, then goes on slyly, "Or if he happened to be otherwise engaged, a nice young beekeeper, perhaps?"

Her insinuation, unfair as it is, comes out of nowhere, and I am winded. And then, because I must not let any chance feelings of guilt interfere with my sense of being fully in the right, I speak, sharply—too sharply.

"We need to finish this. Now."

The witch, I see, is regarding me with new interest.

The Middle's End

She found the ducal palace in a state of neglect. The gates to the grounds were unguarded, the paths overgrown. The windows, in spite of the twilight hour, gaped black, with only the faintest flickering of candlelight here and there. No one came to greet her carriage, and she stood before the front doors, knocking until her knuckles hurt. At last the butler of the once-stately gait let her in; he was old now, and wheezed as he walked. The Duke von Lieber, he informed her, his speech interspersed with bouts of coughing, had fallen off his horse, regrettably with fatal results, two summers ago now, and the duchess, aggrieved by her childless widowhood, discouraged visitors.

Stunned, she stared at the man. Surely, this was wrong. Fairy tales allowed for deaths, without a doubt—but not undeserved or inconsequential deaths, or, hardly ever, deaths from accidents—to say nothing of deaths without issue.

"So you'd best be going now, Your Highness, if it's all the same to you," the butler prompted, not unkindly. "I'd offer you some tea, but our last teapot quit."

She wanted to plead her case, but of course, she could not speak, and her elegant visiting card, proffered at her arrival, had failed to convey the urgency behind her visit. In desperation, she grabbed the card out of his grimy gloved fingers—there was the remembered O of his mouth—scribbled a few words on its rich creamy surface, and, underlining "To your mistress," handed it back. The old man sniffed, blinked, coughed, mumbled in a desultory fashion, and, at last, limped away with a shrug.

She waited. The clock ticked in the corner. The butler, his approach heralded from afar by scraping footfalls, reappeared in the doorway and, the look of surprise now perpetually rounding his mouth, invited her to follow. A step behind him, she walked through rooms that were darker, smaller, shabbier than the dangerous, jewel-bright, velvet-soft places that had haunted her one-time nightmares. At the end of a chilly corridor, he pushed open a door, made a creaking bow on the threshold, and departed with a shuffle.

After some hesitation, she stepped inside.

It took a moment for her eyes to grow used to the dimness. Then she saw the darkened bulk of an enormous bed, and her heart quailed at the recognition. The bed was unmade, as it had been all those years before, but now the rumpled mess of sheets and pillows bore a sad look of squalor rather than the luxurious languor of abandon.

"The maid has run off," snapped a petulant voice behind her. "Bitch."

She spun around. A woman sat at a vanity by the far wall, her back to the room. A single candle burned before her, and in its guttering a multitude of bottles, jars, and vials gleamed dully. The woman's feeble yellow curls, fat shoulders straining against a robe the unbecoming color of persimmon, hands so puffy that a ring could be seen cutting deep into the flesh of one finger, all seemed unfamiliar—but just then, in the mirror, she caught the woman's gaze and felt a jolt. The woman's eyes, that unforgettable shade of poisonous green, stared out of the ruin of her face with frightful intensity.

"*I need to talk to you about Prince Roland?* Spare me!" the woman hissed with startling violence. "Come to gloat, have you?" She swung around in her chair and, snatching the candle off the vanity, thrust it close to her face. "Go ahead, take a good look, why don't you? This is what happens to us. What happens to beauty. This will be you someday—just give it a few more years."

She stared, horrified. Darting light threw into grotesque relief the thinning lips drawn in lurid red, the flaccid eyelids oily with peacock-green paint, the artificial beauty marks glued to three wobbling chins.

The duchess was—suddenly, shockingly—middle-aged.

Middle-aged, and repulsive, and alone.

But surely this, too, was wrong. Those who were middle-aged had always been middle-aged, whether cozily so, like plump cooks and stolid gardeners existing on the margins of every tale, or maliciously so, like cruel stepmothers with striking architectural cheekbones. A charming young woman living at the happy heart of her love story would remain charming, young, and in love regardless of the passage of time—or so she had always assumed, in spite of her own diminished expectations; for were her troubles not unique, caused by a spectacularly evil spell?

"Cat got your tongue, little princess? Too good to address the likes of me?"

The duchess's voice, too, had changed: sharp, rusty springs poked through the threadbare upholstery of the silken, flirtatious tone she remembered. She shook her head, helpless—but even if she could speak, what would she have said? Forever mindful of her manners, she could have never allowed the frantic questions she so wanted to ask to escape into the air that smelled, sourly, sickeningly, of encroaching old age and failed beauty magic: Is this your true face, madam? Do you *deserve* it? Is this your punishment for something, something awful, you've done? Or—are you telling the truth and is this just something that happens?

Will it happen to *me*?

All at once, she felt she understood very little about life.

The duchess was speaking, in hot, angry hisses.

"You think you've won, little princess, and maybe you have, maybe good, boring girls do come out ahead in the end. But you know something? When you're old and your precious little children are all grown up and gone and your eyes are too weak for embroidery, you will have nothing, nothing to think about, nothing to remember, because good as you are, you haven't lived, haven't dared, you've just slumbered your years away in your precious little palace. You want to talk about Prince Roland, do you? Let me tell you about your prince. Your prince was never yours. I knew right away when I saw him at that reception, knew the kind of man he was, the kind of woman he needed. His mouth was hungry, so hungry—and there you were at his side, empty as a canary, stupid daisies in your hair, chirping to my buffoon of a husband about the weather. Oh, I remember it all like it was yesterday. Our eyes met, and he smiled, such a slow, dirty, delicious smile, I bet he's never given *you* a smile like that, and I knew without a doubt, I knew just what would happen when he offered to show me some funny old tapestry."

The duchess was talking, she understood with a recoiling of her entire being, of that long-ago visit—the visit in the third, unblemished year of her marriage. She wanted to protest—more, she wanted to scream—yet she said nothing, could say nothing, and the horrid woman with the vulgar beauty marks atremble on her chins went on hissing spitefully.

"We both knew neither of us gave a hoot about sightseeing, even if the tapestry really was delightful, some faun having his way with a nymph, quite outrageously, too, his red cock smack in the middle of the daft thing! But wouldn't you know, there was a secret room behind the tapestry, and there we spent some delectable hours together. Such a lover he was, so strong, so inventive, with an arsenal of moves that took even me by surprise, tricks he'd picked up from an earlier mistress in some exotic southern land. Of course, then you had to spoil all the fun with your pathetic little suspicions. We never did go behind the tapestry again, and the floor in his study wasn't nearly as comfortable. Oh, but a year later he paid me a visit here, and what a visit that was. Because you know what, little princess? I may be all alone now, youth gone, beauty gone, and that fool of a duke went and got himself dead and left nothing but gambling debts behind—but there was a time when I was *alive*, and your prince and I, we were alive together. The games we played in this very bed, let me just tell you—"

But she was already running, her hands over her mouth.

Somehow, she did not know how, she found her way outside, and into her carriage, and, after a blank ride through the deserts of non-time, was back in her own palace, her own chambers, her own dressing room. There she threw a handful of gowns into a pile on the floor, to reveal a hidden shelf at the back of the closet and, folded on it with great care, the shirt made of nettles. She dragged the shirt into the light, looked at the three pearly buttons along its collar for one full, demented heartbeat, then viciously ripped the third button off.

The nettles, all along the seams, split and gaped.

Her legs gave way. She slid down to the floor, sat frozen for some minutes, her soul near to bursting. Then, all at once hectic, she jumped up, grabbed her sewing kit, tried to repair the damage—to patch up the holes, pull the edges together, close up the wound now gaping where the prince's heart would be—but her hands shook, the needle kept slipping, and the leaves grew brittle and crumbled at her touch.

After an hour of her mutely hysterical efforts, the shirt was ruined.

She stared at it with stark, bereft eyes. There was no time to fix it now. It was not a Monday, there was no full moon, the kitchen was fresh out of nettles. The next day would come and go, and the spell would remain unbroken. A year of her life. A year of blistering, burning fingers, a year of silence, a year of hopes—all gone. Her mouth taut, she swept away the nettle dust, crawled into bed, and slept the heavy sleep of the defeated—slept, as it happened, all through her eleventh wedding anniversary and straight into the twelfth year of her marriage.

When she awoke, everything looked simple once again. Her love for the prince was a bit dimmer, perhaps, but he needed her help, and help him she would. She would spend another year in silence, she would weave another shirt. And this time, there would be just two buttons attached to its collar; but of those two, she was absolutely, resoundingly, certain—as, in truth, she had never been of the third.

For, once she calmed down, she mulled over the duchess's story, and understood that it was not all that unexpected. Indeed, if she were to be unflinchingly honest with herself, the third year of her marriage had not been one of cloudless contentment. She recalled the emptiness she had felt when Nanny Nanny had taken over Angie's care and she had found herself, quite simply, with nothing to do. There had been so many hazy, flat, lonely days— the hours spent listening to that ranting ghost of the minstrel whose bellicose epics she had detested, the battalions of pickles and preserves she had labored over in a swoon of sticky-fingered boredom, the afternoons she had stood before that faded tapestry, obsessively guessing at the meaning of the red spot in its center, willing everything to make sense. She remembered gazing at the prince across banquet tables and ballroom floors, wishing he would stop being so considerate and, her need of rest notwithstanding, start spending nights in their bedroom again. And of course, she remembered hearing the woman's low laughter and the man's soft voice in that tapestried hallway—but she remembered something else, too, something she had forgotten, had made herself forget, until now.

She remembered *knowing*, for a few brief hours.

And so, in a way, the aging mistress's revelations had been a relief, for it was clear now that none of it had been her dear Roland's fault: the prince had already been cursed. And the dimming of that particular stretch of her marriage only made the glorious luminescence of their first two years together stand out all the more dazzlingly in her mind. Devoid of doubts, sure of her purpose, she worked on her shirt with a steady hand, and somehow, without her noticing, the year was over almost as soon as it had begun. On the eve of her twelfth anniversary, she hung the new shirt, complete and impeccable, on the chair by her bed and went to sleep in the full knowledge of a different, blissful life that awaited her in the morning.

She dreamed of wandering in a nighttime wood. Trees loomed, leaves rustled, owls cried above her head. She was lost— there was no path before her—yet she did not mind; she liked the freedom of moving alone in the dark. After a while, she saw lights ahead and walked toward them, and soon came to a row of bright windows hanging on branches like laundered sheets on a clothesline, with no dwelling behind them. She stood on tiptoe and peeked into one, and there was her own blue-and-white bedroom, immaculate like a nun's cell. The window next to it opened onto the palace ballroom; the window beyond, onto the dining hall. All the rooms seemed deserted, but something dashed behind the windows—curtains swayed and teaspoons rattled at someone's passing—and then she heard knocking, as on a door. She glanced about, but there was no door to be seen. The knocking intensified, became urgent, turned into a desperate pounding. She rushed from window to window, her gaze scrambling over satin sofas and flocks of porcelain rabbits, unsure whether she herself was inside or outside, whether whoever was knocking was begging to be let out or fighting to be let in—and the urge to run, the urge to help, was still beating like some wild creature against her chest when she sat up all tangled in the sheets and listened to the frenzied knocking on the door of her bedroom.

She tumbled out of bed, tugged the door open.

Nanny Nanny panted on the threshold, the ruffled nightcap of her own wool askew on her grizzled head, both front hooves lifted. Before she had time to ask—before she had time to realize that she could not ask, bound as she was, for a few hours longer, by her need for silence—the ordinarily dignified Nanny Nanny bleated shrilly: "Angie's been ta-a-aken ba-aa-ad, she neeeds you, she neeeeds you! Run, Your Highness, run!"

She stood for one uncomprehending instant, then, as she was, barefoot, without grabbing a robe, flew down hallways and up staircases, the labored staccato of the elderly she-goat's hooves soon fading into echoes some landings below. As she ran, she tried to recall when she had last seen her daughter, when she had last seen her son—really seen them, really *looked* at them—and, to her sudden horror, could remember nothing beyond a vague sequence of perfunctory homework checks and good-night kisses, delivered and accepted in a cursory fashion, stretching back for silent days, silent weeks.

The door to her daughter's bedroom gaped open. It was so dim inside that for one unbearable moment she thought the bed empty—thought that something horrific, something unspeakable, had happened. Then her eyes adjusted to the light of the bedside candle. Its flame dipped and flared as though gusts of wind were tearing through the air of the small chamber, and Angie tossed in the pillows, her hair plastered like feverish snakes against her moist forehead, her eyes white with fear. She threw herself before the bed, grabbed her daughter's clammy hands in hers. Something was hurting her child, something was wrong with her child, and this was not a fairy-tale side plot, and nothing else mattered, nothing else existed, only this, only her worry, her worry swelling and gusting in the light of the crazed candle.

"Mama," the girl whispered wildly. "Mama, the sofas, the sofas are after me—"

"Where is the doctor, why isn't the doctor here?" she cried. Her voice was hoarse and unsteady, barely recognizable after having been lost for so long, but she did not notice, did not even notice having spoken. "Someone call the doctor now!"

She was enveloped in the smell of wet wool, and Nanny Nanny's soft, milky-white face loomed out of the dimness like a homey moon.

"But she-e-e isn't sick," the nanny bleated. "Shee-e-e had a ba-aa-aad dreeeam, she can't sleeeep, she's been calling her ma-a-a-ma—"

Sinking to her knees, she gathered her daughter close to her, felt Angie's small, anxious heart fluttering against her nightgown. All she knew was relief, immense and rolling like some vast, warm ocean. Not sick, not sick, her Angie was not sick . . . And then she tasted the rusty shapes of the recent words in her mouth, like a gush of blood from a tooth yanked out with great violence—and understood what she had done.

"There, there," she said, and her voice rang dead in her ears.

"The wood, Mama, the wood," Angie muttered hotly. "There were sofas in the wood, chasing me, and the bunnies shattered when I tried to pet them, and—and—"

"There, there," she repeated.

"Tell me a story, Mama."

She pulled the blanket over the child, shifted the pillows.

"You should sleep now."

"I will never sleep again. Never!"

But already, she saw, the girl's terror was draining away and her awareness of her age was returning to her—nearly eleven, she had begun to wear dresses that descended to her ankles, and slippers with small heels that clicked against the marble of the floors in the most satisfying fashion; and a shy page in tight crimson stockings had smiled at her in the hallway only a week ago. The girl's breathing steadied, and her eyes peeked almost slyly through the turmoil of her matted hair. "Unless you tell me a story. Like before. You never come to tell me stories anymore."

And just like that, she felt that her heart would break with the enormousness of her guilt. Had she loved her prince better than she had loved her children? No, she had not, of course she had not—and yet, having spent all this time trying to rescue him, had she not missed so much of their childhood? Because here was another year wasted—a year when she could have played with them, laughed with them, told them stories . . .

A year she could never get back now.

She sat on her daughter's bed, took a breath.

"Well. Once upon a time—"

"There lived a man who had a wife and a daughter," Angie rejoined.

She hesitated briefly.

"No," she said then. "This is a different story. There lived a girl. A beautiful girl who loved to dance. She had these shiny red shoes, and—"

"Ooh, I know this one, too!" Angie interrupted happily. "The girl was naughty, she loved her shoes more than anything, and one day she stepped on a loaf of bread and was punished."

"No," she said again, more confident now, for she was suddenly aware of words—dozens, hundreds, thousands of words—that were beating in the column of her throat, fluttering at the roof of her mouth, all struggling, all demanding to be released. "This is a different story still. This girl lived with the gypsies, and she was a bit naughty, true, but no more than was good for her, and she loved the shoes, yes, but she also loved the old grandmother she lived with, and the young cousins she took care of, and she loved the mountains, and she loved the rain, and she loved the wind in her hair. She traveled with her people from village to village, and wherever they set up their tents, she danced. Her dance was like a summer sunrise, and when dour, stolid peasants watched her, they felt tiny flames of joy start up in their tired hearts. One day a passing horse thief saw her. And even though she was whirling ever so quickly, the girl saw him, too, she saw him standing in the crowd of villagers, because he was not at all like them. He was a full head taller than everyone around him, and he wore a bright red kerchief around his neck and a black shirt unbuttoned all the way to his navel, and when he noticed her looking at him, he laughed, and his teeth were like white lightning in his dark face. So, after the dance, the girl—"

Nanny Nanny issued a slight cough from the armchair in which she had settled with her knitting.

"Is Your Highness certain that this is an appro-o-opriate story for your daughter?"

"Angie likes it," she replied, somewhat curtly. She felt aggrieved at being questioned. Had she not just given up a year of her life for the right to tell whatever story she desired? But when she glanced over at the bed, the child was asleep, her mouth half open, her hair no longer the writhing snakes of a restless nightmare but merely messy tresses framing her peaceful heart-shaped face.

And so she sent Nanny Nanny away and sat by the bed, quietly holding her daughter's hand, until the sky started to fill the curtains with a pale glow. Then she kissed the child's warm cheek, and stood, and walked across the still-sleeping palace, her bare feet soundless against the floors, every bit as though she were a ghost of some long-dead princess haunting the scene of a gruesome matrimonial crime. Back in her room, she unraveled the finished shirt with unhurried hands, first snipping off the two pearl buttons and carefully setting them aside. The orange sun of her twelfth wedding anniversary was just rising above the world when she sat down by the window, a pile of crushed nettles at her feet, and, in an undertone, continued the tale of the beautiful dancer and her horse thief, until the lovers rode off into the wind on a stolen black mustang.

"The end," she whispered then, and, clamping her lips shut, started on the third shirt. Of course, three was the traditional number of fairy-tale trials, and she saw the inevitability of her two failures. The third labor, she knew, would be her last, and she had to accept it, as one accepted the natural order of things. Her work, the third time around, progressed smoothly; her days assumed a certain hypnotic rhythm. True, now and then she felt flashes of uncharacteristic, searing anger—anger toward the nettles stinging her hands, toward the palace walls closing around her, even, irrationally, anger toward the poor prince himself—more, this entire drab, predictable world of repetitious sartorial redemptions, whimsical teapots, and True Love—but such moods passed quickly, and she subsided back into her trancelike state, during which she no longer debated the past, no longer imagined the future, only wove, and slept, and watched her children's innocent pastimes in the magic mirror, and, occasionally, wondered what her stepsisters' days were like or how Brie and Nibbles were faring, and slept again, and wove again.

Three weeks away from her thirteenth anniversary, the shirt

was nearly done, missing only the left cuff, when she ran out of nettles. She picked up her candle and went down to the kitchen to replenish her supply one final time. It was the murky hour before sunrise, and the kitchen lay deserted and still, save for the brownie who was sweeping crumbs into a corner and paid her no heed. She tiptoed to the pantry, and was in the process of filling the pockets of her nightdress with nettle leaves when a deafening crash sounded behind her.

She swung around and, her heart leaping, thrust the candle into the dark.

Arbadac the Bumbler stood hunched over the stove, a spoon frozen on the way to his mouth, the knocked-over pans settling noisily at his feet, a trickle of something viscous slithering down his chin. He blinked at her owlishly for a few moments before a look of recognition brightened his foggy eyes.

"Strawberry jam," he explained with an embarrassed cough, plopping the spoon back into the pot. "A weakness of mine. We're all only human. And you, Your Highness, what sweet craving brings you here at this hour?"

She pointed to the nettles cramming her pockets.

"Ah, yes, of course, the lifting of the curse! I hope it is proceeding splendidly?"

She shrugged.

"Has Your Highness managed to obtain the manticore's mane bristles, then? If you forgive me my professional curiosity?" He beamed at her. Puzzled, she shook her head. "Or the echo of the phoenix's song? No? But you aren't speaking to me . . . eh . . . I hope I haven't done anything to offend you?"

She looked at him reproachfully, gestured at her mouth.

He frowned, seemingly confused. Then his entire face sagged.

"Oh. Oh dear. I didn't, by any chance, tell you that you needed to be *silent*?"

She stopped breathing, stared at him. His prominent Adam's apple jiggled in his bony neck, once, twice. It had grown so quiet that she could hear him swallow.

"Ah. Yes. Yes, so it appears. Well, but of course, that was the working theory for a while, it wasn't like I was suggesting anything unduly excessive. Yes. But I might have been a bit behind the times, you see, what with the dratted clock and this plague of salamanders forever setting fire to the upholstery, it was only last winter that I finally had a free hour to glance through the back issues of *Magic Monthly*, and, well, it seems that in the past century or two, other approaches might have been . . . That is to say, there is a growing concern in the community that women are being deprived of their voices in addition to bearing the brunt of paying for their husbands' and brothers' mistakes, so the imposition of mandatory silence during the performance of preliminary curse-breaking rituals has now been deemed, eh, somewhat unnecessary." He regarded her anxiously. "So, you see, this is marvelous news, because you don't actually have to not speak . . . that is to say . . . Your Highness? Your Highness?"

She was striding away, out of the kitchen, and down the corridor, and up the steps, and past the sleeping guards, and out of the palace, as she was, in her light nightdress and house slippers, nettles spilling in her wake. The nighttime darkness was only just beginning to recede, and the garden lay drained of color, unsteady with shadows. She descended the staircase. The predawn chill was like a slap against her cheeks, but her face remained blank. She walked blindly, ignoring the paths, crossing lawns wet from a recent rain, crashing through beds of wilting daffodils. Two or three marble nymphs gave her looks of alarm and bounded out of her way, the palace gates rushed to swing open and let her through, and frogs in a little pond behind the mill abruptly ceased their throaty chorus of "Kiss me, kiss me!" at the sight of her twisted mouth. She noticed nothing, did not know where she was going, just kept walking, kept walking, driven by some unvoiced urge to leave behind all the places that she recognized, all the thoughts that made well-worn grooves in her mind. She walked until her feet ached, until her fingers turned brittle with cold, until her fury spent itself in physical exhaustion. Then she stopped and looked about.

She stood in a meadow. The world was hazy with the billowing light of a soft vernal sunrise, and the golden fog hummed with manifold voices of invisible bees. There was a small cottage with a thatched roof and a door painted deep blue, the color of her favorite parasol, at the foot of a hill. She had never been here before, yet it was all strangely familiar, like some story heard in a distant past. She rubbed her chilled hands together, breathed on them, waited for something. The door of the cottage opened, and a young man came out stretching, and saw her, and froze.

She went to him, slowly, for there was no urgency left in her now. The young man watched her unmoving. When she stopped before him, he shook his head like someone snatched out of a dream and cried, "But you are shivering, and your slippers are wet! Please, won't you come inside to warm up?"

His speech seemed to have a slight tilt, and the words slid down it a bit awkwardly, as though not completely sure of themselves; like her, he must have come from across the sea.

She met his shy gaze the color of honey.

"I must warn you," she said. "If you offer me a cup of tea, I will scream."

This was the first thing she had chosen to say after a year of muteness, and she meant it. He smiled, uncertainly.

"Your Highness pleases to make jokes. That is Your Highness's right, of course. Alas, I do not possess any tea to offer you, only cider. But I promise it will be good."

Aware of an odd twinge of disappointment at having been recognized, she followed him inside. The room she entered was clean and warm, and had a nice, solid smell about it, equal parts wood shavings, baked bread, and honey. A sturdy table by the window was covered with a blue tablecloth, and on it stood an unglazed earthenware jug with some disheveled red wildflowers. The young man brought out apple cider, and in silence they sat at the table, sipping from two chipped white cups. The cider was spicy, and good, just as he had promised, and she drank deep, with keen pleasure, feeling life return to her stiff fingers and toes. When her cup was empty, she wiped her lips on her sleeve, in a decidedly unprincesslike gesture, and studied the man across from her. He, too, looked eerily familiar, with his cast-down eyes and tousled hair the color of fallen leaves, like someone from a long-ago story—like someone from her own story, she realized then, in the days when her own story had made perfect sense.

"But I know you," she said, sitting back. "You are Prince Roland's courier, are you not? You—it was you who came to me with the glass slipper!"

"I am the beekeeper," the young man said quietly, addressing his cup. Nor was he all that young, she saw, perhaps only a year or two younger than herself.

Undaunted by the finality of his reply, she pursued her half-forgotten memories with rising excitement. "And you brought me all that fruit, I remember, I remember! The exotic star-shaped delights, I waited so eagerly for their arrival. Yes, Prince Roland had traveled to some southern province, but I couldn't go with him. It was the year I was with child." Briefly, she cast down her own eyes and paused, for the sake of propriety, but a moment later was being swept off again on the current of recollections. "And then—then he came back, and I never saw you again. Angie had just been born, and I was . . . well, in truth, I was a little overwhelmed, so I didn't notice you were gone at first, and then I had no one to ask about you, but . . . I did wonder. Did you leave the royal service?"

"That was a long time ago. I am the beekeeper now," he repeated, tersely.

"But why? Why did you leave?"

He shrugged. Still he would not look at her.

"I like bees better."

His tone was brusque. She saw that her questions made him unhappy, and she chewed her lip, frowning. Memories moved through her mind, shifting, shaping themselves, with a slow yet sure sense, into a story with a different meaning. Her nausea and weakness in the early days of her confinement, her sickly inability to reciprocate the prince's attentions, which had been infrequent already and then stopped altogether, the prince's subsequent departure on a diplomatic mission to some southern land and the steady stream of thoughtful gifts that followed, the courier on his bent knee, bearing the tray of overripe fruit, not meeting her gaze, then as now, his childlike mouth drawn in an oddly sorrowful bow, as though in some unspoken apology, the prince gone for days that stretched to weeks, and, preserved in a more recent pocket of wretchedness, the aging three-chinned duchess hissing with bitterness—

"The exotic southern mistress," she whispered, scarcely opening her lips.

"What?"

She looked at his knocked-over cup—and saw everything as clearly as she had seen any number of shameless couplings in her magic mirror.

"You chose to leave the prince's service because you'd witnessed too much on your travels with him. Because . . . you felt sorry for me?"

The cider was soaking into the tablecloth, a blush was soaking into his face, and she understood that what he had felt for her was more than pity. She thought with a sudden certainty: But this is a dream. I know this for a fact, because my past few years in the palace felt like a dream but were real, and this place feels real, so it must be a dream. I never did go down to the kitchen to get more nettles. I fell asleep in my starched, lacy prison of a bedroom, in the middle of drinking another accursed cup of tea, in the middle of weaving another accursed shirt, and all the bits and pieces of my daily miseries congealed in my mind, Arbadac the Bumbler and the sentence of silence and that horrid duchess with her spiteful truths—and now I find myself, still in my nightdress, transported to some imaginary hut abuzz with bees, stripping more meat off the carcass of my marriage while I sit across the table from the youth who belongs to my faraway past, the youth with the golden-brown eyes and quiet words and gentle hands, the youth whose arrival with fruit I once awaited so eagerly. In truth, though—for, asleep, I can speak freely—I never ate any of the fruit. I abhorred those star-shaped monstrosities. I also abhorred plush blankets, and eternally closed windows, and knitting. Oh, I abhorred knitting most of all! I was alone, and I was bored, and I resented the pedantic physician forever telling me that I was too frail, that I needed to keep to my bed, "Prince's orders," and I resented the prince himself, who—quite possibly, fresh from the embraces of some southern slut—would arrive once a month on a scheduled visit so we could exchange halting banalities for an endless hour, while I hid my yawns behind yet another ugly sweater I was making for my kind old father-in-law, my heart beating out a sluggish rhythm: bored, so-bored, so-bored. Because what I really longed for, all through that year, the tedious year until the baby came, the miserable second year of my marriage—yes, what I really wanted, even if I would never dare confess any of it to my waking self—was a hearty plate of herring, a loaf of black bread, and the presence of the shy young man with that childlike mouth and those golden eyes that darkened every time he looked at me.

So here he is now, summoned into transient being from the far reaches of my nighttime fantasies. And since this is a dream, I can do as I please.

And with that, she rose, leaned over the table, and kissed him.

He pushed his chair back, holding himself away from her stiffly, his eyes wide with shock. Then his eyes closed, and he kissed her back.

And even though it was a dream—and it was, of course it was, she was sure of it—the smell of honey in his hair was real, and the taste of apple cider on his lips, and so were his lips themselves, pliant and warm, and his hands, which drew her closer to him, and the darkness behind her eyelids, gentle yet increasingly insistent, so much so that for one half-panicked instant she worried whether this was no dream, after all, and was just about to draw back when she forgot to worry, and simply succumbed, and there they were, the two of them, enclosed in the long, soft, enveloping moment like no other moment in her life, and within its glowing seclusion the world felt surprising and thrilling, yet it also felt solid and good—yes, the world made sense at last—and then trumpets exploded just outside the wall.

She jumped back, he jumped up, his chair tottered and crashed, her cup fell and broke. Fists pounded on the door. They stared at it with a wild surmise. He moved toward it just as it shuddered and flew open, and three or four guards burst in, all chain mail and gauntlets. She screamed, realizing that the blissful dream she had anticipated blushingly was about to become a full-blown nightmare. Upon seeing her, however, the guards started to bow, bumping and elbowing each other in the narrow doorway, and the dream turned harmless, commonplace, and disappointing. They were all speaking at once, and she stopped paying attention, for there was some nonsense about frogs who had seen her sleepwalking this way and her presence required immediately at the palace and the king, the kind old King Roland, dying, dying just before sunrise that morning.

"Your Majesty," the guards called her, bowing, bowing.

She allowed herself to be led outside. The beekeeper stood mute on the threshold, shielding his eyes against the sun, which hung directly over the meadow now, watching them all impassively, as the sun would, while they blundered about on their small human errands of love and grief. She realized that she did not even know his name, and she wanted to ask, but did not—she just accepted a cloak from one of the guards and, meekly obeying the dream's illogic, climbed onto a horse they brought her, and rode away with the men.

In the palace, unresisting, unquestioning, she was dressed in robes trimmed with ermine by maids weeping copious tears, then taken to the grandest ballroom, all marble and gilt, and there placed next to that man who looked like her husband but was most certainly not. Her fake husband's face, she noticed absently, was not like it always was, not sleek and bright and cold but drawn and pained, filled, it almost seemed, with some real emotion. He turned to her and tried to speak, but she did not listen, and when he tried to take her hand, she pulled away, so he grew hard-eyed once again and stared ahead. Courtiers came in a long procession as the two of them waited there, side by side on the raised dais, and the ladies cried and the lords offered their condolences and everyone called them "Your Majesties." She smiled at them with gracious compassion, but her smiles became more strained as the interminable day, as the interminable dream, wore on, for, as she stood there, dressed in the ermine-fringed robe of somber velvet, receiving the line of mourners, listening to the man next to her thank his ministers for their offers of sympathy, she began to feel a bit winded with a suspicion that was tiny at first, a sneaking thought, a flickering, twinging "maybe," but which grew and grew and grew, until, abruptly, she had a sensation that the world was now only a hillock of land with dark waves encroaching upon it from all sides, rising higher and higher, lapping already at her embroidered slippers.

She turned and stared at the man next to her, the man pretending to be her husband.

"Are you feeling well, Your Majesty?" the court physician inquired solicitously at her shoulder. "Well, technically, Your Highness. The coronation is not until next Sunday."

She let out a small, wild cry and, for the first and last time in her life as a princess, fainted.

"Not the *beekeeper*, my dear!" The fairy godmother sniffs. "I must tell you, child, you have positively plebeian tastes."

But I can see that her heart is not in it, and at last I understand her proprieties to be mere gestures of courtesy, kept about her like a perennial clean handkerchief on offer, for the sake of politeness, while her eyes are warm with compassion and her timid hands flutter about me, as though she would like to comfort me, if she only knew how.

"Down to one button, then," the witch notes, and her voice, too, is not unsympathetic. "I'm sensing an unfortunate trend here."

In the graying predawn light, her face has lost much of the hook-nosed, ancient-crone menace it seemed to possess in the harsh blooming of darkness. She is not even that old, I notice with surprise—in her sixties, perhaps—and her features, far from ugly or frightful, are merely weathered and strong.

"This is all very sad, I do agree," the fairy godmother says. "The prince was clearly not the man we all thought him for much of your marriage. But only a short while ago, you wanted to lift his curse—and here you are now, trying to murder him. What happened in your final months together?"

"Why don't we see for ourselves," offers the witch. "Are you ready to finish this, madam?"

I unclench my hand, look at the last snippet of Roland's hair on my palm.

"My child," the fairy godmother says quietly. "There will be no turning back if you go through with this."

"That's the whole point, though, isn't it?" I say, archly.

My defiance rings forced to my ears.

"She's right, you know." The witch gives the brew one final prod. "Not only will this seal your husband's fate—it will also tie your own fate to his, forever and ever. In a way, you will never be rid of him. Not after this. Hate traps you as much as love does. Because hate is not the opposite of love. Indifference is."

"So I'll be indifferent once he is dead," I tell her. And I take a breath, and I take a step, and I stretch my hand over the potion, and then—and then I hesitate. My husband's fate, my fate . . . I assumed that his death would liberate me, once and for all, from the confines of impersonal fairy-tale destiny—but am I fooling myself, am I simply driven to take yet another predictable step in a predictable story? I peer into the cauldron, and its oily black surface readily serves up the reflection of a woman with aggrieved eyes, sharpened cheekbones, and mad, wispy hair. This is not the face I thought of as mine for so long, the unchanging face of a young bride with rosy lips and gaze ever widened in anticipation of conjugal happiness—and yet I see, my heart sinking, that it is a familiar face all the same.

The face of a spurned, jealous wife, the face of a middle-aged villainess.

I take a step back.

"Well, do you still want him dead, or what?" the witch asks.

In my mind, I struggle to recite the litany of hate I used to repeat to myself on many a sleepless night. I want him dead because I hate the smooth perfection of his face, the purposeful nature of his days, the grace with which he charms everyone around him, the ruthlessness with which he discards whatever he no longer needs. I want him dead because I've given him the best years of my life, my youth, my beauty, and he has treated me in such a shameful way. I want him dead because I loved him once upon a time. I want him dead because . . . because . . . I want him dead . . . And then I realize that something is different inside me. The night has burned through like a splinter of kindling, and my anger—my anger has burned away with it. Somehow, without my noticing, the memories of my married years have left me one by one, drowned in the cauldron's darkness, leaving me purged and empty, ready for something else, something new.

I do not want him dead.

All I want is to be free—free of him, free of my past, free of my story.

Free of myself, the way I was when I was with him.

I glance from the doughy pancake of the fairy godmother's face, all soggy with commiseration, to the flinty angles of the witch's face, made hard with wisdom, then look away to the horizon. The sun has not yet risen, but the ink of the night has become diluted, and I discern, beyond the drab stretch of the fallow fields, at the very end of the dusty road, a denser line—the invitation of the woods. And so, I release my fingers, just like that, and, not waiting for the half-hair to spiral harmlessly down to the ground, turn my back on both women and start toward the forest, one foot in front of the other.

As I walk away, I hear the fairy godmother sob once, a soft sob of relief. Then the witch's raised voice hits me squarely between my shoulders.

"If that be the case, madam, have you considered divorce?"

I do not stop running until I burst into the trees.

Part Two

In the Forest Clearing

The wood is just as I imagined it, just as I dreamed it. Leaves have not yet fallen but are already shot through with copper and bronze, and the trees stand tall, like columns in some mysterious autumnal cathedral carved out of gems, wrought out of precious metals, all rubies and amber and gold. Paths crisscross and disappear into the russet-colored dusk. I inhale the smell of ripeness, the smell of rain, the smell of wild things growing, dying, changing freely. It is neither day nor night under the trees, but a lingering in-between gloaming. The path I follow seems to have a will of its own, twisting, turning, always taking me deeper and deeper in. The farther I go, the more ancient the beeches, aspens, and elms, the more pungent the scents, the more solemn the world around me—and the less afraid I feel, as though with every step into the unknown, I am shedding a bit of my familiar past, losing a bit of my familiar self.

The wood is quiet with a profound, churchlike silence, but as I keep walking, I begin to sense stealthy presences all about me, traveling along invisible forest roads on hushed errands of their own. Enormous white moths that look like flowers—or else flowers that look like moths—glide slowly, weightily, from one pool of shadow into another. Glinting eyes stare at me from under misshapen roots, from inside hollowed trunks, yet when I draw nearer, they are quick to blink out of sight or turn into innocuous fireflies that zigzag across my path, winking in and out, before dissolving in the canopy above. The path soon takes me to the edge of a clearing, runs alongside it. I can hear water trickling somewhere nearby. It is dark on my left, light on my right: pale dawn has begun to glow between the giant oaks that line the clearing. I glance over, squinting after the dimness of the forest— and catch my breath.

A circle of slender sprites, translucent like leaves held up against the morning sun, are leading a swaying fleet-footed dance in the grassy glade. Without thinking, almost without knowing what I am doing, quite as if summoned, I abandon the path and rush out toward them.

Then I stand blinking in the brightness.

The clearing is empty, the grass undisturbed by footprints; only a breeze is moving long branches of willows back and forth, back and forth, above a shallow fast-running brook. Oddly, it seems that autumn has not touched this place at all: the grass is verdant here, the leaves vivid, the air full of midday summer warmth. There is a smell here, too, a sharp, clean smell that I cannot name, yet that reminds me of the wild, exhilarating way the night smelled when I walked out of the palace and ran to the crossroads, the now-empty velvet pouch at my hip still filled with my husband's fingernails, with my mother's flowers—was it only hours before?

It feels like another life—or else, a life of another.

A life of someone I did not like very much.

Something swoops over my head with an eerie cry, so low that the wind raised by its wings brushes my face. An owl chasing after the departing night, I tell myself—but when I swing around to follow its flight, I see a long-tailed creature wreathed in flickering fire. It trails sparks across the skies, then vanishes in the gloom of the forest. A firebird? Or even a small dragon? There are no dragons left in our orderly, civilized kingdom, of course, but I have gone so far into the woods that it no longer feels like any place I know, and I am suddenly sure that I would not find this hidden summer oasis drawn, bordered, and labeled on any of the maps my children pore over in their geography lessons.

My heart beating, I stand peering into the oaks that guard the clearing, but all is quiet again; only bumblebees hum, and the brook tinkles gently. All at once, I yearn for a refreshing sip of cold water. The brook is clear as crystal, and its bottom gleams with a pattern of bright pebbles. Too parched to care about grass stains on my dress, I kneel on the ground and scoop some water in my hand.

"I wouldn't, if I were you," a breezy voice says above me.

The water trickles out between my fingers as I meet the gaze of a girl who sits swinging her legs on the lowest branch of a nearby willow. She is stark naked, and her skin has a wet sheen. Perky pink nipples of an adolescent peek through the messy tousle of abundant curls the color of river weeds, and the eyes she has turned upon me are like two forest ponds, dark green and still; as I look closer, I can almost see tiny specks of water lilies floating inside them and tiny streaks of dragonflies darting through.

Looking into those eyes for long is a bit like drowning, and I glance away, dizzy.

"Unless, of course, you want to be a fish," the girl continues blithely. "It's not so bad, being a fish. Some may even prefer it. Not me, though. I enjoy having toes." She wiggles them for emphasis; her toenails look just like the pebbles glistening in the brook's merry current. "Also, I like eating the fish, myself. Girl fish are delicious."

When she smiles, I notice that her teeth are sharp and crowded in her mouth.

Carefully, I rise and edge a few steps away.

"I'm searching for the royal woodsman's cottage," I tell her, then pause for a startled moment: I have not realized it myself until now. I feel a twinge of guilt as I add, "It may or may not look like a shoe. My sister lives there. Well, my stepsister, really. Do you know where I might find it?"

"Oooh, a quest, I love quests!" the girl cries, and dangles her legs faster. "But you must give me something first." She stares at me with her disconcerting eyes. "I've got it! Tell me a secret. Only it has to be a real secret. Something that no one else knows. Just us girls."

And because I am still filled with remorse over my treatment of Melissa, I remember something sneaky, something shameful, from my childhood, something I have never confessed to anyone before.

"When I was eleven or twelve," I say quietly, "whenever I helped with the family dinners, I would . . . I would put things in my stepsisters' food."

"What kinds of things?" the girl asks with interest. "Shards of glass? Nails?"

She grins with anticipation. Her teeth are really quite sharp, filed to points.

"No, nothing like that, nothing to hurt them!" I protest with a shudder. "I just resented them because they were happy. Because they fit in. They didn't have funny accents, and they did well at school. Of course, only Gloria got good grades, but Melissa was popular, she had so many friends. So I'd crush bugs into their soup. Or sprinkle dirt in their hot chocolate. Or do other, even worse things . . ."

I stop. She considers me, her head tilted.

"No," she then says flatly.

"No?"

"No. That was child's play. Give me something else. Something grown-up. And hurry, or I might bite you. Even if you aren't a fish."

She is laughing as she says it, but when I look again at her sharp, bared teeth, I am not at all certain that she is joking. Her features, her voice, her gestures are those of a very young girl, hardly older than I was when I spat in my sisters' dinners, but her eyes, as she holds mine, are old and hungry and savage, filled with some dark, ancient knowledge, and I suddenly feel that it is the wood itself studying me out of the stagnant pools of her irises, weighing my worth, deciding whether to swallow me whole.

I take a deep breath.

"I used to fantasize about leaving my children. I imagined just walking away from them, from the palace, without glancing back. I dreamed of living a rough, bright life on the edge of the world. I'd ride stolen horses, dance with the winds, spend nights with sailors and gypsies, drink, swear—be free. And in those dreams, I never sent a single word home, just let them wonder what happened to me. And I did not miss them."

She worries her lower lip between her teeth.

"Better," she concedes at last. "You seem so nice and simple, but you aren't all that nice and simple inside. Nice is boring. Still, I want something that cuts even deeper. Try again."

And I say it before I even know what I am about to say.

"My husband only pretended to love me when he married me. In truth, he has never loved me. Not one day. Not one bit."

In the fallen hush, the plaintive cry of the bird on fire rises from somewhere far, far away. Up in the willow tree, the naked girl claps and swings her legs.

"Ooh, yes, that will do, that is a juicy little tidbit," she sings out happily. "That will feed me for a day or two." She licks her lips, once, twice, her snakelike tongue darting out in quick, greedy stabs. "You are free to go now."

For some reason, having said what I said, I can no longer meet her eyes.

"Aren't you going to point me toward the royal woodsman's cottage?" I whisper.

"The royal woodsman's cottage? But I have no idea where it is. Not in these parts, that's for sure. No royalty around here. Or don't you know—it may have taken you only an hour or two to get here, but you are very, very far from home, lost little girl. This is my domain, and I eat handfuls of silly princesses like you for breakfast. You should be grateful I have chosen to let you go."

And even though she may be only a thirteen-year-old willow sprite with a wicked sense of humor, some sinister thickening in her voice sends a deep chill through my blood, quite as if all my insides have gone goose-bumped. I walk toward the trees then, quickly, without protestations or questions, not raising my head. The unnatural summer, I see, ends abruptly at the clearing's edge; back in the woods, autumn reigns once again, damp and brown. But just as I am about to reenter the cool dimness, I stop in confusion: where previously one single well-traveled path skirted the glade, there is now a fork in the road, one path going left, the other going right, both disappearing into the forest.

"You didn't think it would be so easy, now, did you?" The girl laughs behind me. "This is still a fairy tale, you know. But you've been braver than I expected from the looks of you, and I am feeling benevolent. Let me see . . . Yes. If you take the path to the left, you will return to your old life, just like you've never left it, and no one the wiser. And if you take the one to the right, you will get an entirely new happy ending. A new, better prince and everything. What color eyes do you prefer?"

I look to the left. I already miss my children terribly.

I look to the right. I am tempted to start anew.

"What if I go straight?" I ask.

"Straight where?" Her laugh is just like the tinkle of the brook rushing over the pebbles. "There is no straight here, dummy. Only left or right."

She speaks the truth, of course. The paths diverge, one veering back, one leading forward, but between them lies a perilous eruption of poisonous briars, a wilderness of weeds, a dark tangle of branches and roots so dense it is impossible to see through it.

I turn to ask another question. The girl is gone. Only the willow branch is trembling lightly, and the brook is still laughing with her young, cruel voice.

For a long while I stand unmoving on the edge of the quiet brown wood, not thinking about anything, just listening to the beating of my heart.

Then I gather my cloak around me and push straight into the briars.

At the Woodsman's Cottage

My hands are soon bleeding, my clothes torn, my face scratched. This is a different kind of wood altogether—no longer the softly luminous, cathedral-like alleys of stately trees, but a snarling chaos of brambles, thistles, thorns, overgrown undergrowth. I cannot see three paces before me as I struggle through the wild brush, and my hearing is filled with the deafening crackle of branches snapping over my head and under my feet. Everything is untamed, everything is hard and sharp, everything is pushing against me. When I tumble into a ravine and find it filled waist-high with yellowing nettles, I almost weep with relief, so familiar does their gentle fire feel against my skin. Yet I pick myself up, clamber onto the other side, and plunge back into the murderous thicket. I do not stop, nor do I turn back—and in any case, I know that even were I to regret my decision and retrace my steps, I would not find the summery clearing with the laughing brook and the two paths diverging.

You are only ever given one shot at a choice in stories such as this.

Creatures in this part of the wood are curious rather than stealthy, almost as though they have never encountered a princess before. Birds and squirrels jump to lower branches to watch me closely as I fight my way past. For a while, a fawn walks gracefully through the brush alongside me, soundless next to my crashing and stomping, the white spots on its skin like round flashes of sunlight in the leaves. Then a wolf springs out of the bushes mere steps away, and the fawn vanishes just as suddenly as it appeared. The wolf stares at me with narrowed orange eyes, then follows me in turn, always keeping the same distance. I have no fear of it.

"Excuse me," I say politely, "but have you seen a house built like a shoe?"

At the sound of my voice, the wolf tenses, twitches its ears, and swerves away, melting into the surrounding twilight. I notice that it has indeed grown darker all around me, as if the day, having only just begun, is already rushing toward evening. I stop to peek at the sky through the brambles, and it seems to me that I do see a star blinking far, far above. Something soft nudges my ankle, and I look down to discover what appears to be a family of plump brown mushrooms gathered at my feet. In the next moment they doff their wide-brimmed hats, and I am surrounded by lumpy, boulderlike creatures with twigs for their noses and moss for their hair.

I crouch before them. Their eyes are like birdseed, beady and excited.

"Pardon me," I say to them, "but do you know where I can find a woodsman's family that lives inside a shoe?"

They twitter and chatter in birdlike accents, then file off, giggling, one after another, into the weeds that reach to my shoulders. I wait a bit, but they do not return, so I press ahead. After another hour or two, it has grown completely dark, but the way has become easier little by little. Stars twinkle gently, their flickering light enough for me not to trip yet not enough to see anything clearly. Sometimes it feels as if I am walking in place, on the bottom of a sonorous well, with the night sky a perfect black circle above me. Now and then I enter colder pockets of drifting mists and guess at vague shapes swirling through them—pallid lilies, grimacing faces, beckoning hands with thin, ghostly fingers—but the fog clears swiftly, and I find myself walking on the bottom of the dark starlit well once again. Once, I am enveloped in a cloud of floral scents sweeter than a powder room crowded with perfumed court ladies, yet with the lightest tinge of rot at the very heart of the smell. It seems to me then that I am passing right next to a crumbling brick wall of some manor all entwined in blooming wild roses, yet I cannot be certain; and when I carefully put out one hand and feel about, I succeed only in pricking my finger on a thorn. Soon I start to feel drowsy, and drowsier still, until I am close to falling asleep on my feet. And perhaps I really do, for as I continue to stumble, to slumber, to stumble through the woods, I imagine a small log cabin striding past me on giant chicken legs, its one window fiercely ablaze, ruffled forest imps squawking and leaping out of its way by the dozen—and a sleek black cat on a golden chain who is singing a wordless song in a pleasant velvety baritone as it winds its way back and forth around an immensely thick oak tree in a blue woodland glade—and a glorious silver-haired maiden who is bathing in a silent forest pool, shining droplets of moonlit water running like pearls down her outstretched white wings—and other, stranger things that shimmer at the edges of my vision, beautiful and wild, yet melt into the dark whenever I turn to look at them directly. And as I walk, as I dream, through the obscure, glowing mysteries of the night, the ground evens out under my worn ballroom slippers, the unkempt brush slowly gives way to the magnificent trees of the morning, and the trees begin to part, and the path widens, and then I do trip, after all, but manage to catch myself, closing my eyes protectively for an instant—only to open them upon a sunny autumnal day, a clear pale sky over a meadow, and, across the meadow, a cheerful house painted bright yellow and shaped like a shoe.

. . .

I blink, half expecting the house not to be there when I look again—yet there it is still, just as solid, with its green roof, its red door, its blue weather vane fashioned like a rabbit. A dozen shirts of all colors, from prodigiously large to doll-sized tiny, flap and billow on a stretched clothesline in the small yard, and a cow is grazing outside the white wooden fence. As I stand there staring, a redheaded boy, barelegged and barefoot, no older than three, bursts out of the door, rushes into the yard, and, screaming with laughter, bends to pick up a handful of mud and flings it at the drying shirts. His aim is faulty: the clod of dirt arcs short of the clothesline and splatters the cow instead.

The cow looks up impassively, chewing all the while.

"Stop it this instant, you rampaging wildebeest!" cries the buxom woman who has just appeared in the doorway. "I should send you and your unruly brothers off to the woods. Not fit for civilized living, the lot of you!" Her apron is askew, her mouse-colored hair coming out of its bun in messy wisps, and there is a wailing baby propped on her hip. "Why can't you be more like your sisters? Come here, you little monster!"

The boy ceases his laughter abruptly and edges sideways toward her, then turns around, a look of resignation on his reddened face, to receive a halfhearted slap on his behind; but her hand freezes in mid-motion when she glances up and sees me running across the meadow toward her.

"Your . . . Your Majesty?"

I throw myself, weeping and laughing, onto Melissa's bosom. It is wobbly and warm, and smells of milk, mashed peas, and infant sleep, and for a few gasps I wish I were a child again, with a child's simple sorrows and joys—and with a mother to right the world with one effortless flick of her wrist whenever the world would begin to tilt off center.

"Don't call me that, don't call me that!" I repeat between sobs and hiccups—and then become aware of the presence of the boy who is clinging to Melissa's apron and the baby on Melissa's hip, so close to me that our noses are almost touching, both children gazing at me in wide-eyed astonishment.

I inhale, straighten, and look down at the three of them. I am a full head taller than Melissa and, I am pained to notice, much thinner, while my gray silk dress, even stained and torn as it is, is infinitely finer than the coarse woolen sack she is wearing.

"I must inform you that I have left King Roland," I tell her in an awkward, formal tone. "Could I impose upon you, please? It will be for a day or two only. Until I figure out what I should do."

Her mouth gapes open, but before she can answer, the doorway behind her fills with a multitude of people, a veritable crowd, it seems to me, and they push and shout and shove until we are propelled into the yard, and there I find myself surrounded by children, children, children, little children, bigger children, children who are only a few years short of being adults, children pulling at the tassels of my velvet bag ("Ooh, Mama, look, look how fancy," a pink blond girl purrs), children pressing their chins into my knees ("So soft!" sighs another girl as she rubs her cheek against the fabric), children touching my hair and my cloak, children looking me over with unabashed curiosity.

"Is this our other auntie?" asks a scrawny boy with scabs on both knees and one finger deep in his nostril.

"Yes," Melissa replies, and her eyes are shining. "This is your auntie the queen. She will be staying with us for a while. For as long as she wants."

And I try to thank her, but just then the yard erupts with noise, as they all offer me their names at the same time, calling out "Tom Junior!" and "Myrtle!" and "Mary!" and "Peter!"—but there are far too many of them, and I cannot keep track, I cannot even count them; every time I start my surreptitious count, six, seven, eight, the red and blond heads bobble, shuffle, dart, dip under my elbows and behind my back, and I must start anew, three, four, five . . . Melissa clucks and giggles and chides, like an immense mother hen in the midst of her brood, then gathers everyone and guides them back inside her house shaped like a shoe. And the house is astonishing—cramped, cozy, mad—filled with odd angles, slanting floors, sharp corners, dipping ceilings, round rooms, narrow rooms, rooms like shafts, rooms like honeycombs, rooms where you can only crawl on your hands and knees, rooms where you must squeeze yourself between the walls, rooms that become chimneys, and for a while, all is chaos, for there are fights breaking out, and three big dogs getting tangled in everyone's feet, and two cats hissing, and I gift my velvet bag to the blond girl (Myrtle, I think), who is so overcome that she will not stop running around, squealing in delight, showing it off to everyone; and milk is spilled, and braids are pulled, and one pillow explodes, so there is goose down floating everywhere. Yet my stepsister, ever so lightly, holds the strings of this merry pandemonium in her capable hands, and eventually order is restored. The boys are sent off into the yard to feed the animals and tend to the turnips in the vegetable patch; the girls busy themselves with sweeping floors, washing dishes, and singing the baby to sleep. Melissa ushers me into a nook below a twisted staircase, sits me down on a chair fashioned out of a tree stump and painted with purple polka dots, underneath a garland of drying garlic that keeps bumping the top of my head, and asks me: "What happened? My dear, what *happened*?"

And I clam up. For what can I tell her? That I almost murdered my husband? That I left the palace without ever meaning to do so, and now I cannot go back?

"Oh, you poor thing, but you must be so tired," she says when I do not reply, and pats my hand. "Why don't I warm up some good mushroom soup and after you eat your fill, you can go straight to sleep. Things will be clearer once you rest."

And all at once I realize how exhausted, how incredibly exhausted I am. How long has it been since I left the witch and the fairy godmother at the cauldron and started on the rutted road toward the wooded horizon? How long was I lost in the trees, talking to beasts, making bargains? It feels like days, if not months—sunshine and starlight, summer and fall. Is it morning or evening now, and what season?

I do not know, nor do I want to know—all I want is sleep, peace, oblivion.

Declining Melissa's insistent offers of food, I follow her up the rickety staircase, pass through rooms upon rooms of slumbering, playing, gossiping boys and girls, navigate a maze of turns and twists to the end of a corridor, then climb the rungs of a ladder to a low-ceilinged loft where luminous dust clouds hang in shafts of light slanting through chinks between logs (it must still be daytime, then), and a bed of sorts is waiting for me—a pallet placed directly on the floorboards, draped in cowhides and wolf furs. Melissa keeps apologizing for the absence of a proper guest room, of a proper bed, of proper linens—"We hardly ever get any visitors here, but Tom will make a good, solid bed for you soon, he's made all the things in the house, it's no bother!"—but I hear her words only with great difficulty as I struggle out of my burr-studded cloak, my gaping satin slippers, my torn, soggy dress. I do not notice when she leaves. A thick woolen nightgown is draped over a three-legged stool painted with lopsided poppies. I put it on—it is several sizes too big and balloons about me like a small tent—and crawl under the hides.

I am asleep the moment my head touches my makeshift pillow.

Birds. That is the first thing I know upon reaching the surface after my long, dreamless dive into the dark. Birds, birds, birds, flapping their wings, shifting, pecking. I open my eyes. Broad beams of the sun are piercing the loft once again, striping it in light and shadow, but coming from the other side now, and numerous birds are cooing somewhere close. When I peek through a crack above my pallet, I see doves, tens of doves, taking off on short sun-dappled flights, landing, spreading their wings, preening, kissing, in a cote just on the other side of the wall. I watch their abbreviated attempts to fly until I am wide awake. My dress, I find, has been cleaned while I slept, and the rips in its sleeves and along its hem mended with confident needlework. I put it on and, humbled by gratitude, climb down the ladder.

Immediately I get lost. All the spaces are odd in this house, all the angles are bent, the windows shaped like teapots, birdhouses, tall hats, the doors hidden behind other doors or inside cupboards. It is like meandering through a wildly imaginative child's drawing. I wander for some time, gaping in helpless astonishment, until I happen upon a round opening in the floor and, edging up to it so as not to crash through, look down into the family kitchen.

My sister is serving breakfast. The table is laden with jugs of cream, platters of forest berries, mugs of milk. The children are devouring stacks of pancakes. The redheaded man at the head of the table—this must be her husband, Tom the royal woodsman—is slathering a thick slice of bread with butter. His shoulders are broad, as are his teeth; he is not at all good-looking, his face seemingly carved with a few wide strokes of an ax, but he exudes solid sense—he exudes goodness. When Melissa passes behind him with another bowl of yogurt, I see her touch him on the back of his neck, see him place his hand over hers. Every time one of the children speaks, he stops eating, swivels toward the child, and listens, and when he offers a few words of his own, everyone pays attention. I am finally able to count their heads, some red like their father, others dark blond like their mother—two, four, seven, nine. Nine children, six boys, three girls—no, not nine, ten, for now I notice the still-hairless baby permanently attached to Melissa's hip. They discuss the health of a lightning-struck linden in a nearby clearing, fish hatching in a stream behind their meadow, the vegetable garden. The children laugh easily.

Wholesome, I think as I look at them. Happy, I think.

They are talking in hushed voices—so as not to disturb me, I realize now—but I do not alert them to my presence. I watch them closely, avidly. At last the man stands, stretches, gathers Melissa to his green-clad chest in a bear hug, and plants a kiss squarely on her mouth, in front of everyone. My entire life, I have never had a kiss like that—solid, certain, open. When he leaves, the children, too, rise; the boys scamper out after their father, the girls start gathering dishes off the table, sweeping away crumbs. And I understand what I will do.

"Melissa," I call.

She looks up.

"You're awake!" she cries. "Come down, come down, I'll make more pancakes."

"Can I have something to write on first?" I ask. "And something to write with."

And then I am seated on another tree-stump chair, before a tree-stump table, with a sheet of paper and a feather quill ("From our beloved goose Martha," Myrtle tells me proudly as she hands it over). For a while I sit frowning. Writing has never been easy for me: there is something about imprisoning my thoughts in neat rows of words on a page that confounds me every time. But my stomach rumbles with hunger, and at last, I dip the quill into the inkwell ("Daddy made the ink out of blackberries," Myrtle has informed me, "and I found most of the berries!")—and start.

"Dear Roland."

But he is not dear to me—certainly not now, and possibly not in years. I tear the narrow strip with the greeting off the top of the page, crumple it up, and try again.

"King Roland."

But queens do not address their spouses as kings, no matter how estranged they are from each other. I tear off another strip.

"To His Majesty from Her Majesty." No. "To whom it may concern." No. "To my husband." No. "To the evil wretch who calls himself my husband." Tempting, but no. As I rip off greeting after greeting, the page is getting shorter and shorter, until I am left with a mere stub, no more than a paragraph's worth, which will never fit all the lofty sentiments about love, faithfulness, and decency that I have planned to include in my long, well-thought-out letter. Myrtle is playing with her velvet pouch in the corner, putting some shiny pebbles in, taking them out, putting them in again, humming softly. When I ask her for more paper, her little face falls.

"But this was the only sheet we had in the house," she whispers.

And so, I consider the tortured, uneven fragment before me, then dip Martha's feather into Tom's blackberries, and write decisively: "Roland. I want a divorce. I want the children, who have never been of any interest to you. And I want half the kingdom." But I do not want half the kingdom, for what would I do with it? I cross out "kingdom," write "palace" above it; but I do not want half the palace, either, for I will never again live under the same roof with that man. I cross out the entire sentence—I trust he will know how to make proper arrangements—and finish simply: "I am staying at the woodsman's cottage with my sister. Please send your reply there." I study the period at the end of the sentence, listen to my heartbeat, and change the period to a comma, and add, my hand somewhat unsteady now: "by a courier." Perhaps . . . But I do not wish to complete my unvoiced thought, not even in the privacy of my mind.

The note rolled up, I go looking for Melissa. I find her in the yard, clipping a new load of laundry to the clothesline.

"I need to get this to the king," I say. "Urgently. I know the palace is far and the way to it treacherous, there are wolves and wicked spirits and—"

But she is already calling for Tom Junior. Another holler later, the boy pops up out of nowhere—a red cowlick, a smudge of mud across his freckled nose, dirt under his fingernails, a sleeve torn over a scraped elbow. She gives him the note and a smack ("You lot must think clothes grow on trees!") and dispatches him promptly.

"But he is too young to go on such a long, perilous quest!" I exclaim as I watch him disappear into the trees at a run.

"Long? Perilous?" She laughs. "See the forest road that starts right over there? It's broad and well maintained, carts travel it weekly. It will take him to the palace in two hours. Three, if he stops to chat with the miller's daughter over at the village. And no wolves around here—Tom takes care to keep them away. And even if there were, Tom Junior could hold his own. A wild boy, like all my sons, not afraid of anything, always full of mischief. Don't know where they get it."

She sounds exasperated and proud at the same time.

As I give her a hand with the laundry, I wonder, silently, about the willow girl at the brook in the heart of the forest and the mysterious path through the brambles that brought me here—but already, much of my journey is fading from my memory, like a shimmering starlit dream. The autumnal air is crisp; the sky, luminous as stained glass, is filled with the flapping of starched white shirts; and all at once I feel hopeful. Perhaps, I think, King Roland will want to be rid of me himself.

Perhaps this will all be over quickly.

My hope, however, will diminish over the next two days, will fade completely by day four, will turn into sullen despair by the end of the week. I help with the chores around the house as much as I can, but I am conscious of Melissa always trying to take all the work upon herself, always giving me the best of everything, always fretting about my discomfort. Late one night, wandering lost about the house again, I happen to pass Tom and Melissa's room and overhear them talking, in whispers, about how best to survive the coming winter on what little they have, what with the appetites of their six sons growing faster and faster, and, too, having to provide for their sister the queen. "But of course, she is welcome to live with us always, always," Tom offers staunchly, and on the other side of their door, my heart breaks a little. I intend to speak to them the following morning, right after breakfast, when our meal is interrupted by a horn trumpeting in the meadow.

I must confess to my breath quickening—but the man who enters the house is in his middle years, with an expressionless face that resembles a door handle, and I quickly pretend to myself that I have not been holding out hope of anyone else darkening the threshold. The courier hands me a parchment with the royal seal (depicting a unicorn in a field of daisies), then doubles up in a series of ridiculous bows and flourishes, and steps aside to wait for my answer.

My hands tremble as I break the seal open.

"My beloved queen," the letter starts. "You have tricked us, drugged us, left us without a word, but your attempt to humiliate us in front of our entire court has failed. We have announced that you will be visiting your ailing stepsister through the end of the year, as befits your charitable nature, and no one shall expect your return before the first snows. We feel that three months of an impoverished existence in a woodsman's shack with no allowance will be enough for you to regain your sense of priorities. At the end of that period, we expect you to return chastened to the palace and resume your spousal duties. As you well know, they do not consist of much, but we require your presence by our side for propriety's sake. In the event you choose to disregard our royal wishes and stay away, we will consider the divorce proceedings initiated, but we promise you that you will rue the day you turned your back on our marriage. You will lose the children and will be left homeless and penniless. The law, as you will be sure to discover, is on our side. Consider this a fair warning. Yours always, King Roland Ferdinand Boniface Frederick Reginald the Fifth."

I read it again, then ask for a quill.

"I beg you, can I please, please, see the children?" I write at the bottom of the parchment. The messenger accepts it with renewed flourishes, pretending not to notice the tears that are streaming down my face, lifts his chin high in the air, and departs. A day, two days, three days pass, but there is no answer.

After another week, I know not to expect a reply.

At the Manor

"My dear, tell me what the bastard did to you," Melissa asks again.

Her nine children have all been put to bed, and the two of us are sitting alone by the fire, warming our hands on mugs of hot milk.

I shake my head, then say, to change the subject: "I overheard you and Tom. Talking about the winter."

She presses both hands to her ample breasts.

"Oh, my dear. You weren't meant to hear that. We are happy to have you. What else is family for?"

I think of all the times I spat in Melissa's food as a child, and flush dark with shame. "I know." And I do know, which only deepens my guilt. "But I want to help with the household expenses." For a moment I stare into the dancing fire. "I believe I would be good at shoeing horses. And—weaving straw bonnets?"

Melissa smiles, then stops smiling. "Oh. You're serious. Alas, my dear. Those are commendable skills to have, even if I can't think how you would have come by them—but the village smith already has three sons to help with the horses. And we don't have much need for fancy hats around here."

"I will not sit with my hands in my lap while you work your fingers to the bone, sister." I frown at the leaping flames in the fireplace—so full of life now, yet in another hour or two, nothing but ash and cinders—and at once the perfect solution comes to me. My mouth twists at the thought, but not a small part of me revels in the bitter irony of its aptness. "Is there someone in these parts who needs a maid?"

Looking stricken, Melissa starts to say no, then hesitates.

"Please. I need to do *something.*" I do not add that, even more, I need to get out of this house where everyone is so welcoming, where everyone is so joyous, where I die a small death every day, every day.

"There might be a lady," she concedes after meeting my eyes. "I hear she is rather odd. And her manor is badly neglected. But I will make inquiries. If you wish."

"I do," I say, "I do"—and she heeds the desperation in my voice, which is why, only two days later, I am walking the forest road with detailed directions scribbled on an oily piece of paper in which Tom brought fish for supper the night before. I soon take a less traveled path branching off the broad track, but the wood remains filled with light, transparent in the way of all autumnal woods, brown leaves fluttering down through the air. As I walk the rustling path, I let my thoughts float where they will. I won-der, not for the first time, about the mysterious life's spark that the witch allowed me to keep at the crossroads. I try to imagine what my children are doing at this very moment. I recall, as I do now and then, the beekeeper with the honey-colored eyes and gentle lips. It suddenly occurs to me that, had I chosen differently at that forest clearing, had I gone right, to a fresh happy ending, he would have probably come back into my life, revealed, no less, as a long-lost son of some distant king, and a perfect new story would have started to unfold, from its enchanted beginning to who knows what (quite possibly grim) conclusion—and, just like that, I understand that I will not see him ever again, having chosen a thornier way. For a few minutes, the memory of our dream kiss lingers, warm and stirring; then I let go of it, and it dissipates in the morning chill, not to return.

I pull my cloak about me and walk faster.

After another half an hour, I detect an unexpected floral scent, rich and sweet, yet with the faintest trace of dampness, of rot, underneath. Presently, the trees lining the path give way to blooming rosebushes, and the lane opens onto the great expanse of an unkempt lawn crowned by a sprawling redbrick manor. Its darkened windows stare blankly through trailing ivy. Rust has corroded the wrought-iron arabesques of balcony grilles, and there is a deep layer of grime on the lion-shaped door handle, as if no hand has touched it in a hundred years.

The instructions I have been given direct me to enter without knocking.

Inside, all is oppressive silence, cobwebs, and obscurity; even the bright morning light invading the foyer has lost its cheer, become somber and dull, after straining through the gray and purple petals of the rosette window above the grand entrance. I move through the unfolding array of hushed rooms, and the echo of my footfalls gets lost, trapped in heavy gray draperies, muffled in thick purple rugs. Everything here, I notice, is gray and purple— the slate tints of veined marble floors, the striped light gray wallpaper, the faded violets of velvet sofas with tasseled lilac cushions, the flat grays of tarnished tea urns, trays, and sugar bowls arranged in fussy clusters on lavender tablecloths, the mauves of artificial orchids and chrysanthemums in prim purple vases, and, presiding over everything, the ubiquitous grays of dust, dust, dust.

This must be the house of a very old lady, I decide as I find my way downstairs and into the chilly, unused kitchen, where, as promised, a sad collection of pails and mops awaits my efficient handling.

I spend that day scrubbing the floors; the next, washing the windows; the third, dusting the knickknacks; the fourth, buffing the silver. The first two floors of the manor are deserted save for a dozen gray birds in rusty gray cages—and the birds, oddly, are always asleep, their heads tucked under ruffled wings. As soon as I arrive in the mornings, I pause by their perches to make sure that they have not died in the night; the scarcely discernible rise and fall of gray feathers never fails to reassure me, and yet I find the sight of these still, headless creatures so unnerving that I try to keep away from their cages as much as I can through the day. For the rest, I soon discover that the job suits me well, which is, in truth, unexpected; manual labor made me restless when I was a moody adolescent waiting for my life to begin. Now I move through the manor, singing softly, transforming the cluttered, dim spaces into gleaming geometries of order, and I think of how much satisfaction this simple work brings me. When I first took hold of the broom, after all those indolent years, I was surprised by the feeling of brisk self-sufficiency, almost of power, that surged from my fingers into my heart. I think, then, of how this might just be the answer—or, if not *the* answer, then at least *an* answer— to the question that used to bother me so during my empty days in the palace: What makes me different from any other starry-eyed maiden dreaming of her golden prince or her golden goose? Raised on the bland, mealy porridge of princess fantasies, I had imbibed the widely held belief that royal idleness was the only suitable reward for past misery and good behavior—but perhaps this one-size-fits-all approach could have never made me happy.

Perhaps I am, simply, someone who was never meant to be a princess. Perhaps I am someone who prefers the daily joy of using her hands.

And for the first time since escaping the palace, I am visited by a feeling that everything may still work out somehow—that everything will be fine.

On the fifth day, I gather my mops and pails and trudge up the carpeted stairs to the top floor. Darkening tapestries of purple parrots poised along silver branches line the long corridor, and when I touch them with my duster, soft clouds of oblivion bloom before me, making the insides of my nose itch. The rooms on both sides of the corridor are all sleeping chambers, the beds like elaborately garlanded four-poster tombs in their undisturbed brocade magnificence, each with an ornate chamber pot hiding coyly beneath the cascading frills of stiff coverlets. In the last room, the curtains are fully drawn, the windows shuttered, and my steps stir graying cobwebs that hang dense upon the air. It takes a moment for my eyes to adjust in the swaying shadows—and then I stifle a cry.

A silver-haired woman in an antique bridal dress gone gray with age is lying stretched out on top of a mauve bedspread.

Once my heart slows down, I see the waxy pallor of her profile in the gloom, the hands folded on the motionless chest, the immense amethysts on the lifeless fingers. The rings are those of an old woman, yet the smooth, slender hands seem young somehow. I do not want to look closer, for fear that, unlike the birds, the woman is truly dead. My face averted, I make a few sweeps at the furriest cobwebs, then tiptoe to the door, forcing myself not to break into a run—and just as I reach the threshold and am about to exhale, I sneeze, and it is not a delicate, ladylike sneeze, either, but the most deafening, earsplitting sneeze of my life, which makes my broom crash onto the floor and my pail explode in a symphony of metallic clangs and rattles.

My blood freezes. I brace myself, steal a backward glance. Her eyes are still closed. Gingerly I pick up the broom and start once again for the freedom of the tapestried corridor—and it is then that the languid, coquettish purr intercepts me.

"My prince!"

Her body has not moved, but the yellowing layers of Flemish

lace on her bodice are heaving theatrically, and her pale lavender lips are unmistakably puckered up for a kiss. I notice a gray glint behind the trembling lashes of her lowered eyelids.

"I am the new maid, milady," I whisper.

The eyelids fly open.

"I know that, I'm not blind," she says loudly, peevishly. "You could have humored me for a moment, of course. But sympathetic maids are hard to come by nowadays. Bring me a cup of tea, why don't you. Plenty of milk, no sugar."

Downstairs, all the birds are awake and chirping madly. When I return with the loaded tray, she is sitting up, propped against the pillows, shuffling a pack of Tarot cards with an intricate cobweb design on their backs. I set the tray down on the bed—a puff of dust rises to meet my face—then move to draw the curtains open.

"Leave it, leave it!" she snaps. "My eyes are too weak for the light."

I bow and hasten toward the door.

"No, stay," she orders. "Cool the tea for me. What year is it?"

"What . . . year?"

In the dimness, it is impossible to tell how old she is. Seen from across the chamber, she appeared young, so young, sixteen or seventeen, no older, and breathtakingly lovely, her silvery hair the palest shade of blond, like the delicate wing of a nighttime moth, her slight, birdlike gestures filled with an ethereal grace. Yet now, as I bend down to blow on the steaming cup, I catch a sour smell of dissolution or ill health masked by some ancient perfume, and her hair has lost its luminous sheen, become a dull gray of long years, while her brittleness resembles the frailty of age.

"Oh, never mind, it makes precious little difference." Listlessly, she drops the pack of cards, scattering suns, moons, and winged angels all over the bedspread, and yawns. Her tongue is like a cat's, neat and shockingly pink, trembling tensely in the dark, hot cave of her malodorous mouth. I shrink back. "Who can keep track? Things are different every time I wake up— sometimes only a little, but I can tell, I am quite sensitive, you know. Once, they replaced all the candles in the house with strange new lamps, gaslight, they called it. Another time, they had a man come who made new, magic kinds of portraits. He did one of me. He had a sinister apparatus on legs, and he covered his head with a black cloth, like this, and there was a bright white flash that blinded me. I cried out—I was quite frightened, I am delicate like that—but the likeness was better than any artist's hand could have made it, only it had no color, it was all gray. I would show you, but my birds pecked it apart. Well, but they are always inventing new things, it's the age, you know. And the maids change. Almost every time I wake up, it seems, there is someone new. Of course, that is to be expected. Sometimes I sleep for only a day or two, but other times it will be five or ten years at a stretch. On one occasion, it was thirty or forty, I myself was not sure how long. True, the same queen was still on the throne, but so much had moved past. You can take the tea away now, I want to go back to my dreams. You will find your wages in the purse with the beaded peacock, over there by the vanity."

When I reach downstairs, the birds are asleep once again, heads hidden under their wings. But the next morning, they are jumping on and off their perches, chattering frenziedly, and in the bedroom the silver-haired woman in her rotting bridal gown is ensconced amidst the dusty pillows, counting out her faded cards, primly covering her yawns with the amethyst-studded hand.

"Are you a princess?" she asks without greeting me first, as though continuing our conversation of the previous day. "I thought so. Born or made? Ah. Well, we cannot all be born princesses. And really, being born to it is not as desirable as I once thought.

There are just so many expectations, you know. The world expects things from you, that goes without saying, but you also expect things from the world. Sometimes, when I feel really blue, I even wonder if my expectations will ever be realized. Of course, I know they will be, because it was foretold, and every time I ask the cards, I always see the same lovely man in my future—but now and then, you know, all this waiting gets to be a trifle tedious. Now, don't just stand there, bring me a cup of tea. Plenty of milk, no sugar, and add a spoonful of sherry while you're at it—you will find the sherry in the drawing room cupboard, unless they've moved everything again. And say 'Yes, Miss Rosa' when I give you an order. And always curtsy."

"Yes, Miss Rosa," I say as I curtsy. But when I return with the tray, she is asleep again, her mouth hanging open, the Lovers card, a naked woman reaching out to a naked man, clutched in her mottled hand, the fusty lace on her shrunken chest stirring faintly with her exhalations—just as I will find her on most days when I tiptoe in to freshen up her stale-smelling chamber, which is entangled in new cobwebs every morning, fat gray spiders busy spinning and spinning and spinning their dreamlike threads above the slumbering woman's face. When awake, Miss Rosa reads her fortune, exclaiming with a somewhat forced delight over the lovely groom invariably promised her in the brittle, graying constellations of the ancient cards, then requests cups of tea with increasingly generous splashes of sherry, and talks in breathless, fluttering monologues. Slowly I piece her story together.

A long-awaited daughter of a long-childless queen, she came into the world beloved and cherished, and her father the king arranged a grand feast to celebrate her birth. Unfortunately, the king cared more for the elaborate ritual of royal dining than for keeping his subjects happy, and thus, having thirteen fairies in the kingdom but only twelve place settings of solid gold, he chose not to invite the thirteenth fairy at all rather than sully his best damask tablecloth with mismatched cups and bowls of inferior silver and risk losing face before neighboring rulers whose offspring might, in due time, serve as suitable candidates for his precious daughter's hand. (He was especially interested in the young son of King Roland the Second who would rule as Roland the Third, for their lands bordered his own.) The twelve lucky fairies marked the occasion by gifting the infant princess with all the customary accoutrements, such as porcelain skin, legible handwriting, and the knowledge of cutlery etiquette. Ten had already given their blessings when the uninvited thirteenth fairy—who, in truth, was more a witch than a fairy anyway and most likely did not belong at a decent gathering—appeared in the doorway, accompanied by bolts of lightning and black ravens tearing through the hall's festive garlands, and called a booming curse upon the babe's head. The girl, she cried, would grow up to be as perfect as a gilded doll—but she would never marry.

"She will die an old maid!" cackled the witch. "A fruitless virgin! A bitter, shriveled-up spinster!"

And she vanished in an explosion of frogs and vipers.

Immediately panic set in amidst the gathering. The king blamed the queen for not keeping a proper household supplied with a proper number of proper place settings, and the queen did the only proper thing in response and died of a broken heart on the spot. The eleventh fairy was then heard to step in and try to amend the curse. She had no powers to overturn it completely, she said with a sigh, but she could make it so the princess *would* marry, and marry for love, and marry happily, which was, after all, the thing that truly mattered—she would just not marry a *prince*. The king, having grown purple in the face, ordered the unfortunate fairy beheaded. The grooms then chased after the last, twelfth, fairy who was attempting to sneak away unnoticed through the servants' entrance. They dragged her before the king. She was young and inexperienced; she had never given a baptismal gift or lifted a curse before.

"Fix it, or else!" the king barked, and the poor thing, trembling, whimpered that the princess would, the princess would, of course, marry a real prince. It might, however, take . . . a bit of time. A while, actually. So it would not be Roland the Third, but it might, just might, be one of his descendants. Or a different prince altogether, but equally royal, no doubt. The king, somewhat mollified, had her dewinged and imprisoned, in case any adjustments to the curse needed to be made at a later date, but at least he allowed her to keep her life.

Princess Rosa, now sadly motherless, was raised by a beribboned and bejeweled flock of court ladies who filled her flawlessly coiffured head with stories of proper royal matches. They told her about the purpose of a woman's life, love at first sight, passionate declarations accompanied by massive engagement rings, dimpled flower girls, personalized stationery, and baptismal lace, then touched, more obliquely, on the interesting subject of conjugal duties. When Princess Rosa turned sixteen—the age of most proper royal marriages—she began spending her time sitting decorously in the window, peeking out from behind the curtains in an attempt to spot the royal suitor as he approached, eager to bid farewell to her girlhood; yet no suitor was forthcoming.

Days became weeks became months, and the princess grew bored and fell into a doze. She dreamed of a blood-red room full of spindles, powerful, turning, vibrating, thrumming. Fascinated, she reached for the largest one—and pricked her finger on its sharp, throbbing end. The pain made her cry out, and the cry woke her. When she opened her eyes, she was disoriented for a minute, for she was lying, dressed in a beautiful bridal gown, or was it a burial shroud, on her bed, her hands crossed ceremoniously on her chest, the room wreathed in mournful shadows, the court physician fussing about her pulse, an anxious crowd of courtiers holding a candlelit vigil around her. They rejoiced to see her awake, for they had nearly lost all hope. They told her she had been asleep for a full year, during which time the king had grown so displeased that he had beheaded the treasurer, the assistant gardener, and half the royal guard. (He had also sent to the dungeons to question the captive fairy, but when they unlocked the last of the rusty locks, they found the cell empty—or almost empty, for there was a small, frightened mouse cowering in one corner. The jailer swore that the fairy could not have fled and therefore the mouse must have been the fairy transformed, but in the ensuing commotion, while the enraged king spewed out spittle-punctuated decapitation orders, the mouse was somehow allowed to escape. Rumor had it, the creature found refuge in the kitchens of King Roland's neighboring palace, where, in another century or two, a clumsy cook slipped and landed on it with her ample backside, putting an end to it, albeit not before it managed to pass its immortal fairy powers to one of its twin offspring, a girl mouseling conceived in mystery and born with the ease of a sneeze.)

Having heard the courtiers' tale of woe and being sentimental by nature, Princess Rosa resolved to stay awake. She filled her bedroom with chirping birds to keep her company and had musicians play violins under her window as she continued to sit, day and night, awaiting her prince. Yet the tedium of her life was overwhelming, and she simply could not help it. The next time she fell asleep, she dreamed of the familiar blood-red room, this time crammed full of not only the whirring spindles but also oblong wine bottles, magnificent mushrooms with meaty white stems, and plump red umbrellas in tight sleeves of crimson satin. When she woke up, she discovered that five years had passed and the crowd around her bed had thinned considerably. Some had lost their heads and many others had fled, for the king was growing ever more irascible. By the time he himself passed away, another decade later, from choking on a fish bone in a fit of anger (Princess Rosa slept through both his death and his funeral), the palace was mostly deserted; only the birds, a handful of devoted old servants, and the court physician remained. When, emerging briefly from a dream of thick-handled walking sticks, buckets entering wells, and trains rushing into welcoming tunnels, she learned of her father's demise, her deepening solitude, and the unceasing rotation of the world, she found that she did not mind all that much. By now, she much preferred sleep to being awake, as waiting for the prince was a thankless pastime and her dreams had become quite involved; nor were her hands necessarily folded over her chest every time she woke up—all alone now, as the last of her maids had died from respectable age, and the physician, borrowing the king's golden inkstand, had departed for lands unknown—for on occasion they seemed to meander deep into her lacy maidenly lap, and pretending to be asleep for a little while longer, she kept them moving there before sighing the final sigh and refolding them anew on her subsiding bosom, just as she drifted off into another dream.

"Except lately," she tells me after her second cup of sherry with a splash of tea, "something strange has been happening. I fall asleep but . . ." She lowers her voice to a dramatic whisper. "*I hardly ever dream.* It's all just black before my eyes. Like nothing. Like death. And sometimes I wonder . . . I wonder if that nervous young fairy really knew how to lift curses. And if I shouldn't have eloped with that nice musician who played under my window when I was sixteen. Oh, I suppose I am still sixteen, I know I look sixteen, I have been sixteen for the past hundred, or has it been two hundred, years. But I no longer feel it. Life has moved past, and I feel . . . spent, somehow. Empty. Old. But back when I still felt sixteen, back when I sat at the window waiting for my prince, I would often catch myself gazing into the ardent face of the first violin laboring with his impassioned bow under my window. He was in love with me, of course, they all were, but he was the one I liked best. Yet I did not let myself love him back, because he was not a prince and he was poor, so I thought he would never make me happy, his splendid mustache notwithstanding. But now I don't know. I wonder if I haven't wasted my entire life, waiting, just waiting. Perhaps I will fall asleep one day soon and simply fail to wake up, and everything will remain black and empty forever."

"Don't talk like that, Miss Rosa," I say quietly, taking the cup of sherry from her unresisting hand. "Why don't you get up and go for a walk in the garden? I will help you find some shoes, help you down the stairs. The air is so fresh and crisp out there. Winter is getting close. Shall we go, right now? Let me open the window at least."

But she has already fallen asleep and is snoring softly, a bit of sherry-flavored saliva dribbling down her withered chin. I wipe it gently, wondering if she truly does not realize that she looks sixteen no longer, that, in fact, she looks like the very old, frail woman that she is. There are no mirrors in her dim lavender chamber to present her with the truth, and I myself would never tell her anything upsetting, for somehow, without noticing, I have come to feel sorry for Princess Rosa, I have come to care for her. When she spends a week without waking, I miss her tipsy chatter; and when I emerge from the woods a few mornings later to find the lawn hopelessly overgrown with brambles and her manor hidden by an overnight eruption of wild rosebushes, so dense that it is now impossible to reach the front door, I feel as though I have lost a friend—and a friend who has not paid me for the last fortnight of work, at that.

I touch my finger to the nearest bush, and instantly pull it away, and watch a drop of blood swell on my fingertip.

"Sweet dreams, Miss Rosa," I say sadly, and turn back into the forest.

At the Log Cabin

The day lies empty before me. I do not want to return to Melissa's house, not yet. They will be finishing their breakfast now; there will be the customary morning kiss from Tom as he rises from the table; their eight children will move in organized, smiling groups, helping with the chores. Seeing them all together makes me miss Angie and Ro so much I am sometimes unable to breathe. When I reach the broad forest road, on an impulse, I take a diverging path, away from the cottage.

Oaks and aspens are fully transparent now, leaves blanketing the ground, birds silent. Every step is a rustle. My solitude is a sadness, but it is also a gift. The woods are beginning to thin, and soon the path emerges from under the shade of the trees and winds along the top of a crest. Close by, I hear a rooster crow, then another. A panting dog bursts from the bushes and runs past me, head to the ground, chasing after some scent, and before I have time to wonder where it has come from, I see, in the ravine below, the slate-gray roofs of a village, spare rivulets of smoke rising from a few chimneys into the cold wintry skies. Mouthwatering smells of baked bread mix with the good, clean aromas of burning yew and birch, trailing after me even as the village falls behind, filling me with longing. I blow on my hands, chilled—and when I lift my head, I see before me, set back from the path, a neat little log cabin surrounded by spruce trees.

The shutters on the cabin's solitary window are painted a cheerful orange, and a few chickens peck in the dust behind a low fence of the same bright shade. As I pause to watch, a stocky woman in late middle age, her gray hair cut as short as a man's, strides briskly out of the door and scatters some seeds on the ground. I realize with a start that she is wearing a loose linen shirt tucked into a pair of britches, tucked, in turn, into weathered leather boots. "Here, chicky chicky," she croons, then looks up abruptly, as though sensing my presence. Our eyes lock.

It is the witch.

"Well, here is a surprise," she says, no surprise in her voice. "You are up early, Your Majesty. Come in, why don't you, I'm about to have my coffee. Oh, and look, my hens have laid me a couple of gifts. How do you like your eggs?"

The inside of the cabin is light and pleasant, and somehow much roomier than the outside led me to imagine. Bunches of aromatic herbs hang around whitewashed walls; sturdy wooden chairs, stained sunshine yellow, circle a table piled high with books. A creature the size of a cat wobbles between the table legs, clicking its tough little claws against spotless floorboards. I stare at it. Its curling green snout is steaming around the narrowly slitted nostrils, and one of its leathery wings trails behind at an odd angle.

"Don't mind Gilbert, he's harmless," the witch says over her shoulder as she busies herself with frying the eggs on a woodstove in the corner. "I'm just taking care of him temporarily for his mother. Once his wing is fully mended, he'll be able to go back home."

The eggs ready, she pushes the books aside, sets down plates and cups, gestures for me to sit. She is both like and unlike the witch of the crossroads: her movements are just as efficient, her tone just as matter-of-fact, and I recognize the compressed forcefulness of her manner—but I hardly recognize the woman herself, with her man's hair, her man's garb, her strong, calm face, her nose shaped more like a potato than a hook, and no traces of warts in existence. Only her eyes are the same, shrewd, piercing, all-knowing. She digs into her food with gusto. I take a cautious sip of whatever is in the cup before me; it is delicious.

"Fresh blueberry juice," she says. "You can call me Gwendolyn."

"But . . . I thought you lived in that cave." I find my tongue at last. "And your hair is short. Also . . . these aren't the right clothes for a woman."

She glances at me sharply.

"The cave, the wig, and the rags are just for show, girl—a way of doing business. Resentful wives expect certain things. Drama, gloom, warts, and perdition. I prefer comfort and simplicity, myself. As for my clothes, conventions are for the weak."

"And . . . and is Gilbert . . ."

"A baby dragon, yes. Eat your eggs, you are looking much too skinny. What brings you to my doorstep?"

"No, I . . . I was just taking a walk through the woods. I've been working for a lady in the manor down that way."

"Ah, yes, Miss Rosa. A very silly woman. I tried to do her a favor once, when she was born, but it was misunderstood. Perhaps I shouldn't have phrased it as a curse, but even I have to follow rules now and then. Still, I was hoping she'd see it as an opportunity."

"The thirteenth fairy, that was you?" I ask in astonishment.

"Hardly a fairy," she snorts, wiping her mouth on her sleeve. "So, then. Do you need help with the divorce?"

My breath stills. "Can you? Can you help?"

"Not for free, mind you. I'm not in the charity business here."

"Oh." I look down at my untouched plate. "I don't have

anything, just the dress on my back. I was earning a little, but my job with Miss Rosa is over now, I think."

"I imagine so. Such a waste." She shrugs. "Well, girl, you didn't exactly get your money's worth with the spell, I suppose, and I still have your trinkets. Why don't we consider them a retainer for my future services, and we'll go over the contract later."

"I am grateful," I start to say—and pause, reminded anew of the mystery that has lingered at the back of my mind for many weeks. I have resigned myself to not knowing, yet here is the witch, mopping up runny eggs with a chunk of bread across the table from me. I could just ask. If I were brave enough. "That night, at the crossroads—"

I hesitate.

"Yes?"

"You wanted my life's spark in payment, but then—"

She winces.

"I've told you already, appearances are in the job description. I wouldn't have taken it, though, I promise, not even if . . . But never mind about that." She presses her lips together, and I know the matter is closed. When she speaks again, her voice is gruff, the momentary note of uncertainty banished. "Tell me what happened between you and your husband in your last months with him, why don't you. The part I don't already know."

I open my mouth—and say nothing.

She studies me in the ensuing silence, not unkindly.

"I see," she says at last. "Well. I know you think you had it bad. And I'm sure you did. But I will tell you a story now. Did you happen to pass a village on the way here? This is a story of a girl from that village."

"Are you the girl?" I ask, suddenly shy. "Is this your story?"

The witch—Gwendolyn—does not reply. She rises to rinse out her cup, puts away her plate, then sits back down, stretches her boots out in front of her, and begins to fill a pipe with tobacco, not spilling a single crumb, deftly, briskly, as she does everything. The baby dragon clambers into her lap, and, once her pipe is lit and clenched squarely between her strong teeth, she rubs the scales on his back as she talks, making him purr and puff and send occasional clouds of fiery smoke into the air through the slits in his long nose. I watch him, mesmerized, for a minute or two, then forget all about him as the story unfolds.

Once upon a time, Gwendolyn starts—some fifty or sixty years ago, at the tipping point of the last century, the precise date is not important—a girl was born in the village. The girl was bright and bold, perhaps overly bold, but not overly pretty, a bit on the chubby side, if truth be told, with a nose rather resembling a potato, and with a meager dowry to boot; her father was the village chemist and his shop, on the main street, was respectable and stocked with many a rare herb, but the village inhabitants were a stolid, healthy, unimaginative folk in scant need of sleeping draughts or nerve-soothing potions. Still, the family managed to get by well enough. The girl, the oldest of four siblings, grew up reading her father's medical journals, playing with ingredients, and dreaming of going away to a large town across the river, where she would study science at a university. She wanted to find out how nature worked—wanted to strip it naked, take it apart, wrest away its secrets, and touch its dark, pure heart with her steady hand, before choosing to put it back together again. Her father encouraged her, but when she was sixteen years old, disaster struck: the chemist perished in an explosion in the barn he used for mixing his more complex tinctures (there were those who whispered that it had not been an accident, that the man had turned rancid with bitterness from his own thwarted ambitions), and her mother informed her that, in their newly strained circumstances, they would not be able to afford her schooling. The family left their comfortable house for much smaller quarters, and two or three years after, the shop, too, had to be put up for sale, to pay off their rising debts. They placed announcements in all the local newspapers, but for months, no potential buyers came to inquire—until one spring day the bell above the shop door jingled and in strode a stranger.

The girl was minding the counter; she looked up in surprise. The stranger was like no one she had ever seen: around forty years of age, he was tall, handsome, and powerfully built, with a short black beard and gold-rimmed glasses, dressed from head to toe in black velvet. There was an air of subtle authority about him; he looked like someone important, someone used to being obeyed. He introduced himself as Dr. Merlin Stone, a science professor at the town university. He had heard that their shop stocked unusual powders and unguents that might be of value in his experiments, he told her. The girl's heart beat violently as she showed him around, answering his questions about the inventory, her head only just reaching his soft velvet shoulder. And so knowledgeable did she prove in her explanations that, upon announcing that he would take their entire supply, Dr. Stone gave her a closer look and asked whether she would not like to come away with him and work as his assistant. He would provide her with room and board in his townhouse, and plenty of pocket money. She could even—if her interests happened to lie that way, of course—attend his lectures at the university, entirely for free, when he resumed teaching in the fall.

She stared at him, then at her feet, then back at him. His eyes, behind the golden rims of his glasses, were gray and intense, and his beard so glossy that, from certain angles, it seemed almost blue. He was waiting for her reply with a look of patience on his face, but his lips were pressed thin and his hands hung too still at his sides, and she saw that he was not a patient man by nature.

"Yes," she cried, "yes, yes, yes!"

And as soon as the first "Yes" passed her lips, she knew that she loved him.

She stuttered from an uncharacteristic nervousness when she asked her mother for permission to go, but the exhausted widow, relieved to have one mouth less to feed, readily gave her blessing, and thus the girl left with the man for the town across the river. His house, she soon discovered, was the grandest in the square, and had she been given to delighting in the world's finer things, she would have found much to admire therein, for the professor, it now transpired, was fabulously rich and in possession of highly discriminating tastes. Yet, having been thrust amidst hitherto unimaginable luxuries, the girl paid no heed to precious old Burgundy vintages in delicately chiseled Bohemian goblets, or poetry volumes bound in tooled Moroccan leather, or luminous Dutch still lifes with lemons unspooling thin golden skins next to yellowing skulls staring out of empty black sockets. Her great, thirsty, indomitable spirit was not fine-tuned enough to be receptive to the fragile beauty of such frivolous human pursuits and enjoyments.

What she sought, in this house of indulgence, was pure knowledge.

A week had not passed since her arrival when she and the professor became lovers. The girl had left the village at twenty, and she was no innocent. She had let the butcher's taciturn younger son tumble her in a haystack behind the cornfield when she was barely fourteen, and since then had had her share of rushed, awkward, utilitarian couplings, had been hurriedly shoved against stove corners or groped on floors behind counters, and had shoved and groped back, taking whatever, whenever, she wanted—yet Dr. Stone was unlike any of the boys, any of the men, she had known. His touch was assured and deliberate, his ministrations thorough and profound, and in response, she discovered her own hidden fire slow to kindle but unquenchable for long, languorous, delightful hours to follow; and if, on occasion, his fingers pinched a bit too hard, his nails scratched a bit too deep, and his teeth tore into her skin with such brute savagery that they left behind jagged blue bruises, she only tingled all over, with a warm, secret flush, pleased that his desire for her was so unstoppable it could turn him into a beast—him, the most civilized, the most refined of all men.

She did, however, prefer him to return to his civilized self soon thereafter; for what she wanted most was to be invited into the hallowed sanctuary of his work.

She lived with him for two or three months, perhaps, when she started to feel troubled. She had not been made welcome by the townsfolk. Whenever she left on some brief errand, to purchase rosemary or sage in the market, to consult a new treatise on chemical reactions in the library, to order a shipment of mercury from the pharmacist, she would walk past the dressmaker's shop, located directly across from the professor's house, and always there would be a flock of women gathered on the sidewalk in the summer heat, women in tightly laced shoes, women with bejeweled little purses, women in ridiculous hats, peeking at her from under swaying ostrich feathers or clusters of silk roses, whispering with hot malice as she went by. She assumed that they were scandalized by her mere existence—a girl staying in an unmarried man's dwelling with no chaperone present; but occasionally she overheard hints of a darker nature. There she goes, the women tittered, tottering in their impossible shoes, a fresh-faced new assistant—but what do you think happened to the other ones, the ones before? That little blond Gretchen, she had such a sweet tooth, the baker adored her? And the voluptuous redhead, what was her name, Elisa, she liked to come into the shop and try on white hats before the mirror, she had such lovely, shiny curls, she dreamed of having a perfect wedding? And oh, oh, do you remember Camille? And remembering Camille, they would smile knowingly at one another.

She brushed off the poisonous gossip, undisturbed by it, for just as she had not been a maiden, so the professor, of course, had had his past diversions. Something, however, had begun to bother her greatly: he no longer mentioned the possibility of her attending his lectures in the fall, and worse, he would not let her into the mystery of his experiments. His laboratory, behind the imposing metal door at the end of the basement corridor, remained off limits to her. She knew that he was working on something extraordinary, something momentous—he had told her as much—but every morning, rising from their passion-tossed bed, he would slap her, at times rather hard, on her naked rump, still reddened and smarting from the blows of the previous night, and say, as he buttoned his exquisitely tailored batiste shirt: "Off to work now, my sweet. Do have the cinnamon ground, and pick up arsenic in town for me, there's a dear. Oh, and for dinner, let us have your delicious rabbit stew, yes?"—upon which he would saunter downstairs, humming a snippet from some opera into his black-blue beard, while she stayed sprawled in the moist (and, now and then, after a particularly vigorous flogging, bloodstained) sheets, staring sullenly at his retreating back, biting her fingernails to the quick, until she heard the great metal door clanging shut in the bowels of the house.

Then she would get up in turn, dress listlessly, and trudge off to the kitchen to grind the powders and cook the meals he required, feeling unhappy. For not only did she love him—she had begun to think of the two of them as partners, as equals. Surely, she mattered more to him than any of his other assistants could have mattered, all those flighty, featherbrained women who cared more for fashions and chocolates than scientific endeavors and who in the end, having grown bored or disenchanted, abandoned him in search of husbands or careers in glove-making? Surely, surely, she understood him better than any of them? Why, then, was there always the sense of an invisible arm outstretched, holding her at bay, whenever she questioned him about the nature of his research? Why did the door to his laboratory, the door at the end of the basement corridor, remain staunchly locked against her?

"All in good time," he would say, smiling down at her over the rim of his glass filled with wine so dark it looked like blood. "I promise you, my sweet, you will find out soon enough."

Another month passed, and the professor announced that he was departing on a short trip to obtain some supplies for his experiments. He would be gone three days. In his absence, he asked her to be a dear and take care of his house. He gave her the keys to all the rooms, an immense bunch whose unexpected weight made her meekly held-out hand dip. He told her she could have the run of the place, could open any door—any, that was, apart from the door to his laboratory, for she had not yet earned the right to learn its secrets.

"This one, right here," he said, tenderly caressing a huge, jagged key of darkened iron. "A lesser man would hide it, but I trust you, my sweet."

She accepted the keys with an obedient nod, smilingly suffered a playful farewell slap on her cheek, so harsh that her skin was branded with four round red marks of his fingers, then, the docile smile vanishing off her face the moment his back was turned, went to the window to watch him leave. She no longer loved him. When his chugging automobile, the first in town, disappeared around the corner, she spat at the window, took the jagged key off the ring, and ran down the stairs to the locked basement door.

The key turned with a surprising readiness, and the massive door opened smoothly, too smoothly, on well-oiled hinges, inviting, ushering her in, then swinging shut behind her. She found herself in chilly darkness, took a step, another. The cavernous echoes of her footfalls made her think of infinitely stretching dungeons, of cemeteries, of eternity. She felt for the nearest wall, happened upon a switch, flipped it. A single weak bulb blinked into faint blue life on the low ceiling.

She looked, her mouth grim.

Broad gleaming tables ran the length of the enormous stone-walled chamber, and on them, between intricate machines that bristled with saw blades, spiked wheels, thumbscrews, and guillotines, stood dozens of bottles and jars, the kind her mother used for pickling mushrooms and cucumbers. In their thick greenish liquid swam glowing, white, bloated pieces of the women who had come before her, their names neatly labeled next to each specimen in the professor's beautiful hand. She saw the heart and the jaw of the chocolate-loving Gretchen—the red hair, once lustrous, now dull, and the breasts, their large nipples like spreading stains of mold, of the fashionable Elisa—the reproductive organs of Camille, who made the townspeople smile. And others, so many others. She read their names aloud as she walked along the tables, and the echoes returned each name manifold, like the last tribute, the final remaining memory tossed briefly between the dungeon walls, then fading, fading, fading, until it was gone in the descending hush.

"Violetta. Helena. Ariadne. Margarita. Isolde. Leonora . . ."

The door clanged. She swung around. Merlin Stone stood in the doorway, smiling with cruel delight into his glossy beard.

"Well, my sweet, this was too easy, I never even made it to the outskirts," he said, his tone velvet. "The others, they were such good girls, tormented by their curiosity for days before they dared to disobey me—but you, you had to know about my work, didn't you? Simply dying to know about it."

He laughed an easy, leisurely laugh, took a step over the threshold.

"So be it. Now is when you get to find out. I am searching for a woman's soul—no more, no less. You see, for centuries, serious people claimed that women had no souls, no souls at all. Men had souls, of course, no one debated that—but not women, they said, for women were more like beasts of burden, good for some things, rather useful, in fact, but not endowed with higher sensibilities. Nowadays, though, many argue otherwise, but nobody knows for sure, for nobody has ever found any definitive proof, one way or the other. A mystery, you see, just ready for a superior intellect such as mine to apply itself to the solution—and what a magnificent scientific discovery it would be, to prove the existence of the woman's soul once and for all. And so many additional questions to ponder!" He picked up a pair of thin black gloves, began to snap them on with the same slow deliberation with which he used to disrobe her, to fondle her, to impale her during their nights of passion. "What physical form would a soul take—a butterfly, perhaps, as some of the ancients believed, or a ghostly reflection of the body, or an electric discharge of sorts, a beam of light? And would it be brought to the surface more easily by joy or by sorrow? Or, say, by terror?" Lightly, lovingly, he ran his gloved fingers over an array of shining instruments, as if over the keys of a piano, lifted one long, long blade, turned it over thoughtfully, set it down again. "And would the soul swell larger if it belonged to a young girl in the bloom of first love?" He met her eyes, smiled; obliviously, she knew, he had mistaken her for a timid virgin during their initial encounter and had thought himself an irresistible seducer, and she had never disabused him of the notion. "Well. I must say, I kept an open mind at the beginning, but now, I have cut up a dozen, two dozen women and have found nothing, nothing at all, so I'm almost inclined to believe that you have no souls after all. Still, a thoroughly dedicated scientist must persevere. Perhaps a soul is simply very small and tucked away, out of sight, hunkering down in some organ, for me to uncover. Now, you, let me see—" He looked her over with care. "Yes, I think I will take your brain. No offense, my sweet, but you just don't have too many other parts to recommend you." He strolled toward her, humming a line from *La Traviata*. "Are you not going to plead? The others did."

She had expected something like this, of course, for, during their last few nights together, she had glimpsed undisguised murder in his eyes. She stayed silent and still, her eyelids lowered, lulling him with her immobility that he mistook for paralyzing fear, letting him come close, closer still. When he was so near that she could smell his tastefully understated sandalwood cologne, could see the wingtips of his immaculately polished leather shoes, she moved with all the speed and certainty of the countless generations of peasants whose blood flowed earth-bound and thick in her veins. With one heavily booted, perfectly aimed kick, she knocked him to his knees.

When she looked at him from above, as he writhed in agony, clutching at his groin, she thought of letting him go—but then she saw the cringing look in his eyes, and understood that she owed him the answer to the riddle that had so consumed him. Back in her village, she had watched the butcher's boy, the one who had taken her unneeded maidenhood, slit the throat of many a pig. She was still holding the great iron key in her hand; now, swiftly, she bent down and dragged its sharp, jagged edge with all her considerable strength against his exposed throat. The blood that welled up from the ragged wound was blacker than the black of his surgical gloves, blacker than the black of his luxurious velvet, blacker than the black of his noble beard masking a weak, ignoble chin. And as he lay dying on the cold floor before her, his life leaking out yet no tangible soul making a scheduled appearance, she knew that, along with the relief of his death, she had given him a more precious gift still—had given him precisely what he needed. For, all along, unbeknownst to himself, he needed to find a woman like her. A woman bold enough to kill a cowardly man—a woman strong in spirit, rich in soul.

Gwendolyn falls silent. The eggs on my plate have congealed into a soggy yellow mess, and her pipe has gone out. The dragon is asleep, snoring cozily, in her lap.

"And . . . then?" I whisper, my throat dry.

"And then I went back to my village. I was quite cured of my desire to strip nature, to take her apart—I saw that there had to be a different, better, way of acquiring knowledge. I was twenty-one years old. I had helped myself to some of the professor's most treasured possessions, and inspired by my new prosperity, the butcher's son was quick to ask for my hand in marriage. They told me that I should say yes, that it was a proper thing to do, especially for a fallen girl like me. I laughed in their faces. With the money I had, I built this little cabin, rented the cave, and set up shop helping women who were not as bold as the girl in my story. Of course, this was all a long time ago, and it may or may not be entirely true. Well, the details may not be entirely true, but the essence is true enough. Most good stories are like that." She starts to empty the pipe, her short-fingered, masculine hands steady, her motions methodical. "Do you want to talk about your divorce now?"

I am staring at her wide-eyed.

"Your husband has many advantages over you, girl. You left the palace of your own volition, you know, so, technically, you are now a derelict mother who abandoned her children. You are unemployed, too, unable to provide a solid home for them, or so it would appear. We need to discuss strategy, but first things first—you must find another job. Since you seem to have a natural aptitude for cleaning, what do you think of starting your own cleaning company? Cinderella Maid Services, how does that sound? It just so happens that I have some clients who are looking for a domestic, I will jot down the information for you."

She is writing names, dates, arranging for our next meeting, at which future steps will be discussed, but I am barely listening, the horrible story she told me weighing down upon my spirit. When, at last, she sees me outside, I am startled to discover that the woods have grown dim, that evening has fallen. The witch—Gwendolyn—has given me a lantern, and, swinging it before me, I quickly follow the path toward the village, toward the sounds of dogs barking and the smells of meats being grilled for the villagers' suppers, all so familiar, all so reassuringly normal. I pause, just once, to glance back at the house in the trees. The cabin itself is almost lost to the darkness of the forest, but its solitary window is blazing bright, and in its cheerful yellow light it seems to me that the whole house is bouncing ever so slightly, dancing from chicken foot to chicken foot.

At the Seaside

In the rosy light of dawn, Melissa is taking down the laundry, stiff with morning frost; winter is nearly upon us. Four of her seven children are in school, two are playing with the dog in the yard, and the baby is napping inside. Pigeons are cooing on the thatched roof. How funny, I think, as I glance over at my sister's cozy yellow house between the billowing white sheets—from some angles, it looks almost like a shoe, the way it juts out on one side and rises on the other.

I am about to point it out to her, then decide against it.

"Good luck," she calls after me. "I hope they work out better than Miss Rosa."

My new employers, I have been given to understand, are a group of twelve prosperous, unmarried, somewhat unconventional young women who are living in a large rented house by the water. To get there, I walk through a sparse birch grove to a rural station, take an hourlong train ride, then, along with a few other domestics of indeterminate ages, clad in sensible, ankle-length skirts and dark, shapeless blouses, board a trolley out to the shore, and traverse the remaining distance on foot, along the seaside promenade. All tints are pale here, bleached by the eternal labor of the waves and the wind, the white sky immense, the ocean rolling in with soothing murmurs, the air so bracing that each breath feels like a gulp of cold water. The house, when I reach it, turns out to be a rambling, airy, many-storied structure with balconies and verandas and a widow's watch tower, its light gray colors perfectly suited to the broad, tranquil perspectives of the sea and the sand; when I climb to the door, the porch steps creak like the deck of a ship. I have a fleeting thought that I will be happy working here. Then, after several knocks that go unanswered, I step inside—and gasp.

Inside, all is chaos. Overturned glasses, overflowing ashtrays, tables sticky with pooling liquors, a cracked mirror, a few lamps on their sides, one bulky lampshade beached nearby like a belly-up whale. A woman's solitary slipper is perched daintily atop cascading cushions, as though poised for flight; when I pick it up, I find its heel broken off and its satin-lined cavity filled to the brim with some sour-smelling liquid, so I drop it in terror and watch the pale yellow stain slowly eat into the filthy white rug. Crumpled papers—letters, photographs, shopping lists, invitations to parties—spill out of a bureau dragged into the middle of the living room and abandoned underneath the chandelier, where wilting heads of lilies stick out of the empty bulb sockets. The grand piano's lid is sprung open, and I see, rotting amidst the springs, a brown bunch of bananas. All the doors between all the rooms are gaping wide, as are half the windows; wintry seaside light pours through the curtains splashed with many-colored splotches, making the devastation I witness all the more shocking. As I follow the trail of destruction through the house, my heart pounds and my knees quiver. I imagine armed robbers still lurking with their loot behind keeled-over armchairs, ready to spring at me, and I finish my inspection at a run, bursting into the upstairs loft as though being chased.

And here, I freeze. Scantily clad bodies of women are strewn at wild angles on beds, draped over settees, crumpled in chairs. I notice a dangling foot in a torn stocking, a nerveless arm tossed off loosely across a table, an apple of a breast fallen out of a soiled negligee, mangled shoes without mates littering the floor—and immediately I think of Gwendolyn's story, of death, of murder.

I realize that my mouth is open, and only then hear myself screaming.

One of the bodies stirs, faintly, and a tousled head appears over the back of a sofa.

"Not very polite of you to shout like that," the head says in a sulky voice, and squints at me through caked, furry eyelashes. "Who are you, anyway?"

The other bodies are now moving, too, shifting, stretching, moaning. I close my mouth with a snap, then open it again to reply. I feel rather shaken.

"Your new maid, miss. I believe you've been robbed."

"Robbed?" Bleary dark eyes blink at me.

"The downstairs." I gesture, weakly. "It's all torn apart, pillows, papers—"

"Well, of course it is," the head interrupts with an irritable yawn. "That's why you are here, now, isn't it? I'm going back to sleep. Wake me up when you've finished, and do be thorough, make sure the vomit is off the curtains, we have some fresh blood coming tonight."

And with that, the head vanishes behind the sofa.

Unsettled, I descend the three flights of stairs and set about the slow, laborious, ungrateful business of straightening the living room, the dining room, the parlor, all equally in pieces. As I move scraping and scrubbing and washing well into the afternoon hours, the hush above my head continues complete, and I am just beginning to worry that I merely imagined the stirring limbs, the spoken reassurances, when a barefoot, barelegged young woman plods soundlessly through the door, a short and none-too-fresh yellow kimono thrown over her shoulders.

"Aren't you an absolute peach," she declares as she opens her arms wide and twirls about the parlor. I recognize the tousled hair, the once-bleary dark eyes, grown vivid and alert. "I fear we've lived in a bit of a pigsty, but young men nowadays, they are just so fast, you know, one needs to keep up, one simply has no time for domestic niceties. I'm Edna. Is there anything for breakfast around here?"

It is nearing four o'clock. Without comment, I go to the kitchen to fry the bananas I retrieved from the piano, make some toast, brew some coffee—the icebox is jammed with haphazardly piled provisions. Just as the smells of morning start to rise through the early-evening air, the kitchen begins to get crowded: more and more barefoot women in slatternly robes and camisoles with the oily shine of tired satin file inside, yawning, running their cocktail-ringed fingers through their messy bobbed hair, rubbing their mascara-smeared eyes.

Edna, who is now sitting on the bar, dangling her strikingly shapely, shockingly exposed legs and biting into her third piece of toast, rattles off introductions in a rapid staccato between zesty mouthfuls: "Greta. Clara. Ginevra. Zelda. Theda. Rita. Barbara, but she prefers Bebe, and rightly so. Anita. Gilda. And, last but not least, the other Barbara, but do call her Bean—we do."

The names all sound like the same name, sharp and fresh, and the women all seem to be the same woman, short-haired, rosebud-mouthed, pretty, indecently young, scarcely into her twenties. I count, to protect myself from being overwhelmed.

"Eleven," I say as I distribute more toast. "That's eleven. But I thought there were twelve of you."

The barefoot women, who have come alive with the imbibing of coffee and are chattering to one another like an exaltation of larks, fall into an uneasy silence, dart sideways glances at Edna.

"There is also Nora," Edna admits with visible reluctance.

She looks just like the rest of them, but from the oddly mature, hesitant note in her voice, I understand that she must be the oldest. "Nora is not here right now."

"She might come by later, though," pipes up one of the others, Ginevra or Zelda. "Hey, you know what, you should stay, too. We're expecting some divine fellows tonight, aren't we, girls? We'll be doing Chinese lanterns, and the music is ever so swell—aren't you just gone on jazz?"

"Yes, stay, stay!" all the others cry, perking up. "We will lend you a dress, and Bean is marvelous with a pair of scissors, she can get your hair looking like it belongs to this century in no time at all. You will have such fun!"

But something about their abruptly restored jauntiness, the artful geometry of their curls, the terrible youthfulness of their eagerly smiling lips, the restlessness in their naked eyes, frightens me. Mumbling excuses and apologies, I gather my cleaning supplies and slip away, just as the child-women start trooping up the stairs to get ready for the coming night, their shrill, excited voices carrying snippets of fashion advice mixed in with misplaced confidences and heartfelt confessions, their dulcet laughter chasing me out into the twilight. As I trudge down the promenade, I feel every single one of my three dozen years weighing on my shoulders, my back aches, and the trolley stop is so much farther away than it was in the morning.

When I arrive the next day, the house is in shambles once again, chairs lying with legs up in the air like so many expired rats, two or three vases smashed, scratched gramophone records hung in an undulating garland on nails freshly hammered all along the living room walls, something pink and sticky gumming up the piano keys, another silken shoe with a broken-off heel filled with sour champagne, the young women out of sight, clearly asleep, strewn all over the loft in exhausted abandon. Prepared this time, I attack the destruction with grim efficiency and manage to escape just as I hear the first creaking footsteps on the stairs above—a cowardly strategy I will follow without fail in the coming days, in the coming weeks, until one Monday in mid-December, at the uncommonly early hour of three in the afternoon, I am intercepted in the foyer by a droopy creature with spiky hair and vivid shadows under her swollen eyes, whom, after a stretch of impolite gaping, I recognize as Edna.

"Rough night," she says with a shrug. "Well, you saw what happened to the potted plants. Shame, really. Tonight will be different, though, we will be meeting some absolutely lovely people. Do stay for the party, it's so much merrier with an even dozen! Did you know they used to call us the Twelve Dancing Princesses? Oh, we were famous, we were! Only now Nora never comes, and it's just not the same . . . Please? Pretty please?"

And whether because her dark, imploring eyes are beginning to glisten, or because, in the last week or two, my sister's sunny bungalow has grown truly unbearable, her six happy children constant reminders of my own shortcomings and failures, I feel my resistance fading.

I hesitate, briefly, then exhale—and nod.

"Oh, will you, will you, really?" She claps, she jumps, she pirouettes; she looks all of twelve years old. "But that's marvelous, marvelous! Come upstairs, we'll get you fixed up right away. No, leave the broom, it doesn't matter, really, it will only be trashed again in a couple of hours . . . Girls, guess who's coming with us tonight! Bean, will you be a dear and grab the scissors, and you, Theda, bring the silver eye shadow, quick!" They crowd around me, talking all at once, peppering me with questions. "What size are you? Do you like pearls or onyx? Say, do you have a beau? But that's perfect, we'll match you up with an awfully nice sweetheart. Don't be silly, now, everyone wants one, and it's just for the night anyway, we always like to keep things moving, don't we, girls?"

And just as I am starting to regret my moment of weakness, they push me into a chair before a three-legged vanity and fall upon me, twittering, giggling, fussing, like a flock of overexcited, maddened children—fall upon me with scissors, tweezers, curling irons, with brushes, perfumes, jars of pomade, with combs, lipsticks, powder puffs—and when, a full hour later, it seems, the frenzy is over and they draw back, spent, I look into the mirror before me and find someone else looking back.

The woman in the mirror is not the thirty-six-year-old mother pining for her children, distraught over her marriage, newly worn-out by the daily labors of scraping off anonymous vomit, her hair tucked away in a somber bun, her face blank like her future. The woman in the mirror is young and enigmatic, her metallic eyelids languid, her bob breathtakingly glamorous, her pink flower of a mouth made for deep moonlit kisses, her whole life in front of her still, one sweet, trembling, mysterious note of anticipation, just like the long, sensuous call of a trumpet that I now hear snaking through the house, emerging I know not from where. Neither do I know how I find myself wearing a cream beaded dress that cascades like shimmering water over my breasts, my hips, rustling and sparkling as I move, my knees defiantly bare; or where I got the high-heeled shoes that produce such delightfully assured tapping when Anita teaches me to dance the Charleston; or how I come to be perched on the piano lid, Greta on one side, Ginevra on the other, our arms linked through, flutes of champagne tipped against our lips, a thin ivory pipe with something dark and viscous inside its carved jade bowl being passed from mouth to mouth.

The smoke smells faintly of burnt flowers, distant lands, and lazy, languorous dreams in which everything unfolds in a warm, hazy, amber-hued harmony, and ever more drowsily, I watch as it curves into flowing shapes—transparent birds, dragons with coral wings, flying arches of medieval cathedrals. But when the soaring stone vaults threaten to rise all around me and my eyelids droop, the chirping children with bright eyes like bits of stained glass and taut mouths of ravenous sinners pull the glamorous young woman who was formerly me out of her reverie and take her up the stairs to the loft and up more stairs to the top of the widow's tower and, somehow, up more stairs still, the steps luminously, inconceivably, rising through the air into the night skies above—and these skies are nothing like the measured, pale, sensible seaside skies of the world the former me left behind. This world is enchanting, and radiant, and full of whimsy; in this world, the air becomes floral scents become strands of celestial music become multiplying serpentine arabesques like the richest tapestries woven with gold threads become trees with entwined crystal branches become blue starlit clouds become infinities telescoping outward, merging with other infinities become boats that float toward us under light-suffused sails of sheer moonlight—and then I see that these truly are boats, drawing closer and closer.

And I count the boats, for numbers seem solid and sane, and I need to distract myself from the dawning terror of knowing that there is nothing but a void beneath my feet. One, two, four, seven, ten, twelve . . . Twelve boats—and I can already discern a beautiful youth standing at the heart of each, leaning on an upright oar like a statue posing to be admired, smiling at us, each smile so full of large, dazzling teeth.

"They are coming, they are coming for us!" the girls cry, and in their excitement they bob up and down on the blue heavenly shore, clicking and clacking their heels, all glittering and hard and jeweled like a plague of exotic, gorgeous insects.

"Oh, won't we dance tonight!" one exclaims, and "Oh, look how hungry they are!" another exhales—and then, turning to the elegant young woman who was formerly me, they all press their hands against their scintillating chests, as if in prayer, and intone together: "Do stay, stay with us forever, we will have dances in the sky every night, it will be glorious, it will be splendid!"

"Please, do say yes," Theda, the youngest, begs. "We will love you, you will take care of us, you will be like a mother to us!"

At this, I sway a little, then totter down one rung of the luminous ladder. Edna's alarmed face is thrust close to me as she struggles to pull me back up.

"No, no, she means sister," Edna whispers. "She means like a sister. A slightly older sister."

But the words have been said, and as their meaning slowly sinks to the bottom of my soul, all the magic of the night seems to catch on their blunt, dull edge and slide sideways off the world. The boats waver, the intense blue of the stars starts to fade, and my desire to have mindless fun, to shrug off my past, to forget my future, if only for a few wild, careening hours—the desire to be young again leaks out of me, and I see myself through the multifaceted, glinting eyes of the insect girls, the girl-insects, I see myself as I really am, a lonely woman on the cusp of middle age, an anxious mother who has already made all her choices, all her mistakes. And now, once again, I remember my children, my own children, my flesh and blood, my daughter who used to love my bedtime stories, my son who used to spend hours conquering imaginary lands with his army of silver forks, my Angie, my Ro, deprived of my love, of my care, for so long, and the thought is like a sharp blade slicing cleanly through the fabric of this illusion, of all the illusions—and as the truth sinks in, so, too, heavily, inevitably, does my heart in my chest, and so do I, sinking, sinking back down through the air, the golden sky ladder disappearing above me rung by rung, the impassive insect faces of the eleven dancing princesses hanging over the edge of the cloud, staring after me, before vanishing out of sight, blinking out with the stars, with the magic.

The gray house meets me with the rickety floorboards of the balcony. I tear off the ridiculous high heels, then run down the widow's watch tower, down past the loft, down past the second floor with its mutilated plant corpses. The first-floor parlor enfolds me in its dim, drafty silence. My head spinning, I hasten to find my old sensible shoes, to gather my bucket, my rags, when a woman's voice sounds behind me.

"You," the voice says, sadly, "are wearing my favorite dress."

I drop the bucket just as a light flares up by the window, and there she sits, unmoving and prim, in the only hard-backed chair in the entire house, dressed all in brown, her hands set in resigned stillness on her squarely placed knees. The sight of her pierces my heart with the recognition of a kindred loneliness; but when I approach, I see that she is not like me, that she is still young, only a little older than the girls in the skies. Her face is heart-shaped and white, her eyes wise with grief. She reminds me of Angie, but something about her seems broken. I stop a few paces away, as my breath dies in my throat: a thin silver chain binds her wrists to the wall, and another chain binds her ankles.

"Are you . . ." But I cannot bring myself to ask what I want to ask, so I ask the question to which I know the answer already. "Are you Nora?"

"Nora, yes," she says in some surprise, as though unused to the sound of her own name. Her voice is uncertain and pale, like the wind in the rushes, like old-age regret. "And who are you? I have never seen you here before. I return to this house every night in my dreams, you know, but it is always empty, my sisters are always away at their dances." She sighs and, not waiting for me to answer, gestures for me to sit by her; when she raises her small white hand, the chain tinkles dejectedly. "I used to be just like them, once upon a time. Bright and reckless and fast. I made up poems—poems about music, about having wings, about boats in the sky—and many said I had a real gift, but I believed all gifts were meant to be tossed away freely, so I never wrote anything down. Every night, we climbed the stairs to the clouds and met with our lovers. Our lovers loved to watch us dance. We had such pretty feet, they said, and mine the prettiest. Every sunrise, in parting, we took off our beautiful shoes and threw them into the air, and our lovers caught them and drank champagne out of them, toasting our joy to come on the following night.

"But our fathers grew suspicious of all the shoes we kept buying, so they threatened to cut off our allowances, and when their threats had no effect, they sent men to spy on us. Men came, with butterfly nets, with magnifying glasses, with church hymnals, with thesauruses, with rulers, and tried to catch us, but we were clever and avoided them all, and some of them fell out of the skies and broke their necks. We watched them fall and cheered at their deaths, and perhaps that was wrong, and perhaps it was for our lighthearted cruelty that we were punished. For, after a while, there arrived a man with a perpetual frown and a white beard pointy as a knife, a man who hid his thoughts under a bowler hat. We heard rumors that he knew how to dissect dreams, knew why some women dreamed of balconies and kings, while others dreamed of wells and walking sticks, and that he would chase us through our dreams until he knew us and, knowing us, trapped us.

"We laughed at the rumors, and we laughed at him, at his arrogant folly, behind our hands, but in the end, he got the better of us. He followed us one night, dark as the night itself, up the golden ladder into the sky, and, once there, took copious notes of everything he saw—and as soon as he wrote something down, whatever it was vanished clean, just like it had never been. I cried for the moonbirds. I cried for the pearl lilies. I cried for the diamond-leafed trees. I knew it was only a matter of time before he spied the magnificent cloud boats with the splendid-toothed lovers.

And so, to save my sisters' happiness, I spoke to him, I promised to come down with him if only he would leave the rest alone. He was glad to have me, then, for I was like a bird in his hand. He took me home with him, and he put these on my wrists and my ankles, for, in spite of my promises, he did not trust me not to fly away. And every day now, I sit chained to his desk and recount my dreams for him, and he dips his dragon-claw pen into his golden inkstand and writes my words down in his thick note-books, and he tears out the pages, and he swallows them after much mastication, and he grows ever fatter with fame. But I have my revenge on him, too, for every day I lie to him. I make up empty nonsense, fill his head and his belly with balconies and kings, wells and walking sticks, while in reality, what I dream of every night is this house, this dark, empty house of my former youth, with the vast blue skies above it and my young, beautiful sisters dancing free and joyous in the clouds. So, whoever you are," and she points a see-through finger at me, jingling the chains lightly, "you are trespassing in my dream. And it is dangerous for you to be here, for the man in the bowler hat may begin to suspect the truth any day now and go back on the prowl through my soul. You'd better leave my dress behind, quick, and return to wherever you came from."

And just like that, as though released from a nightmare, I am back in my own somber clothes, stumbling to the trolley stop through a pale pink morning, my bucket in my hand. On the trol-ley, on the train, my head is pounding, and it seems to me that all the other stern, darkly clad domestics are staring at me with dis-approval. When I limp through the park toward my sister's house, a short man, possibly wearing a bowler hat, darts out from be-hind a tree and flashes a camera in my eyes, and my insides grow heavy with ominous premonitions.

Melissa intercepts me by the front door, her forehead etched deep with insomnia.

"Where have you been, we've been worried sick about you, gone all night like that! Miss McKee is in the living room, waiting to speak with you. You should wash your face before you see her. And what in heaven's name happened to your hair, who chopped it off like that?"

"Miss McKee?" I repeat, my temples splitting at the blazing trajectory that the sun is now drawing across the wintry sky. "Who is Miss McKee?"

Melissa gives me a withering look and strides off into the house, and I meekly follow her inside to discover Gwendolyn the witch sitting on my sister's couch, tapping a pen against reams of paper spread out on the coffee table before her.

At the House in the Pines

"Perhaps I haven't been sufficiently clear." Her tone is stern, and yet again, she looks both like and unlike her previous incarnation, her gray hair cropped just as before but her face made colder, more impersonal, by a pair of glasses poised on the bridge of her nose, which seems to have shrunk even more in its dimensions, a far cry from the potato-shaped bulb of the chicken-legged hut and farther still from the hooked monstrosity of the crossroads. She is dressed quite formally, too, in a tailored pinstriped suit, which makes her look slimmer; or perhaps she has lost weight. "Your position is precarious as it is. Staying out all night, drinking, by the looks of you"—she gives me a chilly glance, the color and texture of steel, over her steel-rimmed glasses—"should not be permitted if you hope to reunite with your children. Now, when does your husband expect you to move back in with him?"

"Two weeks," I whisper, chastised. "But I can't. I won't."

"I should think not. In two weeks' time, then, he will file for divorce, which will give him even more advantage over you. I recommend that we file ourselves before the time is up. We need to pick proper grounds for it, of course. Desertion is out, since you were the one who left him, and as for abuse, well, he was cruel and unpleasant, but he never did hit you, did he? Which leaves adultery, and here, I trust, we have ample—"

"No," I interrupt. "I do not want to file anything."

She clicks her tongue, impatiently. "As your lawyer—"

"No. Please. I do not want to *do* anything." Panicked, I am pleading now, with her, with myself, with him, with the Powers That Be, in whose smooth, impartial workings I used to believe, used to not know not to believe, but which, I now fear, do not watch over me any longer—if ever they have. "Maybe he'll see that parting is the best ending for both of us and agree to resolve everything peacefully?"

She drops her pen onto the table with much clatter to demonstrate the full extent of her exasperation. "The man is a classic bully in love with his own power. He will never agree to a peaceful resolution. Tell me what happened between you two in the last months of your marriage. There might be something there we could use."

I stay stubbornly silent.

"This isn't easy," she says, relenting a little. "Why don't you take a day or two to think it over, and in the meantime set up an appointment with Faye. Talking about things will clear your mind. Do call my office once you make your decision. We should aim to file by Monday. And look, I understand the desire to cut loose when a man hurts you, believe me, we've all been there, but you mustn't forget that your entire future is at stake here. Last night was unwise. Let's just hope there will be no repercussions."

I am, in truth, not entirely certain what happened last night, but a stumble into the powder room revealed frightfully bloodshot eyes, lids painted in black and gray stripes, a glittering pink mouth slanted sideways, red blotches on my cheeks, and an unevenly chopped, bristly mop. After a single glance, I squeezed my eyes shut and would not look again, scrubbing blindly at my eyelids, at my lips, tugging a brush through the remains of my beautiful hair, too frightened to confirm that the dissipated reflection might have any connection to me, to my neat, respectable, hard-working self. And I now feel so distracted by wanting and, simul-taneously, not wanting to recall what precisely led to my riding the trolley at six in the morning, carrying a badly burnt potted hydrangea in my cleaning bucket and bearing an uncanny re-semblance to a not-altogether-sober lachrymose clown, that I let Gwendolyn gather her papers and depart the house before I think to ask her who Faye is.

Once the front door closes behind her, I sit by the window, massaging my aching temples, round and round and round, until I realize that the movements of my fingers have fallen in rhythm with the thin girlish voices I hear chanting some nonsensical rhyme outside, Melissa's three daughters, Meg, Mary, and Myr-tle, playing in the yard, choosing "it" for their game of tag. As I prod my temples, I listen absently to the winding words that reach me through the cracked window.

> *A garden with no flowers,*
> *A summer with no sun,*
> *A forest with no birdies,*
> *A marriage with no fun.*
> *You. Are. Out!*
> *A garden with no flowers,*
> *A summer with no sun,*
> *A forest with no birdies . . .*

I straighten, listen more intently, my heart taking a sudden flight—and before the next girl is out, I leap to my feet and rush from the room, from the house, down the sidewalk that skirts the neighborhood park, shouting, "Wait, Gwendolyn, wait!" after the pinstriped figure in men's brogues that is even now striding briskly toward a gray Packard automobile I see parked across the road.

She looks back at last, allows me to catch up, to recover from a stitch in my side, before asking whether I have made up my mind already.

"It's not about that," I pant—and stop.

It seems preposterous to bring up the stormy crossroads, the threats, the curse, when faced with this smartly dressed, business-like person holding a briefcase of dyed alligator skin and considering me with poorly concealed impatience in the prosaic white light of a clear December day, and I feel a fleeting yet vertiginous doubt, almost as though I imagined that black-and-red night—dreamed it up wholesale to disguise the uncertainty, the terror, of my first divorce consultation with Miss Gwendolyn McKee, Esquire. I inhale and press on. "That time, at the crossroads, when . . . when you wanted to take what you called my life's spark from me, you . . . well, you didn't. And later, in your house, you said you wouldn't have taken it, 'not even if'—but you didn't finish your sentence. What were you going to say?"

"Nothing of any practical use to you. And it might upset you."

"Please. I'm not a little girl. Tell me. Please."

I feel like a little girl standing empty-handed on the sidewalk, begging her for a crumb of some revelation. She sighs, probes me with an even gray gaze.

"I suppose you have the right to know," she says at last. "I wouldn't have taken your spark even if you had it. The thing is, you didn't. You had no spark. No passion. No joy. There was nothing to take."

I stare at her, stunned.

"A garden with no flowers," I whisper.

"Yes, but you used to have it. I could feel the hollow in your chest where it had been once. Someone had taken it from you already. Scooped it clean out."

"Some . . . someone?" My lips feel numb.

"Someone." She shrugs. "Or something. Sometimes it is an act of malicious magic. Other times, it's just—just life, you know. Joy leaks out when there are enough cracks."

"But . . . can I never get it back now?"

Her face, bereft of the steel-rimmed eyeglasses, appears gentler.

"Few things are impossible. Still, let us focus on the pressing matter at hand." She shakes her wrist out of her sleeve in an oddly familiar gesture, glances at her watch. "I have another client, I must run, but if you aren't doing anything at present, why don't you go see Faye. She is quite maudlin at times, but she should be able to help you process your emotions. Here, I'll jot down the address for you if you don't have it handy. Talk to her, organize your thoughts, then call me, yes? We should get the bastard before he gets us."

And it is only after the rather long-nosed chauffeur in a green uniform with flames on the cuffs drives Miss McKee away in her gray Packard that I remember I have forgotten, again, to ask who Faye is. I look at the address on a slip of paper and, dully, walk to the other side of the park, through a neighborhood of neat little cottages rising bright and square and menacing like rows of well-cared-for teeth, until the street ends abruptly and I find myself beyond the town's edge, in a thicket of evergreen trees, on a twisting path carpeted in dry fir needles and leading into a chilly emerald dusk. Some minutes later, I make out a small house through the pines. In another dozen steps, a smell envelops me—the light, sweet, delicious smell of a happy childhood. I have no time to think about it, though, because just then I come to an opening in the trees and, at last, see the house clearly—and it is like no other house.

Its walls are made entirely out of crumbling, sugar-sprinkled gingerbread, and its white roof glistens with frosting. Striped red-and-green candy canes frame the cheerful windows, chocolate hearts dot the door, and the weather vane is shaped like a pink lollipop. I stand gaping with wonder for a full minute, then, cautiously, approach the aromatic door and raise its licorice knocker. When I release it, the sound is the crunch of a cookie devoured by a greedy child, and a voice sweet as molasses calls out: "Just pull the bobbin, and the latch will go up."

The door opens softly, soundlessly, as though on buttered hinges.

Inside, the air is stifling, and it is like Christmas, a confectionery shop, and a doll tea party, all rolled into one and suffused with a warm, rosy glow. Amazed, I stare at the profusion of potbellied teapots, cuckoo clocks, embroidered pillows, needlepoint rugs, porcelain statuettes, plump little lamps with tasseled shades, processions of jeweled eggs along flimsy shelves covered with lacy doilies, everything pink-hued, toy-sized, cozy, crammed—and absolutely suffocating. And I nearly give in to an impulse to dash back out into the woods, when the same saccharine voice exclaims: "Oh, my sweet child, what a surprise, how delighted I am to see you!"—and only then do I notice the round-shaped woman bundled in a multitude of strawberry-colored shawls, seated in a pink armchair under a pink pile of knitting, beaming at me over her rainbow-tinted butterfly-framed eyeglasses.

"Fairy . . . Fairy Godmother?"

"The same, the very same!" she confirms brightly. "But I prefer to go by 'Faye' now, it has a more modern ring, don't you think? Sit down, sit down, have some chocolate with me." Not rising, she stretches her hand to break off a chunk of the wall and, laughing, offers it to me; mechanically, I take it. The puffy pink ottoman I sink into is soft, too soft, and warm, as if someone was sitting there just moments before. "What brings you to my humble abode, my sweet child?"

For some reason, I do not want to mention the witch, or the night at the crossroads.

"I just stopped by to talk," I say, uncertainly.

"Oh, yes, talk, I love talk!" she exclaims, muffled now, her mouth full of chocolate. "You don't mind if I knit, do you, my dear? At this time of the year, with the holidays almost upon us, I am always so busy making socks for the poor town orphans . . . Tell me, and how are your own precious darlings? Doing well, I trust?"

My breath catches.

"Oh, Fairy Godmother! Do you not know? I haven't seen . . . I haven't been allowed to see . . ." And suddenly everything, everything, is too much—the hot, unmoving air inside the sweet pink house, the headache still beating at my temples like a trapped bird at the bars of a cage, the woman's moist, egglike eyes turned upon me in smiling expectation, the chocolate treat I have forgotten I was still clutching beginning to melt, to run down my fingers, the exhaustion of keeping all my deeper emotions eternally locked away while I go about my hopeless task of fighting surface entropy with mops and dustcloths, the bitterness of the knowledge that, unlike all the other fairy tales in the world, mine has proved to be a sham—the old gnawing fear that I will never make sense of anything ever again, the new feeling of violation at having my life's spark wrenched away from me by something, by someone—and more than anything else, the anguish of this never-ending separation from Angie and Ro, days turned to weeks turned to months, and who even knows what is happening to them, whether they are healthy, warmly dressed, properly fed, whether or not they go to bed every night crying for their mama—and now I am crying, too, tears freely streaming down my face, mixing with streaks of chocolate when I attempt to wipe them away with my sticky hands. "I may never be able to see . . . to hold . . . all I want . . . I love them so much . . . and that cruel, hard-hearted man . . ."

My words are turning into jerky sobs, become hiccups before trailing off into wet, incoherent shuddering.

"Oh, dear child! I simply had no idea, no idea!" the fairy godmother cries. She has flown out of her chair and is fluttering about me now, patting my cheeks with her fuzzy pink shawls, petting my back with her plump pink hands. "There, there, a nice long cry is good for you. Here, have a tissue . . . And now, take a deep breath and tell me what's going on. Let's start with what happened in the last months of your marriage, after the poor old dear . . . ahem . . . after King Roland died."

I blow my nose, shake my head.

"Child, it's not healthy to keep things bottled up inside like that."

"You can't possibly understand! How can you, when you yourself never had . . . had any . . . any . . ." Just as the sobs are encroaching again, I choke on a piece of dark chocolate I find wedged in my mouth. It starts sweet on my tongue, then turns so lip-numbingly bitter that I am shocked into silence as I work my teeth around it, laboring to rid myself of its sharp, binding taste.

The fairy godmother is back in her chair, knitting needles flashing in her hands.

"True, I never had any children of my own," she says quietly. "But I know something about the heartbreak of motherhood. Why don't you sit and breathe for a while, and I will tell you a little story. It's a story of a fairy who was not always good."

Surely, not you, Fairy Godmother? I want to ask, but my mouth is too full.

"Hush, child, do not interrupt. Just chew that chocolate, there's my girl."

And as I sputter around the sweet bitterness invading my

mouth, she begins to talk, her needles clicking in rhythm with her words, the lamps glowing warm and pink around us. Once upon a time—the precise date is of no significance—in a nearby kingdom, there lived a fairy. In most respects, she was quite an ordinary fairy, preoccupied with small, benign workings of magic—infusing liquors with enhanced berry flavors, helping with firebird eggs, sewing dresses out of starlight, dabbling in royal matchmaking, and the like—save for the fact that, unlike most of her kind, she was raising two young children of her own. All fairies could have offspring, of course, but most chose not to, for, being obligated in the course of their professional engagements to spend much of their time at christenings and, subsequently, to watch over their godchildren as the spoiled little brats grew into proud princesses who refused to laugh or tyrannical princes who sent countless minions on missions of death in search of talking horses, mute brides, and pairs of comfortable slippers, they knew enough about the pitfalls and tragedies of motherhood to prefer vaulting right over the whole sorry mess on their humming iridescent wings. Not this fairy, though—this fairy had a sweet voice made for singing cribside lullabies and a generous heart made for unconditional love, and so she had produced two babies of her own to share her songs and her love with; and thus it was really quite sad when, finding herself the eleventh in line at a routine christening feast gone routinely wrong, she nobly intervened in a curse placed on some royal infant by a resentful old biddy and, after the infant's father voiced a strongly worded objection to the manner of her intervention, lost her head, leaving behind a ten-year-old fairy boy and a five-year-old fairy girl.

The two children had a miserable time growing up. The hapless fairy's friends took turns raising them, but, being flighty and callous by nature, they could not make up for the warmth that the siblings had lost when deprived of their own doting mother. In spite of the other fairies' meager parenting skills, however, the brother and sister survived to young adulthood and, acquiring sufficient knowledge of their private history, swore revenge. They went about it in different ways. The brother, favoring a direct, blunt approach, as men often would, chose to wreak havoc within the family of their mother's actual murderer. Insinuating himself into the palace under the guise of a celebrated physician, he proceeded to cast a sleeping charm upon the king's sixteen-year-old daughter; then, having gorged himself on the king's rage for so long that his gloating turned to boredom, he ensured the man's death by conjuring a pointy fish bone in His Majesty's throat. At that point, with the royal line essentially snuffed out, the brother took a parting stroll, in the same spirit of gloating, through the slumbering princess's dreams and, unexpectedly, found himself so fascinated by what he discovered in her pure maidenly head that he declared the dreams of impressionable virgins to be the new object of his ambitions, and, bestowing a bristly kiss upon his sister's dewy forehead, donned a bowler hat and left for greener pastures and darker nights.

The sister, on the other hand, possessed of a much subtler intellect and nurturing grander designs, set out to destroy the tranquility of each and every royal family in the vicinity, swearing to render each and every royal child a motherless orphan by the age of five—the age at which she herself had been deprived of maternal love. She worked at it tirelessly, relentlessly, for decades, initially getting the neighborhood queens to succumb to sickness and waste away in a plain, old-fashioned manner, but in time becoming more and more inventive at disposing of the royal consorts, turning some of them into frogs at the precise moment when they kissed their newborn babes for the first time, trapping others in magic mirrors, condemning them to report on the sordid doings of others in all perpetuity, making still others lose their hearts to donkeys or scarecrows or brooms and run off into the sunset with their tragically unsuitable seducers. There was a queen who, in a bout of uncharacteristic insanity, leaped into a well after a golden ball and lived out the rest of her life as a petulant herring. There was another who fled from her spouse and children to join a circus, first as a lion tamer and subsequently (after a local magician known as Arbadac the Bumbler caused an inadvertent accident during a coughing fit at a performance he attended) as the lion. The fairy celebrated each malicious accomplishment with chocolate bonbons and grew quite plump.

The final court she would ever visit appeared similar to all the others—a confection of a palace; a striking queen with eyebrows dark and glossy like strips of luxurious fur; an ineffectual king who dozed on his throne, entrusting the running of the kingdom to his ministers; a joyful five-year-old boy. Posing as a chaplain's long-lost third cousin on a brief visit, the fairy learned the lay of the land, decided on a spell, prepared the groundwork. And then something happened: she found herself procrastinating at the king's court, for a week, another week, a month. She lingered in the company of the queen, who sang sad, tender lullabies to her son, stirring up the long-buried memories of the fairy's own childhood in her hitherto hardened breast; for thus had her own mother sung to her at each bedtime. Then, too, she had to confess to growing quite fond of the king, who was not in the least like other kings of her acquaintance, not irate or oblivious, but mild and courteous, often overwhelmed, and given to occasional bouts of existential despair, which she found worthy of sympathy and, if truth be told, rather romantic. And last, she was—much to her surprise, for she had never shown any affinity for children—drawn to the boy himself. He had the face of a stained-glass angel, a sunny disposition, and a generous spirit. One day, he brought her a present—a watercolor quite advanced for his age, for he had a marvelous aptitude for art. He had depicted a beaming boy standing between beaming parents; the three of them held hands, while a pretty, if slightly plump, young woman hovered above the group on immense butterfly wings.

"This is me with Mama and Papa." He pointed. "And this is you. Because I can see that you aren't just a girl, you are a fairy. A good, beautiful fairy, the kind that grants wishes. And now, will you please grant my wish?"

"And what is your wish?" the fairy asked, smiling, as she scooped him up into her lap and pinched his little chin between her finger and thumb, a trifle too hard. "A new hobbyhorse, maybe? Or ice cream for every dinner?"

The boy's blue gaze was clear and serious.

"I wish for you to stay with us, always. I love you."

And at that very instant her injured heart melted and mended, filling with love in return. But tragically, it was too late. For just as the fairy cried great tears of repentance and relief over the child's radiant chestnut curls, over his drawing of the happy family, of which she suddenly believed herself a part, frantic servants ran through the palace calling for their queen, yet calling in vain, for the queen had vanished. The fairy realized, then, that her spell had been accidentally set into motion, that the harm had been done, that the queen must have somehow chanced upon the enchanted apple and bitten into it—and worse, deep within herself, she understood that she might have meant for it to happen, for had she not, in a supposed fit of absentmindedness, left the poisoned apple on the queen's vanity table only the night before? Had she not, in truth, been hoping to get the sweet-voiced beauty with the sable eyebrows out of the way so she could have the king and the boy all to herself?

Horrified, newly heartbroken, she remained at the scene of her crime for a while after, striving to do what little she could to right the wrong. She failed. She watched the king fall into grief so gray and impenetrable that he became like another ghost haunting the royal cellars. She watched the light leak out of the boy. She fled their palace in shame, swearing to atone for her dark, terrible sins with everything she did forever after, determined to dedicate the rest of her immortal life to performing selfless deeds, dispensing miracles, making sweet little orphans happy. And she tried, and she tried, she tried so hard—but everything she did seemed to go awry, quite as if she were cursed. Her wards were not grateful to receive what gifts she gave, and babes wailed at her approach. She built a wondrous gingerbread house in a shady pine forest, hoping to create a peaceful haven for hungry lost children—yet the only ones who came her way were an ungrateful, boisterous, poorly raised mob of boys, five or six brothers, who treated her abominably, nibbled away half her house, and in the end escaped her tender attentions to return to the woods, where they now led wild, undisciplined lives, swinging from trees, playing barbaric games, transforming into ravens when the mood was upon them, making regular assaults on her sugar windowsills and candy-cane fences, and spreading malicious rumors that she was a wicked witch intent on cannibalism and other unnatural practices. And still, she has not given up—oh, no—she has been knitting socks for the local orphanages, has been turning up at every christening, whether invited or not—"so many godchildren I have, all sweet, motherless orphans . . ."

She trails off.

"But what . . ." My voice is a croak when I find it at last. "What happened to that queen? The queen with the loving boy? What did you *do* to her?"

The fairy godmother wrings her hands in anguish.

"She turned into a chess piece!" she wails. "Such an elegant spell it was, too, a proper, elaborate spell, came with a flash of lightning and everything, a pity there was no one nearby to appreciate . . . That is, of course, it was dreadful, just dreadful . . . The poor dear . . . I found her on the floor of her bedchamber, rolled under a dresser, and I dusted her off the best I could and put her on display with some other knickknacks they kept in the palace library. For all I know, she is still there, I never did have the heart to check when I came back. Because, you see, I did return some twenty years later, when I felt that I'd rehabilitated my character with enough good deeds to earn me a second chance with the king and his son. Neither of them recognized me—true, I had become a bit matronly with time—but perhaps it was just as well. The king was still depressed, so I counseled him, and . . . and I was kind to him in other ways, too, and it did cheer him up, if less than it might have. But the boy—the boy had grown into a man in my absence, and the man was not nearly as nice as he could have been. Cold. A bit shallow. Uncaring, some might have thought. So I decided the best thing I could do for him was find him a perfect bride, the kind who was meek and quiet and patient and would bring out the best in him after a while—and, well—"

She falls silent and, pressing her hands against her chest, stares at me with eyes made enormous by the butterfly frames. I stare back, speechless. I think of the small glass cabinet in the library of my own palace, with its unassuming display of dusty objects—the bleary mirror, the blood-encrusted key, the apple with a bite taken out of its shiny red side, the ivory chess queen, and, in the place of honor, the crystal slipper.

"Do you understand, child? I did it for both of you. I promise I meant well."

And just like that, I understand—I understand everything. I look at the pink china cups, the pink glowing lamps, the pink porcelain cupids, and see all these trappings of goodness and decorum for the mere illusions they are. For the woman before me, the plump, anxious woman wrapped in pink fuzzy shawls, blinking at me through the pink butterfly glasses from the heart of the pink cozy room, is evil, pure evil, a fat, glistening pink spider caught in the center of the web of harm she has been busily spinning for years and years, trapping me and my prince in her sticky snares, all to avenge herself for some half-forgotten childhood slight.

She is no fairy—she is a witch.

An evil witch who ruined my husband's nature, then robbed me of my joy.

Because it must have been her, who else could it have been, it was clearly her.

Wasn't it?

"It was you," I hiss, and as my voice strengthens, so does my certainty. "You were the one. The one who stole my passion. My life's spark. You told me the dress, the glass slippers, the carriage were your gifts, because I was good, because I deserved it—but you lied, they weren't gifts, your magic wasn't free, you made me pay for everything, didn't you? And the price was too high, and it ruined my life, it ruined my marriage, because I never felt completely right, I never felt completely *there*, I knew in my heart that something was always missing, something was always missing in my heart, and now I see what it was! Everything, everything is your fault, you knew just how it would play out, you arranged for all this to happen—"

Swiftly, irritably, she waves her hand about, as though dissipating some bothersome smell. A sudden silence stretches from one wall of her overheated room to the other. She continues to blink at me through her glasses, yet now she looks concerned, and all at once I feel a bit disoriented. To get my bearings, I glance at the framed diploma above her desk, at the box of tissues on the table next to her, at her plump middle-aged figure settled in her ample leather armchair, and the familiarity of my surroundings serves to quiet my agitation, as it always does.

"You are still doing it, I'm afraid," she offers, gravely. "Still blaming outside circumstances for your own actions and short-comings. Yet anger is a healthy emotion, even when misdirected, so I feel we've made progress today." She sets down her pen, gently closes the notebook she holds in her lap, reaches for the tissues, and hands them to me just as her face begins to grow imprecise through the sheen of my tears. "Our hour is up, but we will pick this up next week. And in our next session, I want to work on your sense of self-worth, so let's return to our discussion of your Cinderella complex. We talked about it back in the fall, remember, when you were first considering separation. Why did you think your husband was your benefactor when he married you? Did you believe that he was better than you in some way? Was it just his wealth and your inferior social status, as you perceived it, or were there other reasons, too? I want you to think about these things during the week, and we'll talk about them next Tuesday at eleven. Here, let me write down the time for you, you've been forgetting our appointments lately. Of course, stress *will* make you forget a few things."

She makes a pencil note on her business card, and I take it with a grateful nod, blow my nose, and stand up to put on my coat, and step outside. The cold suburban street stretches as far as the eye can see. I walk in the noonday glare, sliding my finger along the surface of the card, touching the raised letters of "Dr. Faye Wand, Licensed Therapist" embossed in its snowy white center. Just before I reach my sister's home, plumb in the middle of the row of identical working-class houses, I slip the card into my pocket, feeling reassured.

Dr. Wand truly is a miracle worker. She always helps me see clearly.

In the Suburbs

The doorbell rings the following morning.

Melissa's husband has already left for the lumberyard (he has just been promoted to supervisor), and her three eldest—Meg, Mary, and Myrtle—have gone to school; the baby is asleep in the crib upstairs. Melissa has made the children's beds, brought down Myrtle's latest creation to stick to the door of their new refrigerator (the first one on the block, she often mentions in a casual tone, her pride writ large on her face), and poured us each a mug of coffee, which we are now drinking at the kitchen table.

"She's only seven, so who knows," Melissa says. "But don't you think so?"

"Sorry, what?"

"Myrtle. Don't you think she has talent?" She motions to the drawing, sounding a bit reproachful, and I am reminded that I have been sleeping on her living room sofa for nearly three months, and should, if only out of gratitude, pay more attention to the accomplishments of her children—even if it pains me.

"It's very . . . colorful," I say quickly, to appease her, "colorful" being the first word that alights on my tongue—but then I look, really look, and am arrested by the picture's imaginative vibrancy. In the bright green meadow, under the bright blue sky, stands a bright yellow house shaped like a shoe. Its door is red, its roof is green, with a blue weather vane fashioned like a rabbit; doves are flying overhead in a bright white flock, and smiling children, so many of them, lead a happy dance around a short laughing woman in an apron. Melissa, too, is looking at it, and there is an odd, dreamy expression in her eyes.

"It's that Mother Goose rhyme, you know the one," she says.

> *There was an old woman who lived in a shoe,*
> *She had so many children, she didn't know what to do;*
> *She gave them some broth without any bread,*
> *Then whipped them all soundly and put them to bed.*

"The girls demand it every night before sleep. Of course, I change the words when I read it to them, I say, 'She kissed them all gently and put them to bed.' Because, you know, I would never. Although sometimes, God forgive me, I do so want to give them a good, sound smack. Some days are just overwhelming—there are only the four of them, and one still a baby, but I swear, sometimes it feels as if . . . as if I had a full ten." She falters, sets the mug down, slides her worn wedding band up and down her finger. "Can I tell you something? I haven't told anyone, not even Tom."

"Of course. Is something wrong?"

"No, it's just . . . it's this anxious dream I keep having, the last couple of months. Since you've come to live with us, actually."

She stands up to splash more coffee into our mugs as she begins to talk. In her dream, she is herself, and still married to Tom, but Tom is a real woodsman, the kind who chops down trees, a green-clad giant of a man with an ax over his shoulder, and they live in a blooming woodland glade, on the edge of a great, ancient forest, with their great many children. For, in her dream, there are Meg, Mary, and Myrtle, just as in real life, and the baby is there, too; but there are also six boys, six loud, boisterous, tiring, exasperating, wonderful boys, the life and the curse of the house, the pride and the torment of the mother's heart. But they are poor, there is not enough food to go around for everyone, and in a thoughtless moment of frustration, of which she has so many every day, whenever one of her unmanageable sons pulls Mary's braids, or releases piglets inside the house, or flings mud at the cow, she screams that the boys are too much, that they are eating all of them into an early grave, that they would be better off spending their wild, freewheeling days as ravens feeding off the bounty of the land, living at the mercy of the forest. And just as her reckless, dangerous words fly into the wind, her six precious boys, the light of her life, transform into shaggy black birds and, cawing, take off for the woods, never to be seen again.

Or at least this is what happens in some dreams, and she spends the remainder of the nighttime hours pacing her kitchen, twisting her hands, willing her baby to grow up with magical promptness so she could venture out into the gloom of the silent trees and bring her brothers safely home, for the onus of any deed of salvation is ever on the youngest. In other dreams, though, there are no ravens. More heartbreaking still, she and her husband discuss, debate, deliberate, then choose their docile, helpful, artistically gifted, domestically inclined, soft-spoken girls over their savage, bright-spirited, impractical, ravenous, exuberant boys, and Tom, expressionless, stoic, takes the boys deep into the forest, by invisible paths known only to him, and there abandons them to their cruel fate. Occasionally, the slumber gods do take pity on her, and somehow she knows that her sons will not perish from hunger, thirst, and wild beasts but will stumble upon an enchanted oasis of milk, honey, and gingerbread at the heart of the woods, and will cavort in the trees forever after, joyful, free, fed on cookies and candy canes by some benevolent, maternal presence—and that, moreover, this new, unfettered life will suit them much better than their old, small life of chores and chastisement within the four walls of the family home and they will be eternally grateful to her, their mother, for having released them in her endless motherly wisdom.

On most nights, however, the dream gods are not as kindly disposed, and she wakes up just as her husband, his eyes blank, his hands running bloody with the monstrousness of filicide, returns home, and, suddenly aware of what they have wrought, she flies at him in an ecstasy of grief and fury, rakes his cheeks with her nails, screams their lost names into his face, each one torn from within her gut like a curse, like damnation: Peter! Richard! Henry! Arthur! William!—until she finds herself sitting upright in bed, the alarm clock ticking laboriously through the fourth hour of the morning, tears dripping off her chin, her husband snoring next to her in blissful oblivion, the name "Tom Junior" trembling still on her lips.

But it is not always thus—for, more often yet, there are no ravens, and no woods, and no gingerbread fairies in her dreams, nothing dark, nothing magic, nothing to console her with the inevitability of a tale unfolding from its tragic beginning to its fulfilling conclusion. She merely dreams of her life, her ordinary daily life in her ordinary suburban house, and the boys vanish slowly, one after another, each disappearing along with his scant possessions—filthy boots by the door, a small bag of treasured marbles, an infectious laugh, a handful of freckles—along with the room he has inhabited, along with all memory of him. And so their home keeps shrinking, and the rest of them go on as though nothing has changed, nothing has diminished, first mother and father with their ten children, then nine, then eight, until there are only the girls and the baby left in a small house with a white picket fence in a New Jersey suburb with the faintly fairy-tale name of Bloomfield, and Tom has no inkling of anything wrong, no recollection of there ever having been a delightful rambling cottage shaped like a shoe in a blooming field on the edge of a vast, ancient forest, no recollection of there ever having been anyone named Tom Junior, and she herself barely remembers what it is she is missing—she just knows that, on some mornings, she wakes up with a gaping sense of emptiness in her soul, where something else used to be.

She finishes the last of her coffee, worries the wedding band on her finger.

"Just dreams," she says. "Just dreams, I know. To be honest, it's probably all those miscarriages I had, before the girls. But sometimes I can't help wondering—"

And it is then that the doorbell rings.

And since Melissa appears distraught, it is I who stand up to answer.

The short, unshaven man in a cheap brown suit who shifts from foot to foot on the threshold is a stranger, and yet, surprisingly, he offers me my name.

"Are you?" he asks.

"Yes," I reply, a bit experimentally (am I?), and shrink from the swift mirthless smirk that twists his loose, rubbery lips.

"You are served," he croons, thrusts a manila envelope into my hands, and disappears abruptly, as if he had never been there at all.

"Who was that?" Melissa asks from the kitchen table.

I extract a thick sheaf of papers from the envelope.

"Complaint for Absolute Divorce," the black-on-white letters state at the top.

Dully, I leaf through the pages, and out of their stark whiteness words explode like a mob of angry crows startled out of a tree, flying into my face, scratching at my eyes. "Abandonment," "child neglect," "unemployed," "erratic behavior," "long-term

abuse of prescription medications," "history of mental instability," "lived in a rodent-infested room," "unsuited for taking care
of," "no residence of her own," "is currently cohabitating with her
brother-in-law, Thomas Woodley, in an adulterous arrangement,"
"recent evidence of alcohol and drug use (see Exhibit A)" . . . A
photograph flutters out. It is blurry, but I can make out myself, in
crumpled clothes, with a crumpled face, stumbling raccoon-eyed
and windblown through the neighborhood park at dawn, hug-
ging a bucket with a burnt hydrangea to my chest.

The next page delivers the execution order: ". . . hereby request full custody of the minor children, Angelina and Roland
the Sixth . . ."

Slowly I sink onto a chair, the pages falling from my loosened
hands. My heart is like a plague bell tolling in my chest, and my
chest is empty, my mind is empty. It's over, I think, and maybe
I say it aloud. Bustling, scowling, Melissa gathers the scattered
pages, licks her index finger, begins to turn them, begins to
exclaim, my supporting cast intoning the scripted lines of indignation.

"But this is outrageous," she fumes. "These are all lies!"

Are they, though? I myself am not overly sure.

Some of it might be true.

"Call your lawyer," she says, slamming the papers on the table, slamming her fist on the papers. "This makes me furious. I
can't even imagine how *you* feel."

Furious, yes. But also—mainly—frightened: for this blow has
split open a never fully healed scar, and out of the gaping wound
has gushed my constant guilt over not being enough for my children in recent years, perhaps never having been enough, of failing as a mother in so many ways, of clearly, sickeningly, not being
as perfect as fairy-tale princesses are expected to be. And as I sit
there, frozen by horror, watching the lifeblood pouring out of my

heart, all I can think is: Will I now pay for all my faults, my all-too-human weaknesses, by losing them forever, by forfeiting what I love most?

But already, somehow, the telephone is set before me, and Melissa is searching for the number, and I watch the round dial jerk forward and fall back, jerk forward and fall back. And next Gwendolyn's efficient voice is in my ear, and then I am in Gwendolyn's efficient office, and she is telling me we will fight him, king or no king, we will level our own accusations, will prove that I can take care of myself and my offspring, will establish my character, will end by making me a free woman, and a rich free woman at that, here is what I need to do, this, this, and now this—and so I read through this document, and sign here, and authorize that statement, and sign there, and then things speed up, everything slides by so quickly, my tearful farewell to Melissa, Tom, and their girls ("But we are only a short train ride away, we are here for you"), a tiny apartment I have found for rent in the city, my weekly sessions with Dr. Wand, which are beneficial as a matter of record, a string of new employment opportunities (following upon the termination of my contract with the young women of questionable values out on Long Island, who may have proved detrimental to my case), my work taking me out of the city and back to the suburbs, though more affluent than my sister's by far, where I assist beautifully coiffed wives, their short ballooning skirts clenching their wasplike waists, with baking cakes, ironing sheets, and vacuuming wall-to-wall carpets.

I follow my lawyer's strict injunctions not to fraternize with my employers this time, but I watch them closely, for doing so distracts me from dwelling on my own misery. The wives move as though under water, with their immaculately manicured pearly nails and their dainty kitten heels, and at midday their eyes assume a mild glassiness, a bit like the eyes of the fancy dolls in their daughters' rooms. I never meet the husbands (in the city during the day, the wives inform me, at work in their advertising agencies or banks or investment firms), or the children, either (I am not told where the children are), though I am presented with the evidence of their existence in countless prominently displayed pictures. In the pictures, everyone is always smiling, seated over checkered tablecloths at picnics, posing in mid-jump with tennis rackets, lined up by lakes with fishing rods. The husbands' smiles seem offhand and the wives' faintly hysterical, yet the children look sincere, even eager. After a while, as weeks pass and I never see any of the children in the gleaming rooms of these gleaming homes, I fall to wondering whether the wives have not contrived to trap their darling boys and girls inside these framed displays of ideal childhoods and are thus keeping them safely out of the way while they themselves, ever so slightly sedated, navigate the troubled shoals of their marital havens.

Because I can recognize unhappy women when I see them, and these women are unhappy.

They long to talk to me. They act all frosty at first, for the instructional articles they favor in the *Good Housekeeping* magazine have advised them to keep their distance from their help; yet after a while—weeks in some cases, mere days in others—they feel reassured by the fact that I have not made any requests for monetary advances, nor have their precious candlesticks or silver spoons gone missing, so they begin to linger in doorways of dining rooms while I dust their displayed wedding china, and they chat about this and that, and then, at the end of my day, invite me to partake in cups of tea, relaxing pills, and confessions. I take no pills, share no confessions of my own in return, and offer little encouragement, but little is all that is needed, it seems, and I hear their stories. And perhaps the stories I hear are not precisely the stories they tell, but by now I know enough about love and princes to discern, behind the cheery inflections of their genteel fantasies, beneath the cherry veneer of their civilized mid-century dwellings, the dark, heady danger of primitive transformations, the rank odors of beasts prowling through the woods.

There are five of them, one for each day of my working week. The Monday princess, the oldest and most resigned of the lot, met her husband when she was out for a stroll in the park, gathering flowers for her parents' mantelpiece arrangement, and he a stag pursued by a vicious hunt. He bounded over for help, pleaded with her to give him her heart, for only thus would the enchantment be broken, only thus would he resume his true, his human, form, and she felt sorry for him because of the frantic rolling of his golden eyes, the foaming of his blackened lips, and chose to believe him. And once her heart was firmly in his possession, he did make one fine-looking, graceful man; but these days, almost two decades later, she often finds her ceilings scuffed by antlers and her rugs imprinted by hooves, so she has begun to suspect that he lied to her, is lying to her still, that his true form has always been that of a stag and he gladly reverts to his prancing, doe-chasing ways whenever her back is turned, then pretends to misunderstand her tired questions in the mornings—and three or four times now, she has stumbled upon her heart, once his greatest treasure (he said), lying forgotten on windowsills or in kitchen drawers.

The Tuesday princess, by far the richest of them all, is elegant and sleek, slinking about her suburban mansion on feet soft as paws, lying sprawled on sofas in sophisticated silk dresses, grooming herself, her eyes evasive and smooth, stacks of golden bracelets jingling up and down her skinny arms. She takes the longest to speak to me, and even then, she purrs with half-truths and omissions. Still, I learn that in her youth, she was a beautiful white cat, a royal cat, no less, but she fell in love with a broad-shouldered,

happy-go-lucky peasant youth entirely indifferent to her charms—
he was a dog person—and the less he cared, the harder the thorn
of love pinned down her soul. She invited him to live in her palace, gave him fine wines to drink, delicacies to eat, velvets and
jewels to wear, and still he preferred his slobbery romps with
street mutts to an hour of refinement in her discerning feline presence. At last, in despair, she begged him to cut off her head—and
when he did, a lovely woman appeared in place of the cat, so,
rendered dumb by the shock, the youth gave in and married her
right on the spot. And, fifteen years later, they are married still,
but now she often snaps, scratches, and spits at him, for she feels
poisoned by the hateful recollection of the ease with which he
granted her long-ago wish to behead her—a shrug and "Sure,"
carelessly tossed off—and, too, she often catches her ever-gorgeous
husband looking at her with amiable speculation, as though wondering what kind of delightful new being might emerge and grace
him with her effervescent presence if he cut off the head of his
tiresomely nagging, aging wife.

The Wednesday princess, the youngest, married a wolf. He
terrorized her neighborhood for many a season, powerful muscles
rolling under his shaggy pelt, devouring maidens and, on occasion, their mothers (though not grandmothers, rumors notwithstanding, for their meat was too dry for his liking), when she came
dancing across his way one sunny day, a basket of homemade
provisions in the crook of her elbow. He treated himself to her
roast chicken and her rhubarb pie, thinking to eat her next—and
then, somehow, found himself intrigued, for she wore bright colors, sang happy songs, had a mouth the color of burst berries, and
was not a whit afraid of him. And so he brought her home instead, and she was ecstatic at first—she knew herself special for
taming a savage creature of the dark forest—and she went around
his house singing "Tra-la-la!" and cooking delicious suppers. Yet

she soon noticed that if she happened to cease her singing for even a minute or burn even one piece of toast, his eyes would narrow and his tongue would take a few saliva-drenched lolls by his great yellow teeth. The more it happened, the more apprehensive she grew, until her apprehension turned to fear. Some months ago, she happened to meet a young hunter, she confided to me shyly. She is now weighing her options.

The Thursday wife was rescued by her prince from the top of a tree in the heart of the forest, where she sat naked and alone, for what reason she herself cannot recall—it seems like a different life. He had not asked whether she wanted to be rescued. Had she been asked, she is not sure what answer she would have given at the time, yet now—now she misses her tree. But it is the Friday princess, the most beautiful of the five, whose story bothers me most. When she first married her husband, he was a beast under a spell, yet she loved the sad, shriveled seed of a soul that she sensed fluttering beneath his fur and fangs. Devotedly, she followed every last bit of advice she mined from fashion magazines— she perfected her housekeeping skills, splurged on his creature comforts, did not complain about her own petty troubles when her beast came home from work, but listened with avid interest as he grouched for hours on end; nor did she ever forget to take a few minutes to refresh herself before his arrival, putting a touch of lipstick on her mouth and a ribbon in her hair. She arranged his pillows, took off his shoes, and treated him as the master of the house long after he had stopped roaring at her—and, in time, her tender ministrations made him soft and gentle in her hands, a new, caring, sensitive man. Now they should be happy together, but she is getting bored—and gradually, she is beginning to understand that what she loved was not the man himself, nor the beast, but her own near-magical power to effect the transformation from the one to the other. She does not tell me that, not in these exact words, but over a glass of sherry, she whispers that she has undercooked his steak on purpose once or twice, has forgotten to sew on an occasional button, has met him, with some regularity, with curlers in her hair—and even though he has appeared patient and understanding so far, she thinks she might have detected a growl in his voice now and then, and it has made a small flame of excitement flare up in her heart grown lardy on tedium. Who knows what he might turn into next, if only she keeps at it, she says, smiling dreamily into her second sherry of the afternoon. After her third glass, she grows giggly and brings over an instructional book she was given by her mother as a wedding present, *Married Life and Happiness*, penned by a New York physician some three decades ago, and, slurring slightly, recites a paragraph: "Remember that the old idea that a wife is the husband's chattel to do with as he pleases is going out of fashion. The idea that woman has no soul and should be treated on a par with imbeciles and idiots is also becoming antiquated. Women are really beginning to find out that they are human beings, almost as good as we are"—upon which she dissolves into peals of inebriated laughter, and I hasten to excuse myself under a pretext of another cleaning engagement.

I recount these women's stories to Dr. Wand at our next session.

"And how do they make you feel?"

"I would have felt hopeless a year ago. Now I just feel impatient. Because they are all more or less the same story, and they all end quite badly. Are there no happy endings for anyone anymore?"

She muses for a moment.

"In Shakespeare's times, did you know," she says at last, "any story that ended with marriage was considered a comedy. Doesn't that strike our modern sensibilities as ironic? I'd say the ending would depend largely on the beginning, and none of these beginnings seems particularly promising to me. You can't have the right answer to a wrong question, you know. And expectations play a vital part, as well. Are you ready to talk about what happened at the end of your own marriage?"

This question is our weekly rite of passage. I shake my head, so we discuss the approaching meeting with my children instead—now that my court date has been set for the summer, my tough no-nonsense lawyer has arranged for me to see Angie and Ro for an hour every Sunday, under the supervision of Dr. Wand, who, it turns out, is a trusted old friend of my husband's family and, too, specializes in treating childhood traumas. She cautions me not to be clingy, not to reveal my anxieties, not to badmouth their father, and, however I feel, not to cry. When I see them at last—we meet for a walk in Central Park on a beautiful March evening, mere blocks from their home (I can no longer think of it as mine, if ever I did)—I am overjoyed by the sight, by the smell, by the feel of them, the sheer physicality of their presence, and stricken by how tall they have grown in the months we have spent apart from each other, and devastated by the slight formality with which they greet me, the detached stiffness of their first embrace, the awkwardness with which we struggle to find initial topics of conversation—but only for a few minutes, because Ro is already telling me about a puppy his daddy bought him (But I can't compete with a puppy, I scream inside, then try to put the smile back on my face and listen to the sounds of my son's cruel joy), and Angie reveals the gap in her gums where her last baby tooth has fallen out.

"But the tooth fairy forgot to come," she says sadly, and even though she is plainly too old to believe in fairies, I clench my fists behind my back, stabbed by hatred for that self-engrossed, oblivious man.

They show me photos of their Christmas tree.

"But it wasn't the same this year," Ro says.

"Because I wasn't there?" I ask, hopeful.

Dr. Wand shoots me a quick warning look, just as Ro replies, "No, because we had stupid white lights instead of the pretty rainbow ones, like we did before, and it was boring," and then Angie kicks him in the shin and says, "But also because you weren't there." And they talk, and I talk, and we laugh, and we lick and rank one another's ice creams, comparing flavors (Angie wins, as she always does), and somehow, for five full minutes, I truly manage to forget what things are, to stop stewing over their father, and I feel happy, and I feel whole—and then the hour is over, and suddenly I cannot breathe and am horrified to feel tears swelling into my eyes, but Dr. Wand puts a gentle hand on my shoulder, and I remember that in another week there will be another hour—and then a life, an entire life of puppies and ice creams and tooth fairies—and I can breathe again, at least a little.

In the City

This spring, the city is starting to change around me. Everything seems both familiar and endlessly new, as though my way of seeing has altered, my angle of vision has shifted. I look at the same throngs of people I have been passing on the sidewalks of Manhattan for most of my life, and I see stories, countless stories, behind the facades of their faces, just as I see interiors behind the facades of the buildings where I work—and sometimes the stories and the interiors are precisely what one would expect, sad clichés, trite romances with stale endings, princes and princesses leading dreary parallel existences past their happily ever after, vacuous rooms full of imposing furniture arranged in symmetrical flocks for the centerfold pages of design magazines, all in need of perennial dusting; but other times, more and more often as this strange spring draws closer to summer, the places surprise me, the stories unfold and intertwine in patterns that are delightfully startling, until I begin to believe, to hope, that there can be other plots, other joys, other ways of living—because life is changing, and so am I.

By April, the suburban Connecticut wives with their tight smiles, bouffant hairstyles, and handspan waists have faded into their well-mannered, color-coordinated misery, giving way to new city clients I have found, mostly through interventions of my older sister, Gloria, who travels the country as an art consultant to wealthy collectors and knows scores of musicians, sculptors, models, all those "on the fringes of genius," as she likes to call them, half dismissively, half fondly. I clean airy lofts with virtually no possessions other than gleaming African masks or gigantic photographs of flat-chested nudes with sullen eyes. I clean houses with black-and-white zigzag floors and walls that slide open, letting in fresh, heady smells of balmy evenings, of city streets, of freedom. I sweep plastic wine cups and used condoms out of the darker corners of Soho galleries on mornings after openings. I meet people who love well, fully, with passion, but who do not live for love, or not for love alone—they live to create art, to quest after knowledge, to make friends, to walk the world. Not all of these people are happy, but there is an intensity, a vibrancy, an exuberance about them that seems to me better than happiness, or else an altogether different kind of happiness, that reminds me of some long-ago stories I used to hear, or perhaps fantasies I used to have. And though these people's lives are not my life and I stand on the outside, peering in through the veil of my sadness, my worry, my exhaustion, now and then I feel that I, too, can break through, I, too, can will my life into some semblance of theirs, given time, given imagination, given desire, given work.

I meet a gorgeous fortysomething jewelry artist with a penchant for wearing loose, richly embroidered caftans, who, some years ago, was abandoned by her prominent politician husband for a sweet-faced girl with skin white as snow, lips red as blood, hair black as ebony, and the soul of a snake, young enough to be his daughter. Now the older woman lives in a loft with a terrace open to all the winds and seven muscular men for lovers, and they listen to dreamy music and paint flowers all over the walls and throw parties to which the entire city block comes to recite poetry and dance in the moonlight; and when her former husband, having tired of his new wife (who seemed to spend her days gorging herself on sugared fruit and sleeping), begged her to return to him, she smiled with pity and offered him a drag on her joint before her seven lovers escorted him out. I meet a prince whose father kept sending him portraits of suitable princesses and whose mother kept putting peas under the mattresses of overnight female guests, until the heir, fed up, escaped to remote lands (some said, by climbing a beanstalk), and there met a giant who refused to devour the passersby and, as a result, was ostracized by his traditional giant family; the two now share a penthouse apartment with a glass roof and work on making a mosaic map of the sky out of pebbles and crystals. I meet young, lovely witches. I meet old, wise imps. I meet tricky cobblers and homeless elves. I meet cooks who speak in foreign tongues and work magic in the kitchen, beautiful men who wear ball gowns better than any princesses ever could, trapeze performers who truly fly, taxi drivers who used to be kings and kings who used to be shoeshines, fatherless children who tame wild cats, dark-skinned pirates who write immortal verse, young girls who learn the secrets of the universe by peering into telescopes and kissing, then dissecting, frogs. The world is, all at once, so many worlds unfolding within worlds, and as I take Angie and Ro for our supervised weekly stroll, I start to see the three of us as three small spirits holding hands while we make our uncertain, brave, wondering way through the immense labyrinth of marvels and delights—and I want them to grow up to be a part of it, as I myself had not been.

In May, Gloria comes to New York to oversee an installation at a celebrated art gallery, and she insists on taking me out to lunch. I have not seen my older sister since the funeral. She looks much the same, though her edges are harder now, polished by her continued success in life, and most noticeably, her luxurious long hair, the pride of her adolescence, is gone, replaced by a severe rectangular cut that makes her look like a Modigliani portrait. The restaurant where we meet (she is ten minutes late, talking on her phone as she enters at a swishing, clicking stride) is much more expensive than anything I could now afford and much more fashionable than anything I ever cared to frequent; I am humbled by its black-and-white minimalism. Gloria, too, is dressed all in black and white, as though she chose the establishment solely to match her sense of style—and knowing my sister, I would guess that is just what she did. We sit at a tiny table, and shyly I pick at my three or four sprigs of some exotic herb crowned by flowers and arranged with flawless precision in the center of an enormous, barren plate, while Gloria talks of the early days of the feminist avant-garde movement, of Leonardo da Vinci's *Last Supper* re-imagined with women as the apostles, of modern technology influencing art . . . And as I watch her red lips move, watch her black-and-white gestures multiplied by the mirrors, I catch myself puzzling over something. We have never been particularly close—even as a child, I found her formidable ways intimidating—but the lasting chill in our adult relationship, I realize now, has been mainly of my own making, caused by the offense I took at her behavior during my long-ago wedding. She wore a sour look throughout the ceremony, and later, when her turn came in the receiving line, she spoke to me out of the corner of her mouth and spoke to my groom not at all; she never even said "Congratulations." For years, I believed her to have been envious of me, of my brilliant match.

Now, I am not so sure.

"Gloria, what did you have against my marriage?" I blurt out when she pauses to take a sip of her martini.

She raises one elegant eyebrow. There is something of a bird of prey in the spare grace of her movements.

"Let's just say, I did not think you two were a suitable match."

She waves her hand, and I follow the bright red trajectory of her glittering nails. A baby-faced waitress materializes by our table. "Another martini, my dear," Gloria says, lightly touching her finger to the waitress's bare arm, then shifts her gaze back to me. "You were too young. Too young to know yourself properly. Too young to know your fiancé properly. When I was that age, I didn't even know what I liked."

"What you *liked*?"

The waitress sails back across the black-and-white room with the new martini, swinging her hips, and a dozen more waitresses float through the mirrors on all sides of us, their eyes obliquely meeting the eyes of Gloria's manifold reflections.

"Shortly after your wedding," Gloria says, raising her fresh drink to her lips, "I met someone. A prince much like yours. Handsome, rich, all the right parts in all the right places. He wanted to marry me. But something felt wrong, so I just kept saying, 'Perhaps,' and 'Let's talk about it next month,' and 'Maybe after I'm done with my studies next year,' and 'Let me just settle into my job first.' Eventually he got angry, tricked me into a tower, and, once I was inside, walled the door shut. For weeks, I sat by the only window, high off the ground, and his servants used pulleys to deliver my food so I wouldn't starve, but I was allowed to talk to no one, to see no one—and every Sunday, right as clockwork, he would come to my window and shout: 'Will you marry me now?' And then I was angry, too, so there were no more 'Maybe' and 'Later.' I would just scream 'No!' down at him, and he would stride away in a huff."

She pats her dramatic red mouth with a napkin, and immediately the waitress appears by her elbow. "I'll bring you a fresh one," a dozen waitresses promise breathlessly in a dozen mirrors. We wait for her to deposit another white paper square on the table, wait for her to walk away.

"Gloria, I had no idea . . . But you didn't marry him, did you?"

"Of course not. The very thought!"

"How, then, did you get out?"

"Well. Since you ask. One of the prince's servants and I fell in love. We figured out a way to see each other. Remember when my hair was really long? If I let it down from the tower window, it would touch the ground, and she could climb up to me. In time, she managed to smuggle in a rope ladder, and I escaped. We escaped together."

"Sorry." It has taken a few moments to filter through. *"She?"*

Gloria smiles at me, indulgently.

"All part of growing up, baby girl," she says, enunciating as though speaking to a child. "Figuring out what you like. What you are. Which—in spite of being almost forty years old, you know—is something you still need to do, in my opinion."

"Oh." I feel as though I have accidentally walked in on my sister naked, so I hasten to skip over her comment. "And then . . . then you lived happily ever after?"

She drinks the last of the martini, calls out, "Check, please!" and turns her level gaze back upon me. "Sometimes, I just don't know about you. This isn't some fucking fairy tale. Oh, I suppose we had a few good years. Eventually she left me for another woman. An artist I myself had discovered, as it happened, which wasn't pretty. That's when I cut off my hair. In the end, though, I like it better this way."

I do not know whether she means her hairstyle or her life, and I am feeling too embarrassed to ask, so, to say something, anything, I tell her: "I guess all this happened after your mother's funeral? Your hair was still long then."

And now she is looking at me funny, and all at once uncomfortable, I lower my eyes, which is when I see the napkin the waitress brought her still lying on the table, and it is not a fresh napkin at all: the paper square is visibly smudged with the red imprint of Gloria's kiss.

"Hey, she gave you back your own used napkin," I mumble.

"Indeed?" Gloria turns it over. A telephone number is scrawled in one corner. "Yes, I rather thought so." A look of mild yet unmistakable interest flickers through her eyes. "Listen, it was good seeing you. I'll go settle the bill now."

She stands up, tall, elegant, collected, and looks down at me.

"Everything will be all right, little sister. Or maybe it won't be, in which case it will be something else, something new, which may turn out even better once the dust settles. Mel and I are here for you." She touches my cheek, briefly. "But you really need to stop with those Freudian slips. She was your mother, too."

I watch her moving away, as though in slow motion, into the black-and-white geometry of the room, the assured clicking of her heels slicing cleanly through the clanking of silverware, through the muttering of other diners' conversations. There is a sound, a nagging, repetitive sound, like the buzzing of a very loud, angry bee. People at the neighboring tables turn their heads to glare at me, and snapping out of my reverie, I reach for my purse and fish out my cell phone.

It is my lawyer.

"Are you anywhere near my office?" she says. "We need to talk."

What Happened at the End

And so, half an hour later, still reeling, I sit in a glass-walled office high above Manhattan, across the desk from my lawyer, who is telling me that her private investigator has turned up nothing, nothing at all, for my husband is clever and careful, if not actually clean, whereas the evidence against me is solid. There is the family doctor's testimony on the subjects of my depression and my propensity for self-medication and self-harm, there is the recent photograph of me inebriated in the park, there are maids willing to confirm the abundance of mouse droppings and ill-smelling weeds all over my former quarters, and to corroborate my erratic habits and odd behavior, such as my staring into a handheld mirror for hours on end or not speaking for months at a time—and, given the facts, the custody hearing is not likely to go my way. Financially, too, everything my husband owns is either part of his inheritance, to which I have no right, or else squirreled away in offshore accounts and shell companies, equally out of reach, and I have next to no claim on absolutely anything, which she has been trying to get through to me for days, for weeks, but do I listen?

And at last, I am beginning to listen.

"There is the Fifth Avenue apartment, though," I say. "Half of it should be mine. I don't want to live there, but we can sell it and split the proceeds. It would be more than enough to buy a modest place for me and the kids."

She snaps my file closed and sits back, exasperated.

"I've explained. Over and over again. It belonged to your father-in-law. Roland got it through his inheritance. It's nonmarital property."

On the streets below, cars honk, people walk, vendors hawk pretzels and newspapers—life as usual, life as I have always known it.

As Gwen's words sink in, I force myself to breathe.

"But the house on Martha's Vineyard?"

"The same."

"And the furnishings? The artwork? The royal treasury?"

A lonely siren cries somewhere far away. I am starting to panic.

"The same."

"But surely, half of my husband's income—"

"Half of it would be yours, yes. If your husband *had* any income. As it happens, though, he draws no actual salary, he just runs his late father's company." I open my mouth. "Which is his inheritance, and thus nonmarital property." I close my mouth. "On the other hand, Roland's lawyers have just informed me that your own income since your separation—all the money you've earned from your cleaning business, which appears to be doing quite well—*is* subject to the marital division, so they are now demanding half of everything you've made in the past six months."

"But . . . but it's all gone!" My heart is pounding now. "I gave some to Melissa, and I've been paying rent, and there are Jasmine and Alice—I hired them to help out last month, I told you—and then I bought some presents for the kids, and . . . and it was so little, anyway, nothing compared to his millions upon millions . . . They can't do that!" I cry, and in a smaller voice: "Can they?"

"Oh, they can," she says. "In fact, they have."

A second siren has joined the first, and another, and yet another, until half the city seems to be screaming with doom and disaster.

"But what do they want? What does he want?"

"He wants full custody of the kids. And to keep all his money. And come trial next month, he may well get both. Of course, I will do my best. But."

"But he can't do this to me! I'm better at taking care of Ro and Angie than he'll ever be. He won't even bother himself, they'll just have a staff of nannies round the clock . . . Wait—what about Nanny Nanny? She'll tell the court I'm a good mother, she knows, she was there, all the nights I spent by their beds, all the stories I told them—"

"Sadly, Nanny Nanny no longer works for your husband. She hasn't been seen since before Christmas. And I've heard rumors . . ." Gwen lowers her voice. "The family cook served roast leg of lamb at the holiday feast, and—"

"And what? Please tell me."

"And my sources inform me, it tasted more like goat. Like tough, old goat."

For a minute we are silent.

"So, then, what can we do?" I ask, defeated.

She faces me squarely.

"Nothing. There is nothing to do. Unless you are finally willing to tell me what happened between you and your husband at the end."

I look through the window at the city of glass and steel before me, and I think of the last months of my marriage, not so remote in time, and yet belonging to the fabric of some entirely different life, ruled by other laws, held together by other truths, an out-of-time fairy tale with a rosy beginning that promised happiness never-ending, stretching all the way from that snapshot of the blue spring skies protectively enclosing a white-veiled bride as she ran down the grand staircase hand in hand with her beloved, both smiling radiant smiles, to the two of them, thirteen years hence, standing side by side in the dimmed ballroom of their silenced home, clothed in the somber black of grief, jointly experienced and yet unshared, their faces blank, their stiff hands not touching.

After the last courtiers had departed muttering condolences, the fairy-tale princess, about to become the fairy-tale queen, slunk away to her own bedchamber without another look at the man who was not her true husband, who was left all alone, hunched over, in the dark. She was feeling faint and not sure of anything, her reality a mere step away from a dream. Her head ached as though she had not slept the night before, and perhaps she had not. Her feet were sore as though she had recently walked a long distance, and perhaps she had. Her lips bore a faintly tingling impression of other lips pressing against them, and this she could not bear to think about at all, for the kiss, whether real or imagined, had been warm, exhilarating, overwhelming, *alive*, nothing like any of the stilted, close-mouthed, obligatory kisses dimly remembered from the first year of her marriage (there were no later kisses to remember), and the lingering thrill of it, while making her heart beat faster, only served to add to her confusion and misery.

In her room, she sank onto her bed, raised her eyes—and saw two mice, one fat, the other skinny, with whiskers wrapped in golden foil, sitting side by side on her mantelpiece, bracketed by the dusty porcelain poodles.

She gasped.

"Nibbles? Brie? Are you really back? Is that really you?"

The mice nodded, their beady eyes brimming with sympathy.

"We know you are sad," they offered in unison, "and we are here to help you."

(This time, astonishingly, unnaturally, the mice were telling the truth: they were indeed the original Brie and Nibbles of her youth. Their long-dead spirits, snatched from a tranquil afterlife by their dear princess's acute distress, had taken to haunting the dwellings of mice, squealing and moaning, spooking the old out of their slumbers, making the young choke on their cheese, until the venerable Sister Charity, currently known as She with the Immortal Fairy Blood Flowing Through Her Veins, grew annoyed at the hubbub of constant complaints and appeals, and consented to grant the two temporary visibility on the plane of physical manifestations, to "sort out the princess mess," as she told them sternly, turning her piercing blind eyes in the direction of their flickering shapes, "so you can at last rest in eternal peace and I can be left in peace for at least two minutes to complete my important work. Go now."

As it happened, the fairy mouse had recently discovered that there was another world only a breath away from theirs—a much richer, thrilling world full of glorious sewer systems to populate, millions of mice and rats to rule over, and whole alleyways of trash cans positively overflowing with magnificent food—and was currently devising some way to merge the two worlds once and for all. For reasons not altogether clear even to herself, she felt the unhappy woman to be a loose end that needed to be tied up in order for her plan to succeed, but she did not explain her secret purpose to the spirits of Brie and Nibbles, and even if she had done so, her grand future vision would have gone right over their furry little heads.

Dismissed, they found themselves materializing on the familiar mantelpiece and there awaited their friend. They felt rather anxious about their status as ghosts—it seemed best not to disclose the fact of their long-ago demise to the princess for fear of upsetting her, yet wouldn't she be bound to notice that they were ever so slightly transparent? But when she saw them, she did not look beyond what she expected to find, for she was still only a human princess of limited understanding, and grateful as she was for their return, kindhearted and mindful of others as she strove to be in general, she naturally attributed much more significance to her own life than to the lives of simple mice, and would have been genuinely astonished had anyone told her that her one-note, romance-obsessed, cliché-ridden story might not be immensely more important or endlessly more fascinating than the multigenerational, multi-dimensional, magical, militant, philosophical, and culturally diverse saga of the dynasty of Nibbles and Brie.)

And so, overcome by relief at having someone to talk to at last, the princess broke down and told her friends everything—told them about the cruel curse imprisoning the prince since the early years of their marriage, and how she had been trying and trying to get her true beloved back, and how the world had conspired against her, and how . . . how . . . And just as she choked on her sobs, Brie and Nibbles exchanged a dark look, and Brie cleared her throat.

"Pardon us," she said in a tiny voice. "We are terribly sorry to tell you, dear princess, but you are mistaken. There isn't any curse. There never was. We've been watching your prince from the very beginning, and sadly, he is the same prince. The very same prince you married."

She shook her head with such vigor that a headache drummed at her temples.

"No, no, that's not true!" she cried. "It can't be true. Because you don't know. You don't know what terrible things he's done since the curse—"

She blushed, fell silent.

"Believe us, we know." Brie spoke with care. "We mice are small, we can go wherever we please and no one pays heed to us. We've seen . . . things. Many things. Many . . . eek . . . different things. Starting just days after your wedding. A young kitchen maid got lost in the hallways delivering breakfast to the Marquise de Fatouffle's bed, and, well . . . Then, the following week, the marquise herself . . . And others after that . . . Oh, we grew so concerned about you—"

"We argued all the time," Nibbles interrupted. "I thought we should tell you, that you needed to know. Give the rogue the old heave-ho and good riddance, *I* said."

"I disagreed." Brie's golden whiskers drooped. "Because who were we to destroy your happily ever after? You didn't notice anything amiss, and you did seem happy. At first, anyway. Was I wrong? Please, dear princess, was I?"

Her chest filled with a fluttering, as of many birds she could not bear to release, not yet, not yet. She looked at the mice with unseeing eyes, and rose, and walked out of the room. As she slowly went through the palace, she had few coherent thoughts, concentrating merely on putting one foot in front of the other; but she knew, without thinking, that if she happened to interrupt her husband in the midst of yet another copulation, she would not be responsible for what occurred next. But when she threw open the door to the prince's—now the king's—study, she found him alone, sitting at his desk, his head buried in his hands, the painted prince, as before, gracing her with his radiant smile from the portrait above.

The prince—now the king—lifted his head at her entrance, and his eyes were lost, swimming. Then a look dawned on his face, a look she could not place, a look she did not want to decipher. She stood before his desk, straight-backed, still, in her regal ermine-trimmed robe the color of sorrow, her hands folded protectively across her chest as though shielding her heart from any further harm he might try to inflict upon it.

"Roland." Her tone was flat. "Did you ever love me?"

And just like that, the odd look was gone from his face, and in the moment before it vanished, she knew it for a look of hope.

"*Now?* You want to talk about this *now*? My father has just died. Or have you been too preoccupied with your own precious little emotions to notice?"

She chose to disregard the ominous rising of his voice.

"I'll take it as a no. You never loved me. And this portrait. Who painted it?"

"You're unbelievable, you know that?"

He glared at her, and in his glare, she read a threat of looming violence.

She wrapped her arms tighter over her heart.

"Answer me. Who painted it?"

"Who painted it? I did!" he shouted. She forced herself not to shrink back. "I painted it! Imagine that, a prince of royal blood, able to do anything other than sign orders and chop off heads! Imagine me having ideas, having interests, having a life other than the life in which you have me pegged in your own pathetic little world of poodles and teatimes! But did you ever, even for just a second—" He made a visible effort, and his face, his voice, turned cold, turned dead; but his hands were clenched, his knuckles white, as if he was exerting an immense effort to contain something enormous, something monstrous, to prevent it from erupting and subsuming them both. "Did you know that I loved drawing as a child, that I wanted to be an artist, but they told me, when I was only six or seven years old, that I had to follow in my father's footsteps, had to shoulder the burden of responsibility? No, you didn't know, and why? Because you *never asked*. Never asked anything about me. So, let me tell you. I cried for a full week, longer than when my mother had left us, a small, lonely child with no one to talk to. And then I dried my tears and I grew up. I learned to do what was asked of me. Learned to rule my kingdom. Learned when harshness was needed and when to be lenient. Kept my hobbies in check. Married when it was required of me. Produced heirs when it was required of me. You're right, I never loved you—and why would I? I thought, in the beginning, that you had spirit, that you had understanding, that you could be a worthy partner to me, and that, with time, something real might grow between us.

Then I saw what you were really like, what you were really after. All you wanted were balls and roses. Being a sweet little *princess*. You knew nothing about hard work. You knew nothing about companionship. I should have never chosen you. I should have chosen someone with substance, not someone as vain, empty-headed, and unforgiving as you."

Every word was a slap.

She felt the blood mounting higher and higher in her cheeks.

"But none of this is true!" she cried at last, hardly knowing what she was doing as she took a step, leaned on his desk, thrust her flaming face forward. "I wasn't like that at all! I was young, and I was in love, and I tried to make you happy, I tried so hard, I did my best, I wanted to be a good wife to you, it was you—you—you who . . ."

"Who *what*?"

"Who fucked anything that moved, that's what, from the day we got married!"

He appeared momentarily stunned, his mouth flapping loose. Then he was shouting again, their faces so close now she could feel his spittle on her skin.

"Oh yeah? And what would you have me do? And why would you even care? From the day we got married, *you* made it painfully clear that you wanted nothing to do with me, that I repulsed you! You felt no passion for me, it was like I married a paper doll. Have you ever, ever in your life, enjoyed a single kiss? I was twenty-four—and my beautiful young wife was so frigid she couldn't even be bothered to part her lips for me, much less her thighs!"

She recoiled, pressed her hand to her mouth, her lips suddenly, treacherously, burning with an unbidden memory of another man's fiery kiss. A shocked silence rolled over the room, tolling with vast, terrible things that could not be unsaid. Across the ringing stillness, they measured each other, two people wearing the black of mourning, two people who had just lost someone they loved. She knew that, in that moment, he hated her every bit as much as she hated him.

He pushed his chair back, away from her, spoke through his teeth, in control once again. "But here we are, and this is how it is, how it will be, from now till the end, and I will have my little diversions to which you will kindly close your eyes, and you will have your porcelain knickknacks, or whatever else catches your feebleminded fancy, and I will pay for it. I will tolerate this intolerable situation because I need to protect the public face of my company and because you happen to be the mother of my children. I just hope to God they will grow up to be like me, not like you. Now *get out*. I am mourning my father."

The last thing she saw, before turning and leaving the study, was the brilliantly painted man smiling his beautiful, loving, mocking smile into her eyes.

That night, she did not sleep. Transparent Brie and Nibbles hovered above the mantelpiece, trading anxious whispers, but she ignored them. After torching the nettle shirt in the fireplace and stomping the two pearl buttons into dust with her heel, she lay in her starched white bed, staring at the cupid-infested ceiling, her thoughts a feverish jumble of disjointed, whirling images, fears, losses all running together—her children growing up with that man for a father, the beekeeper's kiss, the kind old king's death, the deceitful portrait, the magic mirror, the green-eyed duchess, the duchess's hapless cuckold of a husband and his sorry end . . . It would have been better had you, too, fallen off your horse long ago, it flashed into her mind out of nowhere—but immediately, horrified by her own savagery, she disowned the unworthy thought. Yet once unleashed, it would creep back again and again, as she lay tormented, night after night after night, for weeks on end. For time passed, of course, as was its wont. Her husband was crowned king, and she became queen; they saw each other at official functions, but avoided each other's eyes and exchanged not a word. Her heart broke every time she looked at her son, at her daughter. At night, she would go back to her room, to her bed, and lie there, not heeding the timid consolations of the mice, glaring at the cupids on the ceiling, the same thoughts churning round and round in her head: Oh, if only he had fallen off his horse early on in their marriage—after she'd become heavy with Ro, but before she had time to look into that poisonous mirror and learn the truth about the conception. She was still blind to the man's true nature then, small lapses in their life had not yet joined together into one impassable gulf, and she would have been able to smooth over the more inconvenient incidents in her mind, would have been able to cherish the memory of their love for each other. And instead of wanting to scream "Your father is a monster, a monster!" into her children's sweet, innocent faces, she would be telling her daughter how proud he'd been of her and asking her son to find the bright star that his father had become in the skies, then crying herself to sleep every night with soft, affectionate tears. Her life would be sad yet full of warmth, solid at its heart, *good*. Now it felt hot, not warm, but the heat was hollow, hollow and angry, and she was forever seized with fear for Angie and Ro.

For how, how would they grow up, with that man in their lives?

Spring turned into summer. One especially stifling morning, worn-out by the constant weight of her unhappiness, she gathered her courage and sent a servant over to the beekeeper's cottage with a carefully worded note requesting a jar of honey for her breakfast table (to be delivered by the beekeeper in person). The servant returned alone, to inform her that the beekeeper's place had been abandoned for weeks, his bees dispersed, and he himself gone, no one knew when or where. She tried to hide her disappointment, her apprehension, from herself, tried to forget the taste of cider on the man's warm lips, tried not to worry about her husband's ubiquitous spies, or think about exiles and executions that he meted out with such ready ruthlessness—but all through that day, she felt increasingly aggrieved by what she had come to regard as her one chance at her own small, private joy being wrenched away from her, so unjustly, so cruelly; and that night, all her suppressed emotions bubbled over in one great explosion of scalding fury, and she screamed a silent scream.

I wish he *would* fall off his horse!

Or get eaten by a dragon. An occupational hazard of being a ruler; though not *his* kind of ruler—not the kind who wields a quill instead of a sword—and there are no dragons left in our land, in any case. So instead he might choke on a fish bone during one of his fancy state dinners with the servant wenches pouring wine into his glass while he pinches them under the table. He would bite into his fish, and cough, and it would be a small, delicate cough at first, but then his perfect, gorgeous face would turn red, first red and then purple, and suddenly there he would be, those cornflower-blue eyes bugging out, not so pretty now, is he, mouth gaping, gasping for air, and before anyone even knows what is happening—dead, dead, *dead!*

Or maybe a heart attack. Of course, he is but thirty-eight, but they happen at any age, do they not, and more so if one's lifestyle is so vice-ridden. Or a freak accident, there are always those—a lightning strike, a flash flood, a chance tile falling off a roof just when my husband is passing below, his expensive suede shoes stepping ever so confidently along the sidewalk . . . But no, I do not wish him ill, I'm not a vindictive person, I'm kind and good, all I want is justice, only justice, I want him to pay for depriving me of any chance at my own happiness, for marrying me when he knew he didn't love me, for cheating on me with impunity from the very beginning, as if there were nothing at all wrong with it, as if I—I!—forced him into it myself, but of course I did not, I was so very young and I loved him, I loved that man, once upon a time I loved him, I did my best to love him—but not dead, of course I do not wish him dead.

Although—if he *were* dead—all the memories of my miserable years as his wife, all my humiliations and mistakes, all my poor choices, would die with him, and that would be just, that would be well deserved, being granted a clean slate like that, having a future again, unburdened, unmarred, haven't I earned it after everything he's put me through? Because I hate what our marriage has made me, a small, mute, unloved thing. If he were dead, she, too, would die with him. So, perhaps, I do want him dead.

I want him dead because I hate the woman I am when I am with him.

Oh, and my children, my children would be so much better off without him. Because, of course, I would be doing it for my children, not for myself. Not that—not that I would actually *do* anything, ever! Although hasn't the magic mirror mentioned a witch who helps unhappy wives with their marital problems? There would be no harm, perhaps, in going to see her. Just to talk, nothing more—I wouldn't have to follow through with anything. In truth, I couldn't, for isn't a lock of hair always required for such spells to work, and how would I get a lock of his hair, I'm never close enough to him, I would have to pretend to a reconciliation, force myself to sit down to a private dinner with him, distract him enough to slip a sleeping draught into his wine, then, worse, feign passion, trick him into my bed . . . But I would never do any of that, would never go that far, that would be so base, so treacherous, so shameful, I would never, and even if I would, he wouldn't go along with it in any case, he wouldn't be interested, would he, not after all those hateful things he said to me, none of them true, because I loved him once upon a time, I did love him, of course I did, so I couldn't, I would never.

So, then, just a consultation. One brief little consultation with the woman. Just to hear what she has to say, just to explore my options, just—

My lawyer's voice, kinder than usual, reaches me as if from another place.

"Tell me what happened at the end," she says.

And I meet her eyes and, at last, tell her the truth.

"Nothing. Nothing happened. I understood some things, that's all. Hard things. Ugly things. Things I haven't felt ready to admit to anyone."

"Such as?" She is gently insistent.

"My marriage was not as I thought. And Roland may not have been the only one to blame for things ending. And also . . ."

"Yes?"

"Nothing," I say, firmly. "Can we talk about the trial now, please?"

And also, I was far from the innocent fairy-tale princess I had believed myself once.

The Fairy-Tale Ending

"Divorce is not unlike temporary insanity," my therapist observes. "You can't judge yourself too harshly. You can't judge him too harshly, either. Believe me, life will go back to normal by and by."

This is our last session before the trial, which is set to start on Friday.

"But he is doing all these awful things!" I cry. "He wants to take the children away from me, he wants to give me nothing and rob me of what little I have . . . And I—I did nothing wrong, you know. I tried to be a good wife. Never lied to him. Always did my best to help him. Put my marriage first."

Dr. Wand jots something down in her notebook, ponders briefly, and crosses it out. "You feel betrayed, and that's understandable. Consider his point of view, though. He gave you everything he thought you wanted, he took care of you and the kids, surrounded you with luxury—and you ran away from it all and would now rather be cleaning other people's toilets than go back to him. And to be frank, you never seemed that involved in his life while you were together, either. Do you even know what precisely he does for a living?"

"Whose side is she on, anyway?" Melissa says loyally when I repeat the conversation to my sisters the following night, as we sit in Melissa's living room drinking Gloria's expensive Bordeaux.

"Oh, I don't know," Gloria muses. "Everyone has his truth. Roland may see things differently."

Melissa turns on her.

"Whose side are *you* on, then?" she says fiercely.

"Don't get me wrong, I don't like the asshole, never did." Gloria shrugs. "All I'm saying is, I bet he's not the villain in his mind. Everyone is a hero of his own story."

Everything seems so ordinary, so peaceful—Melissa's cheerful living room with its striped couches, floral pillows, polka-dotted curtains, and her daughters' framed drawings on the walls, the company of my sisters, so easy to slip into, even after all these years, like some old, stretched cardigan—and yet I know that everything is about to change. The trial is only two days away now, and my anxiety is such that I cannot sleep, I cannot eat, I can barely think straight. I notice Melissa glancing at me with concern. When she notices me noticing, she smiles, a bit too brightly, and says, in a clear ploy to distract me: "Speaking of stories, remember that book of fairy tales we used to love, the one in the red leather binding? I found it in the attic the other day, and now the girls don't want anything else before bed."

"I never liked it," Gloria announces.

"You did, too!"

"No. I never did. The women in these stories are all wimps and ciphers. No feelings, no thoughts of their own. No *balls*. All they want is to get rescued and to get married. Artifacts of masculine oppression, the whole bunch."

"Not true," Melissa says. "Most fairy tales are subversive. Feminist, even. No, don't snort, listen. These are stories women told to other women, old wives' tales, spinners' yarns, right? And who are their heroes? Women again. Snow White, Rapunzel, Little Red Riding Hood. Girls who run away from home, choose husbands, escape wolves. They have names, they have characters, they have adventures. But the men? Just nameless blanks, the lot of them, and some are downright evil. Did you know, there is a version of Sleeping Beauty in which a married king comes across her, rapes her in her sleep, then goes back to his wife. She gives birth, still in her sleep, and it's actually her baby who wakes her up trying to suckle her. And I'm sure the storytellers knew exactly what they were saying. And the Cinderella prince, what a dolt! First he takes one ugly stepsister to the palace, then the other, and he can't tell they aren't his true love until someone else points out their feet are bleeding? Not exactly the romance of the century! But Cinderella, she knew what she was doing marrying the guy. It never says she was in love. She just wanted to be a queen, and it sure beats washing dishes . . . Hold on, let me tiptoe upstairs, I'll get the book from Myrtle's nightstand."

She brings it down, and the three of us sit on the couch and look through it together, Melissa in the middle, turning pages, and Gloria, unconvinced by Melissa's rhetoric, making dismissive noises as each new wide-eyed princess floats into view. Inwardly, I find myself inclining to Gloria's opinion. The illustrations, though, are beautiful and unexpected, with the familiar tales of Charles Perrault and the Brothers Grimm set by the artist in Victorian manors filled with glowing gas lamps and grandfather clocks, in Jazz Age mansions full of bobbed flappers, in oppressive suburban mid-century homes, all beige-tinted bourgeois comforts. My memories of the book are vague at best—as the youngest, I did not always share in my sisters' pastimes—and yet, as the next picture comes into view, I seem to recall seeing it before, and am studying it with mild interest when Gloria takes the book out of Melissa's hands.

"French Baroque is appalling." Only she is capable of infusing so few words with so much disdain. "Methinks we've had enough of regressing." She shuts the book firmly. "Shall we now do something more age-appropriate and open the third bottle? By the way, remember how, when you were four or five, you went about talking with some ridiculous made-up accent, sniffing some precious bouquet you unearthed somewhere, drinking milk with your pinkie stuck out, and pretending you were an adopted child of some foreign grandee and we your evil stepsisters?"

"I did *not!*"

"You most certainly did."

"You did, you know," Melissa chimes in, smiling.

"No, did I, really?" I had honestly forgotten all about it. "I must have been a horrible sister," I say, half laughing, half repentant. "But it was hard growing up as a follow-up act to you two."

"Nonsense, you were always the prettiest," Melissa says.

"Maybe so, but it didn't count for much with our mother, did it? I mean, Gloria, you were tough, you had brains and ambitions, and you, you were so outgoing, and you had that laugh, everyone liked you. But what did I have, apart from my silly blond curls? I wasn't good at anything, Mom said so all the time. Not good at anything other than mopping dirty bathroom floors, that's what she told me, over and over, until I really couldn't stand working in that hotel. You two were always her favorites. Even the name she gave me, I always hated it, the most boring name of the lot . . . Well, I guess I just needed to get away from home so badly, I had to marry the first suitable man who asked. And Roland was certainly suitable. Of course, we all ran as far and as fast as we could, though in very different directions, no?"

"What a load of horseshit." Gloria pours more wine into her glass, then, after a moment's hesitation, mine. "Mother never played favorites. Hers was tough love with all of us, you don't know half the stuff she said to me and Mel. Every time I brought home a less-than-perfect grade, she told me I'd die drunk in a gutter. 'Just like your father.' That's what she said to me. Every single time. There were days I was sure I would always hate her. Well, what did I know then, I was fifteen. So, fine, she wasn't easy to live with, but she worked herself sick for us and she raised us the best she knew how . . . And there is absolutely nothing wrong with your name. It was our great-grandmother's name. It's beautiful. And it suits you perfectly."

Melissa is frowning at me.

"But you loved him, right?" she asks. "When you got married? Didn't you?"

And just like that—whether because of all the wine I have drunk, or the relief of speaking to my sisters after the decade and a half of near-estrangement, or the coziness of Melissa's home, her girls' happy drawings on the walls, her good, stolid husband asleep upstairs, or Gloria's matter-of-fact, plainspoken vulgarity— something in me breaks loose, something vast and cold slides away, and from below, released, the emotions swell, and the truths, their dark, warm, salty flow much like the sea tide, much like weeping, and I see what I have been afraid to see, what I have hidden from myself for so long behind the story of an innocent lovesick wife put upon by a heartless man who tricked her into a marriage without a spark.

I did not love my husband when I married him.

I never loved him—and deep inside, I must have always known it.

Oh, of course, I was infatuated once—more, I was smitten, for he was handsome, he was brilliant, he was worldly, he was rich, he was ambitious, he was generous, he was absolutely every-thing a sad young girl with clouds and dreams for feelings could have wished for. And yet I did not love him, not in the deep, true sense, not in the way Melissa loves Tom, not in the way I love my children, not in the way our stern, no-nonsense, widowed mother loved the three of us. But as a child, I had often found her love heavy, demanding, disapproving, damaging even, so I had come to long for a different kind of love to find refuge in, to escape to—an easy love, a pretty love, a fairy-tale love. There is no easy love, of course, but at twenty-one, at twenty-two, I could not have possibly known it, and when something much like it came dazzling into my life, all my future selves, all my unrealized chances, all my untold stories seemed but a paltry price to pay for it—and a price I paid gladly. No one had robbed me of anything—I myself made the choice to give away my freedom, to give away my fire. And it never even occurred to me that I could say no, because how can you say no when fate singles you out, raises you out of the common muck as someone special, someone deserving of an ideal life, a life in which everything is easy, everything soft, everything gentle, and no one ever barks a harsh word, and no one ever slaps you, and no hard-drinking fathers die of heart attacks at the age of thirty-eight, and no hardworking mothers, old and gray before their time, cry nightly at the kitchen table before growing grim and estranged. But in this ideal life, everyone glides with the oily predictability of porcelain figurines in a decorative music box, one-two-three, one-two-three, and your days are like a never-ending teatime, everything polite and elegant and gilded just like some picture of a smiling princess in a powdered cake of a palace in a fairy-tale book. And maybe this life has no depth, and maybe it has no spark, that may be true, everything may well be somewhat flat, everything slightly dulled, even kisses may well taste of dust and ice, because proper fairy tales do not need any depth and you yourself tossed passion away when you married a seemingly flawless man whom you never loved, whom you were not in love with, whom, in truth, you never even wanted to take to your bed, for there had always been something in him, something too slick, too cold, too perfect, something that you disliked, something that held you off. And yet, at the time, it all made such sense, and you were like a young hopeful fly carried away by a luminous drop of sweet nectar, intoxicated, blinded by the luster, not knowing that the fresh-smelling sap would soon calcify into hard amber and you would be trapped in all that suffocating golden light, you would be trapped, trapped, trapped—

"It will be all right, everything will be all right," Melissa is repeating, holding my shoulders as I weep, speaking to me in that soothing tone I have heard her use with her daughters.

Gloria sets down her glass, abruptly.

"I wasn't going to tell you," she announces, "but I'm a tad inebriated now, and you're bawling anyway, so what the hell. The cad hit on me when I met him. Put his hand under my skirt. The last time I ever wore a skirt, I believe. Remember that gallery opening I invited you to? You'd only just gotten engaged. I didn't tell anyone because I thought you loved him. I should have, maybe. Probably. But I was young. We were all so fucking young. Look, I'm sorry, all right?"

"Oh my God. He hit on me, too. At the rehearsal party, the night before you got married." Melissa releases my shoulders. "He followed me into the ladies' room and tried to kiss me. I was mortified. That's why I acted a bit funny at the wedding. And why I never liked visiting you in later years. I felt horrible. Just horrible."

"Oh, me too," Gloria says. "Me too."

The three of us look at one another across the widening hush.

"Would it help in any way," Melissa begins, tentatively, "if Gloria and I testify at your trial? I mean, it may not be much, but all the same . . ."

And then everything speeds up again, the way things tend to in my life when something momentous is happening, and I am too overwhelmed to focus on any one instant for long, so everything runs together, in a stream of blurring snapshots, from the late-night, somewhat slurred, telephone call to my lawyer, to her conversations with my sisters, to the rushed meeting arranged for the very next morning, only one day before the trial is scheduled to start, where I find myself, bleary-eyed, with an incipient headache and my heart in my throat, sitting at a blond-wood conference table across from a sleek-suited man representing my husband, his cuffs crisp like abstract sculptures, his golden cuff links blinding, and my own lawyer, dumpy in comparison yet formidable and calm, is issuing demands, and the man is fuming and bustling and whispering into his phone and then subsiding, retreating, until, hours later, yet somehow all at once, numbers are thrown about, and days of the week are bandied back and forth, the talk of summer vacations, college payments, and suddenly there it is, a stack of papers crisp before me, still warm from the printer, the divorce agreement. I sign, here, and here, and here, and the sleek man disappears with the stack as I sit at the table, gasping a little, stunned by the magical speed of the events unfolding—and when the man returns, his cuffs seem less crisp, dampened with sweat, and my husband's many-angled, spiky signatures darken all the pages underneath my own tremulous scrawls.

And just like that, we are done.

And oh, of course, there are details and clauses to pore over, weekends when the kids will stay with him, modest financial concessions granted to me—all of which I will process later, later. This is the bare substance, this is what I know right now: There will be no trial. He will keep all his money. I will have Angie and Ro.

I walk through the evening city happier than I have been in my entire life. I feel light as a feather. I feel like singing. I feel as though my feet are not touching the ground. All clichés, and all perfectly true. I am going home, to prepare for the children, who will be returned to me tomorrow, tomorrow, tomorrow . . . And so what if my neighborhood is far removed from the cool, rarefied heights of Fifth Avenue, so what if my apartment is small, my building shabby, my furniture secondhand—none of this is important, and all the important things I have in abundance. I fly home through the darkening streets, and am already fumbling with the keys at the front door, so happy, so happy, when a voice hits me in the back.

"Jane."

I freeze, the keys clutched in my hand.

"Jane."

I inhale, turn slowly.

Roland.

My former prince.

He stands on the sidewalk, hands shoved into his pockets, slightly out of breath, as though he has been running after me for some blocks. His haircut is expensive, his suit immaculate, his shoes shine like mirrors, and yet he seems disarrayed, he seems nervous, his figure not nearly as imposing, his face not nearly as handsome as I remember it. I have not seen him in months, but it feels like years. In fact, it feels almost as if I am now seeing him for the first time ever—seeing him in real life, outside my memories, outside my fantasies.

And he is not as I imagined him.

"What do you want?" I ask. "Are we not done?"

He begins to talk, his mouth sneering, his voice harsh. Everything, he tells me, has worked out just as he willed it, because I am a fool and he had me where he wanted me from the very beginning. He never intended to have full custody of the children, he has no time for it, he has a business to attend to, demanding it was just a trick to make me give up all my financial claims. I could have walked away with millions, but instead I left everything, everything, on the table, so easily manipulated, so naive, did I not realize that he would have signed away so much to avoid the publicity of the trial, there was never going to be any trial anyway, I played right into his hands . . . And he talks, and he talks, and I can tell that he wants me to grow angry, wants to stomp out the happiness he must see in my face—but oddly, whatever words he says, they seem to have no effect, for I hear, am surprised to hear, other words moving just beneath them, words of uncertainty, words of hurt.

Why did you make me believe, right at the end, that there might be some hope for us, after all? That night, the night you left, why did you kiss me? Why were you not there for me when my father died?

Why did you marry me if you felt no passion for me?

And as I look at him, standing crumpled and angry on the sidewalk, his mouth working around barbed words, his eyes pained, I realize that I, too, will have to face the wrongs I have committed. With time, I may even be ready to acknowledge the truth behind his cardboard cutout in the shape of a storybook villain. Perhaps my ever-so-sage therapist will tell me that his clumsy passes at my sisters before our wedding were his own cries for help, his own attempts to escape the fairy-tale marriage that fate was driving him into yet which he felt wrong in his bones— and someday, perhaps, I will even listen to her. Someday, but not today, for it is still too early to be magnanimous.

I want this night for myself.

In the middle of his tirade, I move to the door, turn the key in the lock.

"Jane, wait!"

Someday, but not yet.

Without looking back, I step inside, and the door creeps closed behind me.

The foyer is stuffy and dim—no liveried concierges, no visitor log books, no flower arrangements, no mirrored expanses here. As I stride across to the mailboxes, I glimpse something scuttling across the floor. A cockroach, I think at first—I have seen a fair share—but no, it is much too big to be a roach. I stop to look. A rat, or maybe an unusually large mouse, hobbles toward me across the lobby. My first impulse is to scream and run, as incoherent exclamations flash through my mind—my poor children, they aren't used to this kind of thing, this place is worse than I thought, but of course it's only temporary, I will work hard, I will work so hard to get us out of here—and then I am arrested by the sight of the creature's white, staring eyes.

The poor thing is blind.

And in that instant, while I hesitate, the mouse, or perhaps the rat, rises to its full height, slowly, laboriously, twitches its whiskers, squeaks at me, and lifts its right paw, looking for all the world as though it is giving me a solemn benediction, a benevolent blessing—or else thanking me for something. I gape at it, openmouthed, about to burst into a jittery laugh ("history of mental instability," the divorce papers said), when a small secret door unlocks somewhere deep, deep within me, swinging open just a crack, just for a moment—but a moment and a crack are all it takes.

It floods back, it all floods back—the fairy godmother, the glass slipper, the blue-and-white palace, the chatty teapots, my friends the mice, the vile potions, the treacherous mirror, the nettle shirts, the witch, the curse. And as I stand in the middle of the dim foyer of a rent-controlled building in the lower reaches of Manhattan, I hold the immensity of both realities in my mind, and I say to myself: Perhaps all of this is the same story, only seen from two different angles, like one of those trick paintings—birds if you look from one side, horses if from the other, both if you move far enough away to take everything in at once.

Because maybe, maybe, I simply could not face the darker facts of my marriage—my discomfort at being a rich man's idle wife, my constant guilt over not doing enough for my children, my postpartum depression, my brief addiction to pornography, my longer addiction to prescription pills, my unacknowledged attraction to one of Roland's underlings, my obsessive spying on my husband along with my pathetic attempts to explain away his philandering, to shift the blame from him at all costs, to myself, to his women, to anyone and anything, my growing desperation to forget the bitter truths of so many awful, shameful moments—oh, such layers of self-deception I practiced, possibly out of some nebulous notion of ideal love, but just as possibly, only so I might go on living with my own cowardly choices . . . And all the years I spent sifting through, shaping, reshaping the past, trying to pinpoint the exact moment at which our marital happiness dimmed, embroidering upon the myth of our perfect romantic beginnings—until the kind old Roland Senior died and I found his papers and learned of the clause stipulating that Roland Junior needed to marry before the age of twenty-five in order to come into the ownership of his trust. Then, at long last, our screaming confrontation, and my therapist trying to dissuade me from drastic measures, and my subsequent visit to a lawyer who frightened me so, a shrill, man-hating witch—or so she first appeared to my eyes—droning at me, "Law is not strictly a science, it's more of an art," her professionally suppressed yet palpable excitement at the realization that my ex-husband-to-be was the wealthy heir of a windowsill empire, the first mention of the word "divorce" striking me with the force of a lightning bolt blazing out of the dark stormy sky . . . They say, do they not, that divorce is akin to insanity, so perhaps all these other truths I now remember are only stories I once told myself to keep sane, to mask the crude ugliness of things ending, to transform the chaos of pain into some semblance of order, of higher sense. And maybe that is what all fairy tales are, at their heart: generations of unhappy women throughout history who lost their mothers to disease, fathers to violence, daughters to labor, sons to hunger, who were beaten, abandoned, exploited, orphaned, collectively trying to dream themselves into a life that made sense, spinning tales of man-eating ogres, crystal shoes, poisonous apples, and true love—thinly veiled metaphors of everything gone wrong and everything hoped for on lonely winter nights.

And then again, just as likely, it might be the other way around. Maybe, once upon a time, I was indeed an ordinary fairy-tale princess, like many other such princesses, a princess with her cardboard love for a cardboard husband, living a cardboard life in a cardboard palace, stuck within the confines of a predetermined tale, going through predetermined motions, a fate akin to death, a fate worse than death, yet all the while, in my gilded porcelain teacup, in my beautifully curled blond head, dreaming of another life, of another place—a place full of surprises, full of choices, a place I could sense, glimpse, almost touch now and then, in my rare moments of non-cardboard, transcendent emotion, whether genuine joy or genuine pain. Perhaps, then, when my heart was kindled once and for all by a real love for a real child, for two real children, I managed to do something truly magical—to break through the theatrical decorations, to will myself out of my one-dimensional prison and into the three-dimensional world, this world around me, this life, this city, this moment.

And whatever the truth—whether once upon a time I was a wretched housewife distracting myself with fantasies to while away my empty days or a depressed princess battling the tedium of stale fairy-tale coupledom—I have never felt more clearheaded, more awake, more present, more ready to jump into the thick of life, than I do now, and no other place has ever seemed more thrilling, more unpredictable, more crackling with possibilities—with real magic—than this dim lobby with an old cranky elevator and a blind mouse, before which I stand amazed, overwhelmed, holding both lives superimposed in my mind, one balancing the other.

The elevator thuds as it arrives, and its door shudders and creaks. My next-door neighbor, an ancient lady wrapped in bundles of gray and brown shawls, makes her unsteady way out into the lobby, and sees me, and stops.

"Are you all right, dearie?"

"I . . . yes, I . . . I thought I saw something run into that corner."

Together we peer into the shadows.

"Ack," she says. "Must be rat." Her strong accent has a whiff of the Old World about it, strange places, dark stories. "Shameful, state of this hovel. Someone should call exterminator. Good day to you, dearie."

She sounds like a fairy-tale witch, I think, amused; looks like one, too, with her hooked nose and the warts on her chin. Mesmerized, I follow her precarious progress toward the front door, then, shaking myself awake, press the elevator button. As I step inside the poorly lit box, I am touched by a fleeting feeling that I was thinking something important, maybe even something vital, a mere moment ago, but the thought remains uncaptured. I may remember it later, I tell myself. For now, there is so much to do: the children are coming tomorrow, tomorrow, there is no time to waste.

My place is small, but I spend hours cleaning it until it shines, cleaning late into the night, cleaning as I have never cleaned anything in my long life of cleaning. When every last doorknob is gleaming, every last dust bunny banned, I sit down by an open window and look at my city, the magical city that never sleeps. I look at the wide night sky with a scattering of pallid, urban stars, and the shining rivers of headlights streaming below, and lamps coming on and blinking out in other windows, illuminating or concealing other lives, other stories—and only a stone's throw away, there are dogs, and sirens, and boys, and flowers, and women young and old, and lovers, and beggars, and poets, and pretzel carts, and wine bars, and bookshops, and laughter, and sadness, and triumphs, and losses, and kisses, and fights, and miracles, and quests, and discoveries, and heartbreak, and life, life, life.

That night, when I go to bed, I dream of being a witch. I dream of being a sleeping beauty. I dream of being a gingerbread house. I dream of being a prince. I dream of being a falling star, a rushing wind, a rustling forest. When I wake up in the morning, the sun is pouring through my window, and everything looks unexpected. Perhaps, I think, I have finally dreamed myself into a new story, a story with no commonplaces—an entirely different, as yet unknown story that will be a new beginning after the familiar end.

The Beginning

Acknowledgments

As a child, I loved the traditional fairy tales—Alexander Afanasyev, the Brothers Grimm, Charles Perrault. As an adult, I questioned them. Hundreds of stories, read and reread, and years of wondering about them have formed the foundation of this book. My indirect debts are simply too many to acknowledge, but in the course of doing research, I was influenced by many fairy-tale scholars, interpreters, and storytellers, most notably A. S. Byatt, Italo Calvino, Angela Carter (*The Bloody Chamber* is a masterpiece), Robert Coover, Neil Gaiman, George MacDonald, Cristina Bacchilega, Ruth Bottigheimer, Maria Tatar, Marina Warner, and Jack Zipes.

A few direct borrowings must be mentioned: The phrase "wild surmise" originates in a John Keats poem, then makes its way to the ultimate line of Angela Carter's novel *The Magic Toyshop*, before ending up in my beekeeper scene. The children's counting rhyme is my paraphrase of a saying attributed to Oscar Wilde: "Keep love in your heart. A life without it is like a sunless garden when the flowers are dead." The quotation about women having souls is, astonishingly, real, and comes from a 1922 book, *Married Life and Happiness*, written by William Josephus Robinson, a prominent New York physician and early birth control advocate; I used it verbatim and only omitted one comma in deference to modern punctuation.

Research and literary influences aside, this book would not have been possible without the help of many people I am lucky to have in my life. Special thanks are due to Warren Frazier, my wonderful agent, who has always been there for me with his guidance and friendship. I am also deeply grateful to Ivan Held and Sally Kim, for their generous support and faith in my work; to Gabriella Mongelli, my editor, for her unflagging excitement about the book and her fine judgment; to Anna Jardine, once again, for her painstaking attention to the written word; and to everyone else at Putnam who worked to make *The Charmed Wife* a reality.

Several astute readers have seen the manuscript in its various stages and offered wise suggestions: Moses Cardona, Annie Kronenberg, Bill Reiss, and my two oldest friends, Olga Levaniouk and Olga Oliker. Britton Sauerbrei, my partner and first reader, provided me with invaluable advice on mouse behavior, found the perfect epigraph in a Timothy Steele poem, and made me very happy throughout. And, as ever, I am grateful to my family—my mother, Natalia Kartseva, who has sustained me with numerous pieces of cabbage pie and maternal wisdom, and my children, Alex and Tasha Klyce, who prefer stories quite different from the ones I myself loved as a child and who never stop teaching me new ways of seeing the world.

Last but not least, prompted by my daughter, I must mention Brie, Nibbles, and Nibbles Junior—the three orphaned baby mice who were not with us for long, in spite of a number of sleepless nights I spent feeding them milk-diluted peanut butter from an eye dropper, and yet whose brief existences inspired the ongoing mouse plot of the book, in particular the idea of mice substitutions. There had been only two mice to start with, Brie and Nibbles—we found them squealing in our basement one spring evening, their mother likely caught by the neighbor's dog. The original Nibbles died in the night, and I was just debating how to break the sad news to my children when, providentially, I happened upon yet another blind mouseling crawling in the basement. I tried to pass him off as Nibbles in the morning; my children, however, were more observant than the oblivious princess of my story, and, my ruse soon discovered, he became Nibbles Junior. Odd are the ways in which life finds its way into literature.